THE THIRD APOLOGY

This paperback edition published in 2025 by Tweedlecoate.
tweedlecoate.co.uk

Cover Design by Calvert Creative

Back Cover Photographs (left to right):
Protest in Toulouse © André Cros
Couple by the Pool & Hitchhiker sourced from Dreamstime
Paris Résistance reproduced under Creative Commons License

Printed and bound by CPI Group (UK) Ltd, Croydon, CR0 4YY
ISBN 978-1918316001

THE THIRD APOLOGY

D A Adamson

Tweedlecoate

In memory of Tim
A fellow traveller

Chapter 1

France 1944

They both heard the distinctive crunch of jackboots on the stone ballast of the railway track and the sound of dogs barking. Damn it, thought the Agent. She heard the soft click as the boy released his gun's safety catch as they lay in a hollow next to the line. At the same moment they both sensed the rails starting to vibrate. Three flashlights moved towards them from the Rognac junction. The other hidden partisans' orders were not to open fire until the Germans were nearly on top of the explosives. The clanking noise of the steam engine was close as it dragged its heavy load up the incline towards the ambush point. Suddenly, there was a shout in German, followed by a burst of automatic fire and a cry. The young man heard a thump as a body fell to the ground. Comrade or German? The boy trembled with fear.

He tried to move. 'Stay there,' hissed the Agent, as she waved him to stay down. By now the heavy locomotive was nearly upon them, slowing as it approached their position. The driver, had spotted the patrol's flashlights, and applied the brakes. The heavy train rumbled forward, followed by the first of the carriages packed with troops. Above the hissing, creaking noise of the train they could hear more shooting, but it was closer now. The young man could see the head of a soldier leaning out of a carriage window looking to see what the commotion was about. The Agent thrust down the detonator plunger, for a moment the boy thought the charges had failed and a momentary wave of panic gripped him. Almost instantly he was deafened by a tremendous explosion, the ground shook immediately followed by a second blast. The boy's ears rang as he felt the pressure waves briefly lift his neckerchief, it was quickly followed by a shrieking sound of escaping steam and an earth-shattering crash as the train lurched off the rails and started to career down the embankment. They both leapt to their feet and ran into the safety of the wood as the carriages and wagons peeled off the track in a slow motion descent of grinding steel and breaking glass.

~

It was mid April 1944, the SOE Agent had been parachuted into occupied Provence to work with French Résistance cells and organise RAF ammunition and arms drops to aid their clandestine work. Their first mission was to derail a train at Rognac junction on the Marseilles to Avignon line as it travelled north in readiness for the anticipated Allied invasion. Its cargo of armaments, ordnance and troops was a rich target. The ambush had gone like clockwork just as they had planned it back at the remote barn near Rognac ten days before. The Agent's instructions had been meticulously followed by the nine partisans in her charge. For the boy it had been his first active involvement since his promotion from intelligence gatherer and messenger.

On the night of the raid as the light had faded a dew descended on the Agent and the boy's hiding place in a hollow next to the railway line. The boy's fingers had become stiff with cold and he fretted about correctly attaching the fuse wires to the detonator. He was anxious to perform his duties well and he thrust his hands inside his coat pocket to warm them and tried not to think of the humiliation of letting his comrades down. As he shivered in part nervous excitement, and part cold as he smelled the forest awakening from its winter slumber. The only sound to be heard was a blackbird singing its last chorus before nightfall hidden somewhere among the holm oaks and pines, oblivious to the carnage about to be unleashed.

The Agent also heard the bird and was reminded of walking with her father in the Miochowskie woods outside Warsaw, and she remembered why she was here. Her shimmering reverie vanished as she sensed the young man's restlessness, one moment his hands were in his coat pockets, next they stroked his rifle as if he was calming a cat.

'You okay?'

'Yes,' he muttered, in a barely audible voice, ashamed by his manifest nervousness.

'It's normal to feel afraid, just concentrate on what you have to do,' she said.

The boy was comforted by her words, but the pit in his stomach still felt hollow and his mouth was dry as a baguette. He could scarcely believe where he was and what he was about to do as he lay in shrub grass next to the British agent. He had been impressed by her near faultless command of French countered by her masculine workers' tunic which could not disguise her underlying beauty. He thought he was acting in a scene from a cinema newsreel.

The Agent's briefing in the barn had been thorough and commanding. His fellow partisans had listened intently and were at ease taking orders from a girl barely older than one of their daughters. Occasionally one of the group asked a question. The boy, the youngest and nimblest member of the group, had been assigned to assist the Agent in attaching the charges to the railway line and run the fuse wire back to the detonator. He had been entrusted with a key role in the sabotage plan and was infused with patriotic pride, fuelled by a ferocious hatred of "*les boches*" occupiers. He understood the consequences of being caught: torture and certain death.

The train was due at nine twenty. 'Remember what I said, when connecting the fuse wires keep as low as possible so no one can see your silhouette,' said the Agent. A little before nine o'clock the pair slipped quietly from their hiding places and scrambled up the grassy bank onto the railway line. In intermittent moonlight they began to attach the detonators and two RDX explosive packs, one on each rail about ten yards apart. While the Agent was attaching the plastic explosives, the young man forgot his fear, and quickly ran the fuse wires under the rails. In no time, he was sliding back down the embankment, the wires spooling behind him while he did his best to hide them in the damp grass. Soon they were both back in their hiding places. It had taken a little over four minutes to secure the charges unobserved.

~

The cacophony of death rang in the boy's ears as they fled through the dense wood. The sound of splintering trees as the groaning rolling stock crashed off the tracks accompanied by the screams of injured soldiers was punctuated by automatic gunfire as the partisans raked the train with bullets. He thought the noise would never end as he ran with the Agent, his damp hand in her gloved hand. As they careered through woodland he could barely keep pace and she pulled him, stumbling over exposed tree roots and through bramble-thick undergrowth until the orchestra of destruction faded behind them. The boy's chest hurt as he fought for breath, his pent-up excitement was blighted with horror as he realised the carnage he had helped cause.

Eventually, the Agent stopped; the boy was amazed at the girl's stamina, she appeared calm as if she had just taken a strenuous woodland walk. 'Do you think anybody noticed us as we left?' he said.

'No chance, the spectacle of the train crashing would have distracted the Germans. Don't worry, the most important task now is to return home undetected.'

'What about the others?'

'Each one has his own escape plan prepared. We'll have to lay low for a week or so as the Germans will be hunting for us.'

'Reprisals?'

'Of course. You can expect them to be severe.'

The Agent turned towards him and gripped his shoulders with both hands, it was as firm as any man. Even in the semi-light of the wood the boy could see her brown, almond shaped eyes, glinting. 'You did well,' she said. 'Now go as fast as you can, be very careful, the German patrols will be out in force, and hide your weapon well.'

'I will.'

'Tell no-one and try to forget everything you've seen.' She bent her head towards him and gently kissed him on the lips.

The boy gasped in surprise.

Chapter 2

North of England 1968

'Your results.' Angus Mcintyre's clergyman father was standing at the garden gate. He was waving a piece of paper. His dog collar gleamed white matching the white handkerchief in the breast pocket of his charcoal grey suit.

Angus dismounted from his old bicycle and wheeled it towards his father. It was clear he was in a rage. Angus saw he had opened his letter from the matriculation board that contained his 'A' level results.

'You've ruined your chances of getting into Oxford,' he said, in his gruff Scottish accent. Two 'Bs' and only one 'A'. Before Angus could utter a word of protest his father continued his rant. 'What have you been playing at? These results are an utter disgrace.' He thrust the piece of paper at Angus. 'You have been spending too much time with that wastrel, Peter Jagoda. Listening to pop music and heaven alone what else.'

Angus smiled.

'What are you grinning at? You have let me down, and the school. I know, as your headmaster, that you are capable of getting straight A results. His father turned on his heel and strode into the presbytery, throwing his arms around and muttering as he went.

Angus stood and looked at the letters: History A, English B, Maths B. These were just what he had hoped for. They were enough to get him into a good university as far away from Leeds as possible. He did not want the exclusive atmosphere of Oxford that his father so desired. He wanted a more cosmopolitan environment, not a hot house of privileged elites. Any place down south, far away from his father's oppressive religiosity.

Angus had purposefully taken the brakes off his swotting. He knew his father was dead set on him getting into Oxford, *his* old university. He was damned if he was going to satisfy his whims over his own preferences. These results were a personal victory for Angus.

'Bad luck, darling,' said his mother, when eventually he went into the house. He threw his long arms around her and bent down and gave her a long hug. 'You are so tall these days,' she said. 'I can hardly recognise my little boy Angus. I do wish you would get your hair cut, it is as long as a girl.'

'Oh mother. I'm eighteen now. Long hair is the fashion.'

'I know, I just haven't got used to it yet.'

'Father is in a rage about my results.'

'I know. He'll get over it. He always does. He shouldn't have opened your results. I told him off but as usual he took no notice.'

'I don't know how you put up with him.'

'Years of practice, dear,' she said, with a weary smile.

'Not very Christian.'

'He can't shake off his Presbyterian upbringing. His father was an even bigger ogre. Strangely enough, he and I got on well. But let's not talk about the Macintyre family. Have you heard how Pete got on?'

'I have just been with him. Predictably he got an 'A' in maths and two 'D's. He's not going to uni, I think he wants to train as an accountant. He's an ace with numbers, very quick-witted. You know Pete.'

'Don't I know it. If you heard your father go on about him you would think he was the devil incarnate.'

'I was surprised father let him come back to the school to take his exams after his expulsion.'

'That was down to you wasn't it?'

'Partly.'

'You *are* a kind boy, Angus.'

'Sometimes, Pete can't help himself.'

Chapter 3

'Have you finished your studies?' said Mrs. Jagoda, gently knocking on her son's bedroom door. Pete put down his Mickey Spillane novel just as Mike Hammer was about to punch a pimp. Pete liked his heroes to get things done. Mike Hammer was that sort of guy.

'Still hard at it Mum,' he said, as he slipped the book under the bed cover and picked up *Double Entry Book Keeping*. When his mother opened the door wide she saw a writing desk sprawled with accountancy tomes. The scene was a subterfuge of studiousness.

'It's time to put your light out now, you'll never be up in time for the office,' she said.

Felicja Jagoda was an upright, handsome looking woman with a broad Slavic forehead and large, glittering brown eyes. Pete was in awe of her inner steeliness that belied a loving nature. Before he had time to give her a goodnight peck on the cheek she had sat down on the edge of his bed. Pete knew it was a sign that she wanted to talk. It was only recently she had started to open up about her early life growing up in Poland.

'It's important that you study hard and make a good career for yourself,' she said, fidgeting with a gold signet ring that had once been her father's. 'We don't have the wealth I had as a child. The Nazis stole everything we had... including my family,' she said, and lowered her head, unable to look her son in the eye. Her hand moved to some beautiful pearls around her neck which she wore every day, whatever she was doing. Pete remained silent and waited for her to continue. Although he had heard many of the stories before, he loved to hear about her past. He suspected her nostalgic anecdotes about her long dead murdered family were heavily censored. She had lost so much in the war it was difficult to imagine how she had managed to build a new life for herself. Her reminiscences were as much a therapy for her, as an aural history lesson for him.

'My Papa had clothing factories and shops. He was a shrewd, hardworking businessman, you remind me of him sometimes. Your own father is just a skilled tailor, a good man, an expert cutter, but without the ambition and drive of my father.'

'Don't be hard on Dad, he loves his work and he's well regarded. You're forever telling me he has a great reputation, the top business people in Leeds come to him for their schmatter,' replied Pete. He hated his father being belittled.

'You should hear him complain about his customers,' said his mother. He says they never pay him enough, or they're not satisfied with the beautiful suits he's made. "Alter this Mr. Jagoda;" "This cloth is a bit heavy Mr. Jagoda;" "*How* much Mr. Jagoda?"'

'How did you meet Dad?'

'Not until after the war. He had left Poland before I escaped. His family were tailors like him, they lived in Poznań; it's a big city in the south. All his family were wiped out, they all perished in the concentration camps. He never discovered how they died, or where. There were no traces. The Nazis burned the records at the end. I don't think he's ever got over it.'

'I can't imagine it. It's too horrible.'

'He came to England in 1937 and joined the RAF. It was fortunate he never had the aptitude to be a pilot, despite trying. But he was always good with his hands and he became an aircraft mechanic. When his pilots did not return after a raid he worried if they had engine failure. Silly man!'

'You told me once you worked for the War Office during the war.'

'I could speak fluent English, German and French. It proved useful, I had studied at university in Poland. My Papa wanted an educated daughter. I think he probably had plans for me to run his business one day. I had no brothers, just two younger sisters.'

'What happened to them?'

'Murdered with the rest of the family.'

'Oh Mama, how awful.'

'I travelled with my father in Europe, buying cloth for his factories.'

'You were his interpreter?'

'Yes, kind of. Papa did speak some English, and German of course.'

'So what did you do for the British?'

'The authorities said they could use me in an office in London. I had to move down there. It was frightening in the blitz. I read intercepted German military messages. At my interview they described the work as dull, but of course it wasn't. Typical English understatement. I felt I was getting back at the people who had destroyed my family.'

'How did you manage to get out of Poland when you were Jewish?' Pete said.

'The Germans hadn't invaded by then, but we knew it would happen one day. Travel in Germany was near impossible, especially for Jews, so I went by boat from Gdansk to Scotland and then by train to England.'

'What a journey for a young woman on her own.'

'It was exciting. My clever father had business contacts in Yorkshire. He arranged for me to see the owner of a big textile mill in Huddersfield. My father's factories were making uniforms for the army by then and he needed cloth badly. It was the spring of 1939, six months before the war began. Ostensibly I was sent to England to select the right cloth, place an order, then come home. I suspected something was afoot when my mother gave me her pearls and my father's signet ring.'

'How long were you meant to stay?'

'I had a seven-day travel permit, but of course I never went back. It was a plan hatched by Papa. It was typical of him to think of me first. Nobody had any idea how bad things would eventually become. It was beyond everybody's imagination. When I discovered Papa had tricked me, I was furious. I had no idea that when I said goodbye, it would be the last time I would ever see them.' His mother's eyes filled with tears.

'Oh Mama, that is so sad, what happened next.? You were in a foreign country, a young girl, alone, and vulnerable.'

'I did think about trying to go back, but Papa was one step ahead of me. My passage was one way. It had been arranged for me to stay with Polish friends of my mother's who lived in Leeds. They were very kind and treated me like one of their own. I think my father sent them money for my upkeep until they vanished.' His mother gulped back more tears. 'Enough of this silly talk, it's long ago. Now I have you, my little boy.'

'I'm twenty Mum!' Pete said.

It made Pete think how he could restore his parents' status instead of living in this miserable terrace house. He stored the ambition somewhere in the back of his mind.

'Are you behaving any better? I hope you have given up your underhand schemes. Sometimes I think you *are* still a child. You have to grow up and pass your accountancy exams,' she said, and patted the books on his desk to emphasise her demands.

'Oh Mum, don't go on at me. You sound like Dad.'

'He worries about you too, it's only natural. We only want the best for you.' His mother got up from the bed with a sigh. 'Promise me, lights out soon,' and she bent down to kiss Pete, her pearls brushed his chin, and he felt the cool touch of them on his skin.

As Pete's mother carefully descended the steep attic stairs, she thought about her intelligent but wayward boy. At a very young age he had been caught selling tapes of pop songs recorded off Radio Luxembourg to his school friends. At secondary school he had sold filed down aspirin tablets as fake "uppers" to his fellow pupils. It was this ruse that got him expelled.

It was fortunate that Mr Jagoda had persuaded Angus' father to allow him to return and sit his 'A' levels. It was also typical of Angus' kindness that he had also lobbied his stern father too. Pete's passes were not good enough to get him to university, but they were sufficient to be accepted as a trainee in a large accountancy practice in Leeds. It was one of the happiest days of his mother's life when he received the firm's letter of acceptance.

Once the sound of his mother's footsteps faded away, Pete picked up his paperback, he did not like being reminded of his own shortcomings: quick to learn, easily bored. Accountancy had proved fascinating but he hated the studying attached to gaining the qualifications. Pete's impatience churned him up inside. There was so much going on in the outside world that was out of reach. He felt isolated in his garret bedroom, tied to his studies and the tedious office. Meanwhile, his best pal, Angus, had left to live the high life at university.

He threw down his novel and placed a Supremes' LP on his Dansette record player and waited for the wailing exuberance of Diana Ross, as she sang, "*Baby Love*." He lay back on his bed and thought about his father, working assiduously in his little Chapel Allerton tailoring shop. He knew so little about him. He rarely mentioned his dead parents and relations. Pete suspected the memories were too painful for him to discuss. Occasionally, he would repeat a joke he'd heard from a customer and would chuckle as he recounted it at the dinner table. They were often quite funny. It revealed a rare glimpse of a different father, someone foreign to him.

His mother was equally opaque about working for the British government during the war. He wondered how his parents suppressed their anger about how the Germans had destroyed their lives. They had stolen their businesses, homes, entire families. Such cruelty was difficult to fathom, he felt weighed down by a deep sorrow for them. He really should learn more about the family story, a history that was in danger of being purposefully forgotten.

Pete stared up through his bedroom skylight, the streetlight outside casting an ersatz orange glow over the flaking paintwork of his bedroom ceiling. The nagging feeling of dissatisfaction with his own lot returned as the record needle scratched its way to the centre of the LP. He could hear shouting and laughter on the street far below, young people returning from the pub.

His thoughts returned to Angus, it must be their differences that had made them close. They were unlikely companions: Angus, studious, with an intelligent dry wit. He was sure there was an undiscovered side to Angus. Occasionally, he had glimpsed a vein of anarchy coursing its way underneath his mild public persona. On occasions, Angus had acted as a stooge for him at school to legitimise one of his dodgy schemes. Angus' authority was so authentic that if he gave his endorsement others followed. And he never asked for a cut. That was a failing. He was also aware Angus had secretly lobbied his unsympathetic father, to allow him to sit his 'A' level exams. It was an unasked-for kindness.

Now his old friend was in his second year at university and he missed his company. Although they caught up between terms, he sensed their old bonds were atrophying as they went their separate ways. He was also secretly jealous of Angus' free-wheeling, academic life - partying and being surrounded by attractive, brainy females. It also irked him that if he had worked a bit harder he could have been with his old mate. This stoked the embers of urgency to break his office drudgery and evenings stuck in a pokey attic bedroom.

He turned out his light and cursed out aloud.

'That boy is talking to himself again,' said his mother, from her bed on the floor below.

'Go to sleep, Felicja, you worry too much,' said her husband.

Chapter 4

'*Work hard, keep to the path of the Lord and the Lord will look after his own*,' was one of the Reverend Macintyre's many homilies.

His Scottish accent reverberated with Presbyterian tones of stricture and it was within this claustrophobic atmosphere that Angus and his sister Fiona were nurtured.

His father did not threaten eternal damnation but non-compliance of the '*Macintyre Word*,' hinted that catastrophes could befall them involving fire, brimstone and other assorted horrors. The Reverend Macintyre ran his school in a similar vein. His old fashioned views became the butt of jokes within the school and between Angus and Fiona.

'We moved to England for your benefit Angus, to give you the best chances in life,' was a phrase he trotted out with monotonous regularity. Angus saw through the hypocrisy, his father's move from Fife to an English school head's position primarily benefitted Macintyre senior's own career. His selfishness for his own success was boundless. However, he did share aspirations of high achievement for his son, but not with his more academically gifted daughter.

As Angus reached his teenage years respect for his father had become eroded by his constant demands to do better and better.

'Father, why can't you recognise that Fiona is much brainier than me,' he said one day, while seated around the Sunday lunch table.

'What is it with you boy, always questioning my judgments. What Fiona does with her life is not important. She'll have a husband one day who will look after her.'

'Not if he meets you. You'll frighten him away. Gretna Green will be her only salvation.'

'Angus, don't,' said Fiona. She giggled in half-fright that her father would have one of his rages.

'Oh come on father, we are in the 1960s, not 1860s. Fiona could be a doctor, a lawyer, a scientist, she's capable of more than you have ever achieved.'

'Don't be so damned impertinent.' The Reverend's face went puce, the contrast with his white dog collar was alarming. He was stung into brief incomprehension by his son's barbed remarks. For a moment Angus thought his father would get up and hit him, like he did when he was a small boy. Angus secretly hoped he would try. He was ready with his hands curled into fists under the table. He would love to give his father a good punching. It was well overdue.

'Hamish, control yourself,' said Angus's mother, placing a restraining hand on the clergyman's arm. 'The pair of you, stop this minute.'

'You have succumbed to the evil influence of Peter Jagoda. He's a bad apple, always has been from the day he came through the school gates.'

'You've never liked him because he wouldn't go along with your pious religious views. That's what wound you up.'

'How dare you.'

'Pete's an atheist. He doesn't believe in any religion, not even that of his parents.'

'Exactly my point. He's heathen, Godless.'

'Why can't you accept people with different views to your own? You've tried your best to break up our friendship for years.'

'Hardly. I allowed him to sit his exams back at the school didn't I?'

'You told me you felt sorry for Pete's father when came begging at your door,' said Angus's mother. 'Anyhow, I think he is a nice young man. What his parents went through in the war is beyond belief…'

Privately, the suffering of the Jagoda family questioned Mrs. Macintyre's belief in a redeeming Christ, in a God at all. Such thoughts she did not share with her husband.

'That never stopped him being a disruptive, lazy rebel,' said the Reverend.

'How was it he won the maths cup every year?'

His father got up, slapped his linen napkin on the table and stormed out of the dining room.

~

Angus first remembered meeting Peter when they were new boys at his father's grammar school. Angus immediately identified "Pete," as he was forever known by his acquaintances (but never his own family), as a rebel. At least his father's assessment was correct. But he had chutzpah, and Angus had never encountered anyone like him before.

The pair had not spoken for the first three weeks of term. One day, Pete was taking bets from a group of boys that he could climb to the top of the horse chestnut tree behind the cricket pavilion. Angus was meandering around at the back of the throng of excited pupils, they were keen to see the outcome of their wagers. Pete had collected nearly three pounds in two-shilling bets from his classmates. Pete was already halfway up the tree when he was spotted by the new physics teacher.

'That boy, come down immediately,' ordered the teacher.

'Sir, Sir,' said Angus. 'Jagoda is just collecting conkers for the annual competition. It's a school tradition.' Angus' honest demeanour, and his status as the headmaster's son, persuaded the sceptical physics teacher that Pete's mission had some legitimacy, if hazardous. He suspended punishment but forbade any further climbing. Despite the collective groan from the boys, Angus' unasked for intervention was the signature that sealed his bond of friendship with Pete.

Chapter 5

It was late March 1968, not long after Pete had been wrestling with his own thoughts in his attic bedroom, when Angus unexpectedly 'phoned his house.

'Fancy a pint or three?'

'Can't wait,'

'Regent, Chapel Allerton.'

'The best Tetley's in town.'

When Pete met his old friend he could not fail to notice Angus' dishevelled appearance. His hair was a black mass of curls resting on his shoulders and he sported a grubby white T-shirt emblazoned with: "STOP THE WAR," over an image of a burning Vietnamese child.

'I forgot to ask, why the hell are you here at all? Doesn't your term finish in another three or four weeks?'

'Guess what?' said Angus. A sheepish grin spread across his handsome face.

"Come on, what is it?" said Pete, putting down his pint.

Pete knew his old friend too well. He realised this was something serious. Angus was not given to grandstanding.

"*I have been thrown out.*"

'Of home?'

'No, *university*.'

'You *can't* be fired from university...can you?' Said Pete, amazed at what he was hearing. 'Angus, you were always such a goody-two-shoes. How have you managed that?'

'Simple: not attending any lectures or tutorials and drinking too many of these,' said Angus, holding his pint of beer up in the air before downing it in one long swig. He wiped his arm across his lips and continued with a hollow laugh. 'You see, I scraped through the first year by the skin of my teeth. But this year I couldn't be bothered to get down to anything. In fact, I have done bugger all work this term. It all got too heavy man, more bloody studying. I got a job in a pub and shacked up with a barmaid.'

'Angus, I can't believe it. *You* of all people.'

'It's true. As of yesterday, I'm O-U-T,' he said spelling the letters. 'I was given the gypsy's warning at Christmas and told to get my finger out, or else.'

'So, you carried on doing sweet FA?'

'The "or else" happened.'

'What about the barmaid?'

'She ditched me out when her old boyfriend came back on the scene. He'd done a short spell at her Majesty's pleasure.'

'What had he done?'

'Dunno, but he looked nasty.'

'Bloody hell Angus, you've become a rebel without a cause, eh?'

'No, I have plenty of cause really. You know I have been studying my arse off for the last six years. Talk about "*Great Expectations*." My father never stopped breathing down my neck. Then my university tutor and finally, the bloody Head of the Faculty. It was too much man, I've had enough. I never want to read another classic English novel, Shakespearian play, or a Beowulf poem. Sod the lot of them,' he said, slamming his pint glass down on the table with a bang. The noise was loud enough for the landlord to peer over the bar to see if there was a fracas erupting, his hand hovered nervously over the panic button that summoned the cops.

Pete was astonished at Angus' uncharacteristic behaviour. It suddenly dawned on him how little he knew his old friend. 'Your parents will go up the wall. You know what a stickler your old man is about education.'

'It's *him* that's the problem. He's still living like a nineteenth century Kirk Elder. He hasn't got around to acknowledging it's 1968, I don't think he gets the "my *ggg…generation* bit. They both laughed out aloud as they imagined Mr. Macintyre meeting Roger Daltrey.

'It's the same with my mum and dad,' said Pete. 'They just don't get it. My father was moaning the other day when one of his younger customers asked for flared trousers on his suit. If it wasn't for the female company in my office, I couldn't stand another day. You cannot imagine how boring my work is.'

'It's numbers all day long. Pretty mind numbing.'

'Spot on,' said Pete. 'I presume you've said nothing to your parents yet, otherwise your father would have nailed you upside down on a cross by now!'

'You know my God-bothering father too well, Pete. To be honest, when I got home, I just couldn't face it. I told them I got study leave.'

'Crikey! My advice is to tell 'em how you feel and take the heat now. They are bound to find out from the university soon.'

'You're probably right.'

'Anyhow, once the brown stuff has hit the fan, then what?'

'Well, that's what I wanted to talk to you about. Another pint?'

~

'Marrakesh,' said Angus.

'Isn't that in Arabia?' Pete said. Geography was never his strong subject.

'North Africa, you ignoramus, it's in Morocco.'

'Sounds miles away.'

'Not that far. We'll hitchhike to somewhere like Marseille in the south of France and pick up a boat heading for North Africa. We'll pile out at the first port then head for Marrakesh.'

'Hey up, what's this "*We*" business?'

'Of course, you'll come with me. You keep telling me how fed up you are working in your dull office.'

'Well, I am going, anyway. I told you, I spent last term working in a pub instead of going to lectures. I've saved up enough money to get by on.'

'You *are* serious about this. You make it sound dead easy, just throw up your job, or in your case, uni, stick your thumb out and you'll be in Africa in no time.'

'I've been doing some research: once we get to North Africa, we can take buses or trains, it will be safer than hitching. It's dead cheap.'

'Could we hire a couple of camels?'

'Don't be daft. We're bound to team up with people going the same way. Some mates at university went last year in a beaten-up Land Rover, they said it was fab.'

'Did they come back?'

'Not all of them, one of the girls got caught selling drugs. She's still in clink. You just have to watch your step and be sensible.'

'Will they let us in?'

'Oh yes, but we'll need some stamps on our passports, and a few jabs in case we are bitten by dogs, mosquitoes and what not.'

'Hell Angus! You've been doing plenty of homework. When are you going?'

'You mean when are *we* going?'

Chapter 6

Predictably, there was hell to pay in Angus and Pete's households when their plans were revealed.

'The demon drink has invaded your mind boy, I'm 'phoning the Bishop,' said the Reverend Macintyre. 'We'll all be praying for you to come to your senses.'

But it was a new, determined Angus that saw him through the family rows, cajoling and threats of excommunication. 'But father, it will help my French,' said Angus. This lame answer did not wash with Macintyre senior. His father was not listening. The Reverend saw his son's betrayal in ecclesiastical terms: the young man's mind was being controlled by unseen, evil spirits. In other words it was all Peter Jagoda's doing.

Angus recognised this was the moment he had to stand up to his bullying father. He was not going to be bamboozled by the Reverend's outraged religious piety, or give in to his dictates, what he referred to as "*God's plan*."

His sister Fiona came to his bedroom while he was packing. 'Gus, you rotter. You are leaving me to fight my battles with Daddy all on my own. It's not fair of you clearing off like this,' she said. 'I can't wait to get out of here too. I am afraid it will leave poor Mummy to cope with *him* all on her own.'

'It won't be long before you're off to Oxford,' said Angus.

'I've got to pass my exams first.'

'You'll walk them,' he said. He gave his sister a long hug. Fiona cried silently, her head cradled into Angus' bony shoulder.'

'You *will* come back, won't you?' she said.

'Of course. I'll be there to attend your graduation, I promise.'

Across town, the news was taken with equal fury in the Jagoda household.

'You're robbing me and your mother,' said Pete's father, his voice choking in disbelief, as the news of Pete's accountancy resignation sank in. 'You're selfish... you don't care about the sacrifices we've made to give you a good education.'

'You're throwing away your opportunities through wicked wilfulness,' said Pete's mother. In her eyes, giving up his hard-won accountancy job was commercial suicide, an act of vandalism from which her beloved son would never recover.

Of course, Pete didn't recognise this, he was an eternal optimist. To Pete it was not an abdication of responsibilities, rather an opportunity to see the world through a different lens. One of his own design.

The final departure for France was traumatic. Pete's mother remained mute, stoical. She thought back to the dangers that she'd been exposed to at a similar age. She could understand a youthful desire for adventure, but that was in wartime. Then she had a mission to fulfil. Her son's reasons were hedonistic and selfish.

Pete's father was blunter: 'You're finished. Don't expect to come home again and sponge off us,' he said. 'You've wasted your education and your career prospects.' Throughout this hail of harsh words and wasted arguing, Pete's mum lovingly ironed her son's shirts and underpants in preparation for the trip ahead.

The senior partner in Pete's accountancy firm tried to apply pressure. His dry arguments about life as a successful chartered accountant did not cut any ice with a headstrong twenty-year-old. 'You're throwing up a great opportunity, you've a flair for the work and one day you'll be a partner in this great firm,' he said, throwing out his arms as if he was Satan on the Mount of Temptation. He could not understand why, after offering this young man the world, he would not kneel and worship at the accountant's calculator.

Recognising his arguments were not having the transformative effect he had hoped, the senior partner dealt his trump card: 'And of course, do not forget your generous retirement pension.'

Retirement? In Pete's mind, pensions were meant for dead people. He had a life to lead, and he wanted it now.

'I'll be back in a year or two,' said Pete to his mother. 'I am not being drafted to Vietnam.' His mother kissed him lightly on both cheeks and whispered in his ear: 'Keep safe my darling, and give my love to France.' Pete was mystified by the remark, perhaps it was the memories of her travels with her late father. He soon forgot about it in the excitement of departure.

Up until the last moment, Angus' departure was no less eventful. His father disappeared early to church, believing his final prayers would bring about a miraculous intervention and save his son from eternal damnation and an unfulfilled academic education. Angus was relieved he did not have to face his father. Angus hugged his mother and held his sobbing sister in his arms on the doorstep. Mrs. Macintyre believed Angus' adventures would be the making of her son once he was unburdened from the shadow of his father. She knew instinctively that Angus' kindness, common sense, and surety of himself would see him through any eventualities. They were her comfort as she watched her tall, handsome son as he closed the presbytery gate; he waved briefly before he strode away until she could no longer see his bobbing grey backpack.

Angus was passing the church when his father emerged from the east door at a pace. Angus' spirits fell, he had hoped to outflank a last parting from his nemesis.

'Ah, Angus my boy, caught you before you disappeared into the wilderness.'

'I'm going to North Africa, father, not the Amazon jungle.' His father ignored the jibe.

'Take this with you,' he said, thrusting a tiny bible into his hand. 'I meant to give it to you last night. It will be a shield against danger you may encounter on your travels.'

'Thank you father. Don't worry, I am not going on a crusade,' said Angus, as he slipped the deterrent into his jacket pocket. 'I have to go now, I'm late. Goodbye.' He quickly shook his father's hand and walked off down the road before any further words could be exchanged. He did not look back. If he had done he would have seen his father standing, head bowed, hands steepled in prayer.

Angus resolved to dump the bible in the nearest bin he could find, the last thing he wanted was memories of his father to haunt his adventure.

Pete, like Angus, had hoped to make his departure as quickly as possible but was diverted by an unexpected offer from his father: 'I'll drop you off at the "Boot and Shoe" pub on the Great North Road. It'll give you a good start.' Pete hesitated as he wanted to make a clean break, but felt he could not turn down his father's kind gesture.

They drove to Leeds bus station and picked up a surprised Angus at their appointed rendezvous. The journey was painfully slow. Mr. Jagoda was not a natural driver. He saw many non-existent hazards and missed genuine ones. There were frequent violent swerves and fierce braking incidents, each accompanied by an uncharacteristic stream of Polish invective. Eventually the Austin Cambridge bumbled to a halt at the pub drop-off. Angus was first to get out, lugging his heavy rucksack onto the roadside. As Pete went to open his door, his father turned towards him and put a hand on his arm. 'Son, you should know your mother secretly wished she was going with you. She's always been a bit of a romantic... read too many Mills and Boon novels,' he said with a small smile. 'She wanted you to have this,' and he shoved four ten shilling notes into his hand accompanied by his grandfather's signet ring. It was wrapped in an exquisite lace handkerchief. 'She asked you wear it, she believes it will protect you.'

Pete was speechless at his mother's kindness. He slipped the ring onto the smallest finger of his left hand, it fitted perfectly. It had the initials of his grandfather: "AMJ." He was even more astonished that his mother was envious of his adventure. Pete leaned over and kissed his father on the cheek, something he hadn't done since he was a child. His father flinched, and Pete saw his father had large tears slowly rolling down his cheeks.

'Good luck to you both and remember to send us plenty of cards,' he said, as Pete clambered out. With a half-wave, his father shoved the car into gear and the Austin jerked off towards Leeds. Suddenly, overcome with emotion, Pete fought back his own tears as he waved at the disappearing vehicle, its brake lights flashing on and off.

'Look what my mother gave me,' said Pete, opening his hand to reveal the notes and the gold signet ring.'

'I hope you are not going to pawn it.'

'Never.'

'Come on, let's get going,' said Angus with a smile. He patted Pete's back as they walked towards a lay-by. They didn't have long to wait before a car stopped, and Pete's melancholy soon lifted. They both thought about their contemporaries slogging through tedious audits or trying to keep awake in stuffy lecture theatres. It was if a sudden lightness pervaded their senses and they smiled to themselves, both lost in their own private thoughts.

As they travelled south, Angus chatted to the driver, exuding his usual reassuring calmness, his hair was washed and combed, his jeans and T-shirt spotlessly clean. Pete was glad of his company. He needed Angus' unflappable common sense, meanwhile his stomach churned in fearful anticipation of what lay ahead. They had agreed before setting off that there would be no pre-set timetables. Marrakesh was the ultimate goal, but they would follow the tides of the moment, and where circumstance washed them up, they would hang out until boredom, love or poverty drove them onwards.

Their ideals were curiously portentous.

Chapter 7

'So much for the famous white cliffs,' remarked Pete as the "Maid of Kent" ferry steamed out of Dover harbour bound for France. A cold, swirling sea fog shrouded their view of the legendary chalk edifices as they pulled on heavy tweed jackets and wind cheaters.

'France, here we come,' said Angus.

'Let's have a beer,' said Pete.

Pete had never been abroad before and his disillusionment with foreign travel quickly became apparent. Their first night was spent sleeping in a field. The night was clear, their resting place a grassy undulation, the remains of a WW1 trench. It had become warm and the pair were tired and could not be bothered to erect their tent. 'We are under the care of the starry heavens, think of it as our sanctuary,' said Angus, in his usual poetic vein.

'More like purgatory,' replied Pete, as he curled up in his sleeping bag and tried to turn his lumpy rucksack into a make-shift pillow.

Next morning, they staggered stiffly into a café overlooking the curved east end of a beautiful medieval cathedral. 'Where the hell are we?' asked Pete.

'Soissons.'

'Nice church, if you are into that sort of thing.'

'My father would have approved. On second thoughts, maybe not. Too ostentatious, very Catholic High Church, it was another of his pet hates.

'Your dad had a lot of those.'

Pete lit up his third cigarette and forced down a tiny cup of bitter coffee. His ham baguette had scoured the roof of his mouth. 'Ouch. Bloody French bread, my mouth feels like I have been chewing razor blades.'

'You'd better have a croissant next time.'

Angus ignored Pete's moaning. 'We'd better get on the road,' said Angus, with quiet enthusiasm. It wasn't long before a small Renault Dauphine pulled up and a middle-aged man jumped out. 'Hop in boys,' he said, in good English. 'Where are you headed?'

'Paris,' they said in unison.

'We sound like the Everly Brothers,' said Pete, as his spirits rose.

'I can take you some of the way,' said the Frenchman.

The friendly driver explained he taught English in a French school but had trained in England. The man's attractive wife spoke some English and she told them they had just dropped off their son in Lille where he was starting his first job. The couple were heading home to Reims, and although the boys' destination was Paris, they decided to accept the diversion. After all, what was the rush?

Pete spoke no French, normally he remained mute and offered around his *Gitanes*. However, spurred on by the presence of an attractive, English speaking French lady, he leaned forward from the back seat to engage her in conversation.

'French clothing is so chic, ' he said, attempting to exercise some of his persuasive savoir faire. He burbled on about French dress sense and kept dropping 'Chanel' into his sentences as it was the only name he knew associated with French clothing. When he had exhausted this theme, he veered into French art cinema, a subject which he knew nothing, but he was determined to hold the good looking woman's attention. She smiled at him in a bemused way as she barely understood a word that he said. Her husband did some of the translation. After muttering uncomprehendingly about "*cinema verité*," and Brigitte Bardot. Pete remembered seeing a striking film poster somewhere for the film "*God Created Woman*." After that he dried up.

As Pete floundered, Angus came to his rescue, and diplomatically changed the subject and asked about the couple's son's new job as an engineer. Temporarily thwarted in his charm offensive, Pete slunk back in his seat and stared moodily out of the window at the rolling fields of Aisne.

They arrived in Reims at six o'clock. By now they were all on Christian name terms. Jacques and Adelene invited the pair to sleep in their garage which had a soft gravel surface, ideally suited for sleeping bags. The pair were invited inside for a supper of delicious soup and bread, cheeses, copious salads, and fruit. This was followed by some foul-tasting white stuff, called Danone, their first experience of yoghurt. They drank several bottles of red wine, 'Too much wine and I cannot teach,' said Jacques, and with a '*Bon nuit*,' he retired to bed.'

Angus, also tired out, disappeared with his sleeping bag to the garage. Adelene, now tipsy and flattered by the attention of the charming, dark-haired Englishman, was happy to flirt with her young admirer in the spirit of French *entente cordiale*. When Pete eventually crept into the garage sleeping quarters, he declared to a sleepy Angus, that he took everything unflattering he may have said back about the French.

The following day, Adelene drove the pair to the best spot to hitch to Paris. On departure, much to Angus's embarrassment, Adelene unashamedly kissed Pete on the mouth. Angus made do with a peck on both cheeks, '*Bon voyage*,' she said, with a broad smile.

'You're behaving like Sid James from a *Carry-On* film,' said Angus, as Pete waved at Adelene's car as it disappeared towards the city.

By a combination of two truck rides and a dodgy-looking character driving a vast Citroen Safari station wagon they reached Paris. This time it was Angus who was attracting attention as the driver kept winking at him in the rear view mirror. It was fortunate that for once, Pete was in the front seat.

By now it was early evening and the streets were bustling with people. Pete was fascinated by water flowing down the gutters at the road side. 'This place pongs a bit,' he said.

'French sanitary arrangements are not up the standards of home. You'll get used to it,' said Angus. It was only by a miracle of Angus's metro map reading and his basic French language skills, that they found their way to the Bois de Boulogne camp site. Tired beyond caring, they half-heartedly erected their shabby, Army Surplus tent, and crawled in, exhausted.

~

They were awoken next morning by a tramp who had untied the tent flaps and was feeling around for anything he can lay his hands on.

'Oi, what the hell are you doing? *Cochon*!' said Angus. "*Allez, allez!*"

He pushed at the smelly figure with a hefty shove of his large feet, still pinioned in his sleeping bag. The cushioned blow sent the miscreant rolling backwards uttering foul expletives.

They planned to spend a few hours in the French capital as tourists but they found some of the streets of Paris were like a war zone. The student riots were in full flow with vast, chanting crowds and street cobbles being ripped up and thrown at the riot police.

'We'd better get the hell out of here, before we get arrested,' said Angus. 'Our long hair will make us targets for the cops.'

'What are they rioting about, it looks bloody violent?' Said Pete.

'They don't like De Gaulle's repressive government, they want educational reforms and better social justice, and of course, every student wants to stop the Vietnam war.' They jumped on the nearest metro that was still running, and headed for the most southerly *porte*.

Leaving the metro station, Angus took out his compass and found the first road in a southerly direction.

It was not long before a large cement wagon picked them up and they jammed themselves into the noisy cab. Pete performed his newly learned French phrase, '*fumez-vous, monsieur*,' and handed out *Gitanes*. Angus made small talk with the grubby-vested driver. After about ten kilometres they were dropped off at a building site in a small Paris suburb.

The pair trudged off and reached the city boundary where they found themselves marooned on an endlessly straight, poplar-lined road. The early May weather was unseasonably warm. Angus stripped down to jeans and a T-shirt and Pete donned a checked, sleeveless shirt, which looked incongruous next to his heavy, twill trousers. During the next three, fruitless, hours, the two twenty-year-old Englishmen were sworn at, spat upon and they narrowly avoided being run down. Hitch hiking outside Paris was clearly an unpopular pastime, particularly if you looked like students.

The fashion for long, unkempt hair had not permeated mainstream French culture. They were being mistaken for rioting Parisian revolutionaries, or worse, German youths. One elderly 2CV driver mounted the grass verge in pursuit of Pete who had to throw himself into a ditch to avoid disaster. 'You'd think they would have more respect for the sons of their wartime liberators,' he said, as his patience finally ran out. His warm memories of his encounter with Adelene had quickly evaporated.

'Let's go back and find ourselves a café and have a break,' said Angus.

'Yep, it's too bloody hot standing out here,' said Pete. They slowly retraced their steps to the last suburban habitation and found a place of refuge in the form of a typical, small, café. There were a couple of customers leaning on the bar jabbering away with the patron. The boys threw themselves down at an empty pavement table. *Le patron* grimaced as he spotted the weary-looking, long-haired, youths. Probably student troublemakers by the look of them, he thought. He hesitated as he contemplated throwing them out, but business was slow and he needed the trade. He was well versed in ripping off strangers. In happier days, he'd owned a café in the Boulevard St. Michel in the heart of Paris's *6th arrondissement*. That was until his wife and business partner ran off with all the cash from the safe. The pair had even emptied from the till the day's takings. This injustice had done nothing to curb his irascibility.

'*Deux cafés et deux bières pression, s'il vous plaît*,' ordered Angus. The pair were slumped in skinny metal chairs, their damp clothing stuck to the seats. They both lit up cigarettes and sat in brooding silence, wondering if they could ever get out of the city. The smell of coffee and Caporal tobacco mingled with the distant murmur of French conversation helped them regain their equilibrium. They stretched their tired legs and cooled off in the shade of the striped awning. *Le patron* delivered the drinks, banging them down on the metal table top. He placed a pencil scribbled bill under one of the glasses. They both consumed the strong coffee before moving onto the cold beers. After a few minutes, Angus leaned forward and casually picked up the bill. He studied it and smiled quietly to himself before returning it to the table. Pete stretched forward and read it. 'Bloody hell, twenty-five new francs,' he said. Angus looked at Pete, then at the bill. Pete gestured with his thumb that it was time to do a runner.

'Let's finish our ridiculously expensive drinks first, and keep nice and calm,' said Angus. 'Then we'll scarper.' Once they'd drained their beers and the café owner was safely ensconced behind his counter chatting to his customers, they pushed back their chairs and bolted down the road, their rucksacks flapping as they ran. The pair darted into the first street they could find which merged into a busy open-air market. They giggled with guilty laughter.

'This town ain't big enough for the two of us,' said Pete, in a faux cowboy accent. 'Let's skedaddle.'

Chapter 8

Angus fished out his compass and they found an N-road leading in a south easterly direction. Refreshed, but anxious about being picked up by unfriendly gendarmes, they walked quickly away from the town.

As they were about to resume hitching, they noticed a busy fair in full swing up a side street. The street opened onto a dusty square full of roundabouts, dodgem cars and stalls. 'This looks fun,' said Pete. 'Let's have a look-see.'

'This looks better than the fairs we have at home,' said Angus, as he clambered on to a garish rollercoaster. As the roundabout gathered speed his fare was taken by a saturnine Romany, who showed off his acrobatic skills as he darted with ease around the rumbling, undulating surfaces, collecting fares. The handsome young man still found time to flirt with the girls with whom he showed off his ballet-like artistry. Angus hoped Pete didn't try to dodge his fare, fair ground people were best avoided when it came to getting into an argument.

Later, Angus found Pete as he was getting into a dodgem car. 'Where did you go, did you pay up?'

"Nah, I jumped off before he could get me,' said Pete.

Angus watched as Pete drove his dodgem with wild abandon. It only took a couple of minutes before he was involved in a heated argument with a young Frenchman in another car. At the end of the session they got out of their respective dodgems and squared up. A punch-up was about to kick off when the French boy was struck by another dodgem and sent flying. Angus grabbed Pete's arm and dragged him away. 'Pete you're a bloody liability!'

As they were hastily leaving the fairground, Angus spied a fortune teller's tent. 'I'll just pop in here for a few moments,' he said. 'No point in you going in Pete, you'll not understand a word said. Just wait here, and please don't get into any more trouble.'

'Okay, okay, I'll be a good boy. Anyway, I don't believe in any of that stuff. You're flushing money down the toilet.'

Angus's strict Presbyterian upbringing gave him an inherent fear of anything that smacked of the dark arts. Normally, he would avoid an encounter like this but somehow, he felt drawn into the fortune teller's tent. Meanwhile, Pete lay down on a small patch of dusty grass in the sunshine and lit up a cigarette.

Angus ducked down and pulled back the tent awning. He saw a young woman with dark hair and large gold dangling earrings seated on an old wooden stool at a low, round table. Angus noticed the stool's carved legs, a damask cloth covered the table that featured colourful signs of the zodiac sewn into the fabric. His first impression was it looked like a stage set. The table was complemented with a large, shiny crystal ball. The young woman smiled and looked up revealing a gleaming set of white teeth, save for one solitary gold fang in her lower jaw.

'*Dix francs, s'il vous plait, monsieur.*'

Angus pulled a crumpled ten franc note from his pocket and placed it in her heavily ringed hand. Immediately, she took his left hand and ran a finger across his open palm.

'Sit down,' she said. Angus could tell her accent was not French, perhaps Eastern European. Uncannily, she read his thoughts. I'm Turkish, and you are, Dutch, Danish?

'English,' said Angus, withdrawing his hand.

'You are a sensitive man but are capable of great anger. Show me both your palms.' She studied both hands for a full minute in silence. Then she pulled out a pack of tarot cards from somewhere under her voluminous, dark-coloured dress. Angus looked alarmed.

'Don't be afraid, I never use the death card.' She punched out the cards on the table assorting them into three separate piles. Angus recognised the joker card sitting on top of one of the stacks, he knew this signified optimism or trust in life. On the top of two other stacks were the lovers and the devil card which he did not understand. The cards' presence sent shivers down his spine, he could hear his father's strictures echoing in his ears on the evils of the '*unbelievers*.'

Angus sensed her prescience as she spoke slowly to him: 'You'll eventually find happiness, she hesitated, 'but you'll have to seek it out… I see children and a woman… there will be a foreign person in your life who is difficult to see. Friends will cause you problems, particularly with love. You like learning…but you are sometimes blind to see what is within your grasp.'

'Will I live in France?'

'No.' There was no hesitation. She pulled the crystal ball directly in front of her and stared at it intently. 'You're an interesting person, thoughtful and receptive to the channels. Your mind is open. Many people's are closed, they lock out the other side.'

She placed a scarlet shawl over her head and raised her hands above the ball. It appeared to have a life of its own, casting green and orange shadows across the tent canvas. Angus wondered if this mumbo-jumbo was an elaborate hoax. The girl began humming, rising to a dirge-like drone, tears began coursing down her cheeks. Oh hell, Angus thought, whatever she tells me I'm going to believe every bloody word. Why the hell did I come in here? He was about to get up and go when she put a hand on his and squeezed it tightly. He remained rooted to his stool.

The fortune teller's mutterings ceased. She threw off her shawl and wiped her streaked cheeks with a multi-coloured handkerchief. She turned and looked directly into Angus's eyes. The fortune teller did not blink. Angus experienced a sensation of someone searching inside his brain, he began to feel faint. It felt as if she had taken control of his mind, he heard her speaking as if she was a very long way off. 'Everything I see will not necessarily come true. Your fate is in your own hands,' she said.

Suddenly, Angus came back to his senses. It was as if he had awakened from a dream "Why were you crying?' he asked.

'Because sometimes I see things that make me sad.'

'What things?'

'You have to take control of events and not be led by others. Be careful of people close to you, they will cause you heartache and sadness.'

She turned away and said no more, the session was over. Angus got up to leave. 'Thank you, it has been an experience I will not forget.'

She returned him a faltering smile. 'Take heed of my words young man,' she said. 'Be determined to seek your destiny, it will not just come to you.'

Chapter 9

Angus stepped hesitantly out of the tent into the daylight, he blinked, felt light-headed as if he'd smoked a joint. Pete was lying on his back on the grass, his eyes were closed as he puffed on a *Gitane*, "Have you seen the future?' he said, without opening his eyes.

Angus said nothing as they plodded their way out of the noisy square, leaving behind the fair's flashing, tawdry, lights. Angus was thinking about what the medium had told him and ran over her words in his mind. He tried to banish the fear she had instilled in him. He thought about his father who would dismiss the medium's predictions as pagan nonsense.

It was five o'clock and too late to begin hitching again. Dark clouds were replacing the day's warm sun as they slogged along in a desultory fashion. They were very hungry and bought some radishes, saucisson and a baguette from a small grocery store. They squatted on the kerb to consume the contents. Later, they entered a tiny auberge and ordered beers and contemplated their next move.

'We'll have to find a place to pitch our tent soon,' said Pete. 'Fat chance in these urban surroundings, no sign of any parks anywhere.' They downed their beers and reluctantly ventured out and walked towards the outskirts. By now it was drizzling warm rain and they quickly become soaked. 'I never thought it rained in France,' said Pete. They walked for another twenty minutes until they came to a small twenty-four-hour petrol station. Dog-tired and in need of a proper wash, rather than relying on rainwater, they crept around the back of the forecourt building. They spotted a weedy patch scattered with used tyres, empty oil drums and assorted litter. It would have to suffice. They entered the filling station to buy some chewing gum and Angus asked the manager if they could pitch their tent out the back.

'There is an empty van on the front you can use if you like,' said the manager. He pointed to a Peugeot D3 van on the forecourt. 'There's room for the two of you to sleep in the back. If you give me five francs each you can use the petrol station's toilet and small shower room.' The boys quickly handed over the ten francs with grateful thanks to their saviour of travellers.

They both slept well, despite the hard metal floor. At a little after six thirty the following morning they woke up to the sound of the van's engine being started and the sensation of the vehicle moving. It took a few moments before they realised what was happening. As the van picked up speed, they could hear a radio loudly playing jazz music in the driver's cab. They looked at one another and started to giggle. They banged on to the driver's partition wall, but the driver was oblivious to their hammering. The vehicle continued to speed on its way.

There was nothing they could do so they sat back and waited for the van to reach its destination. 'Do you think we're being abducted by the gendarmes,' said Pete. 'They've clocked us after the café caper. I thought that station manager was too accommodating.'

'Nah,' said Angus. 'Stop worrying Pete. We can jump out when the van slows down.'

'Sounds too dangerous to me.'

Angus had taken out his compass and calculated they were going in a south westerly direction. 'Not too bad,' he said. 'At least we're not going back to Paris.'

They had been travelling for nearly two hours, speeding along undulating roads, they were occasionally thrown against the van's metal sides as the vehicle swung around corners. They peered out of the small back door windows and saw they were on a busy road with cars and wagons going in both directions. The rain from the previous evening had been replaced by warm sunshine and it was getting hot inside their tin box. They felt thirsty and hungry. Eventually, the van slowed down and they glimpsed out of the window a beautiful medieval city with painted houses. The van rattled as they drove over cobbled streets. Angus calculated they had gone about eighty kilometres when finally, the van slowed and turned off the road onto a paved surface and came to a halt. Angus leaped to the back of the van to look out of the window. He could see they were in the forecourt of another garage. There was piles of tyres stacked up and a man was driving a noisy forklift truck loaded with old worn canvases that he was wheezing around to the back of the building.

The driver's door slammed, and they heard muffled greetings from someone inside the depot offices. Quietly they opened the double doors and jumped down and made their escape. They darted unnoticed to the rear of the building. The boys could hear more voices, Pete peeked around the corner of the building and saw the driver return to his vehicle. He looked around in surprise as he found the van's back doors were wide open. He looked inside and found a cigarette packet with some cigarettes inside. He put them in his pocket.

'Blast! We should have shut the damn doors,' said Pete. The baffled driver looked around, searching for the phantom door openers. They heard him muttering to himself as he shut the doors with a bang. He backed the van into a bay and loaded new tyres into the rear of the van. It was hard work, one of Pete's *Gitane* fags was pursed tightly in his lips. Then Pete noticed the van driver had two large hearing aids, one protruding from each ear. When the vehicle was fully loaded, the deaf driver went back into the garage office, he emerged after a couple of minutes with a piece of paper which he stuffed into his overall pocket. Then, he jumped back into the van and roared off, none the wiser of his outward journey's human cargo.

The boys stealthily emerged from their hiding place to discover a small café adjacent to the depot and they slipped inside and ordered much needed coffees. 'Where are we?' Angus asked the proprietor.

'*Troyes, monsieur*.'

Angus purchased a new, more detailed map. The owner pointed with an oily finger the road they were on. Angus studied the map and after a moment, he looked up stared out of the window. There was an attractive auburn haired girl sitting on the kerb, she was obviously hitch hiking.

'I spy a fellow traveller,' he said. 'And beautiful with it.'

Chapter 10

Paris. Autumn 1967 - Spring 1968

'I'll see you at the Café Albert,' said Jean.

'I'm going to visit my Great Aunt this evening.'

'You never mentioned it.'

'I don't tell you *everything* I am doing every day,' said the girl, clicking her finger and thumb in annoyance.

Françoise was tired of her boyfriend's incessant needing to know her whereabouts every hour of the day.

She had started her foundation course at the fashion design college the previous September and her all important degree level studies in fashion at the Sorbonne would begin that autumn. Françoise lived in a tiny apartment in the *rive gauche* paid for by her controlling father. She did not want to be in halls with other young students and had badgered her father to rent the apartment. 'I want to be my own person,' she had said to her parents.

It was in the bohemian quarter of Paris, just off the Boulevard Montparnasse, in keeping with her proposed profession. In times past it had been the hang out for artists, writers, and philosophers. Compared with her hometown of Aix-en-Provence in the south of France, this was an exciting new world for an eighteen year old. She loved the isolation which had given her time to study without interruption, although initially, she had been home-sick. The only person she knew was her mother's aunt. That was until Jean arrived on the scene. Now she regretted hooking up with him as he clung onto her like clam.

'You look well,' said Françoise, to her great aunt.

'Well, I try to use the stairs when I have the energy,' she said. 'The old lift in this building is often broken, so sometimes I have no choice.'

'Doesn't the concierge look after the lift for you?'

'He's older than me and probably the lift. If he's not asleep he's reading a lurid paperback. He's a waste of time. If your Great Uncle was still alive he'd have sorted him out. Anyhow, enough of my old lady's complaints, how are you my dear?'

Françoise found her elderly and spirited relative much easier to talk to than her own parents, who told her only what she needed to know. In many ways her Great Aunt was more in touch with the modern world than her parents. 'Fine, thank you. I'm enjoying my little apartment on the Rue Notre Dames-des-Champs. It's very convenient for college and there are shops, cafés, and everything I really need nearby in Montparnasse. And when the weather is warm, I sit in the *Jardin Du Luxembourg* and read and draw.'

'You must be careful my dear, you're very pretty, like your Mama, when she was young, but good looks often attract the wrong type. Boys can be an awful nuisance and you need to concentrate on your studies, you'll have plenty of time ahead of you for all that nonsense.'

'You're right, Aunty, I do seem to attract the clinging type of young man. They can be very claustrophobic, always pestering me.'

'Oh, you must get rid of any like that. They end up being more trouble than they are worth. The secret of successful relationships is having *mutual* respect. If it's lop-sided it never works, my dear. Take it from me. I had an admirer before I met your Uncle. He used to *fawn* so, *he* got on my nerves. He was quite well off, his family had paper mills, he was desperate to marry me. I turned him down of course. Imagine having to go to bed with someone like that for the rest of your life!' she said, roaring with laughter.

'Oh Aunty, you're outrageous!'

'Now tell me, how is your Papa? Is he still as bad tempered as ever? I know I shouldn't say this, but I never understood why my sister's daughter ever married your father. I know he's been successful with his painting businesses, but he never seemed happy, even when courting your poor mother. I often felt your mother wasn't his first choice.'

'Who was?'

'I really don't know.'

'How sad, poor Mama.'

'I am sorry if I'm being indiscreet my dear, but your father can be such a *misery*!'

Françoise smiled at her Great Aunt, she recognised the kernel of truth in her comments. 'Yes, he can be grumpy sometimes, but he is always kind to me. I think he would have liked to have another child, a boy, if he could. It is a taboo subject at home. Maybe he feels he's a failure?'

'No. I think it was something deep-seated in him that's been there since the war. He was very brave when he was in the Résistance and I think that might have affected him.'

'He never talks about the occupation. There is a conspiracy of silence about the war, too many hidden secrets in our family, it really annoys me. My generation is much more open and prepared to discuss their emotions, my father and mother are so uptight.'

'Sometimes it is better to let the past stay in the past. The time we were invaded by the Germans was horrible for everyone, most people want to forget it ever happened. We were brought up to be private and get on with life as we found it.'

'But what about our famous philosophers here in Paris, they expressed themselves, talked about their feelings?' said Françoise

'They were the exception,' she said. ' Most people never understood them, or ever heard their views. It was confined to the intellectual elite and some of the middle classes, many of whom were shocked by their lack of morals and nihilism. After all, we were a Catholic country, the priests tried to keep us in check, but that never really worked. Many people deep down are selfish hypocrites.'

'Your father and his older brother, Philippe, were always squabbling when they were young. They were forever getting up to mischief, they drove my sister mad. Your father and uncle were brought up on your grandparents' farm in those days. When I got married I went to live in Paris, and I would go and stay with them for a few weeks in the summer. The 1930s was a wonderful time, Paris was lively and fun, but I missed the beautiful sea and the warm sun of the Mediterranean.'

'Sounds idyllic.'

'Then the war came along, and we had the Germans here.... it was very difficult, family loyalties got divided. It's a shame to see your Papa, only happy when he's shouting at your mother or someone else.'

'He worries about me too much, he can't understand I want to lead my own life. I think Mother sees my point of view.'

'She's a woman, she understands these things better.'

~

'Where were you yesterday?' Jean said. He was waiting outside Françoise's apartment door on the second floor of her building. 'We were meant to be going to the cinema to see the new Jean-Luc Godard film, '"Weekend."'

'I had to complete an assignment and stayed late at college. Come on Jean, we only had a tentative arrangement. You must not get so het up, you are getting more like my Papa every day.'

'I'm sorry Françoise, you know how I look forward to seeing you.'

Françoise took him in her arms and stroked his hair and face and comforted him like a mother calming an angry child. Jean was given to outbursts of petulant anger, but she knew how to calm him with a few kind words. 'We'll go another night. Let's arrange it for next week. Is it a date?'

'Okay, but you won't let me down again?'

'How were your law your studies today?' said Françoise, ignoring his wheedling remark.

'Oh you know, so, so,' he said, still trying to elicit sympathy.

Françoise had got used to his behaviour and ignored his whining. 'It's such a lovely evening, let's walk by the Seine at Notre Dame and have a drink somewhere? We could pretend to be tourists,' said Françoise.

'I want go to the Jardin du Luxembourg and then Café Tournon,' said Jean. Françoise could not be bothered to argue with him and let him have his own way. It would be a little victory for him and boost his inflated ego.

As they strolled hand-in-hand along the dusty pathways of the gardens Françoise mulled over her Aunt's comments in their recent conversation.

'What are you thinking about?' Jean asked.

'Oh nothing,' she said.

She had only started to date Jean soon after arriving in Paris when she was lonely. Now, she wished she had not encouraged the relationship. She was never especially attracted to him. He was a good two inches shorter than her, despite his Cuban heels. They had met in a bar near college, at first glance, he looked American preppy, close-fitting trousers, neat shirt, and leather loafers. On getting to know him, her initial attraction slowly turned to disappointment and more recently disillusionment. He had turned out to be self-obsessed, and like her father, a control junky.

She had tried to ration the number of times they met to twice a week. Then he got in the habit of turning up at her apartment unannounced. She had not the heart to turn him away. When she was reading or drawing, he would sit in a chair and stare at her silently. It was very disconcerting.

'Jean, will you *please* stop looking at me like a needy poodle.'

'I can't help it. I love looking at you. You're so beautiful and talented...'

'Oh, for goodness sake be quiet. I can't concentrate.'

Since the beginning of the January '68 there had been frequent student protests at the college. Demonstrations against the Government's education policy and the Vietnam War were some of the topics. Graffiti appeared on lecture room walls and outside the university buildings. It had started to get a little frightening.

'Students are here to study, not to foment revolution,' said Jean. They're anarchists who want to overthrow the Republic.' He was ultra conservative in his views and pontificated as if addressing a jury. Françoise had not given a lot of thought to the issues until they had been thrust in front of her since arriving in Paris. Despite her ambivalence, on principle she followed the student line as much to antagonise Jean. By early spring, Françoise was fed up with Jean's constant, controlling presence. She heeded her Aunt's advice, and told him the relationship was over.

Predictably, Jean whined in protest, then got angry and aggrieved. Françoise had to change the locks on her apartment door, as unbeknown to her, Jean had made a duplicate key. She only found out when returning from college she found him lying in her bed. She threw his trousers and shoes out of the window and told him if he did not stop pestering her, she would call the police. 'That won't do much for your chances of becoming a leading advocate,' she said. 'Now get out.'

In May the student protests escalated, and lecture theatres became occupied. The trades unions joined in solidarity and street riots started. The protests spread across France, it was near anarchy. The speed and strength of the discontent became alarming as workers occupied factories and then there was a general strike. The country ground to a halt towards the end of May. Because of the worsening situation, Françoise's father wired her money and demanded she return home. Her college shut down, meanwhile, Jean continued to stalk her, parking his car on the street close to her apartment. Finally, she decided to take her father's advice, and at the same time, shake off Jean for good.

Françoise bolted for home.

Chapter 11

France May 1968

'We are just outside Troyes. We need to be heading towards Dijon,' said Angus, as he brandished his new Michelin *routière* of France that he had just purchased in the petrol station. He had discarded his father's hopeless RAC map that only featured the major cities of Europe, and not much in between.

As they left the small café they decided to say hello to the attractive young girl sitting on the kerb waiting for her next hitch. A lift that would not be long in coming. She was sipping from an Evian water bottle and sunning herself. Pete sauntered towards her while Angus tagged on behind it was just like being back at school, Angus thought, Pete making the moves.

The girl had high cheek bones and straight, dark auburn hair that gave her a passing resemblance to Françoise Hardy, the singer of melancholy French pop songs.

As Pete edged closer to the girl Angus realised Pete had not the faintest idea what to say beyond 'Hello' in English. Angus grasped the initiative: '*Hi, ça va?*' he said.

'*Ça va bien*,' she replied. Her radiant smile made Angus's tummy flutter.

'*Comment vous appelez-vous?*' Said Angus, in his less than perfect schoolboy French.

'*Françoise.*'

'*Comme Françoise Hardy?*'

The girl laughed at Angus's flattering remark in his clumsy French.

'I'm just a fashion design student,' she said.

That figured thought Angus, looking at her chic, casual clothes. Angus introduced both of them. He guessed she was about eighteen or nineteen years old. She exuded a morning dew of youthful beauty, newly minted, her only blemish was a mole on her left cheek. She unfurled her long legs and rose from the kerb. She was tall and slim, her hair tied back in a knotted green band. The skin-tight, light blue jeans were cut off below the knee, a la mode. Angus noticed the white Sorbonne university T-shirt tucked into her jeans which was held in place by an expensive-looking, snake-skin belt. At her side was a bright red duffle bag stuffed to the brim. She pulled out a pair of stylish sunglasses and placed them on her forehead, her ensemble completed.

'We've just had a secret ride in a van,' said Angus. Françoise raised her eye brows in a questioning look, and Angus saw her flashing dark brown pupils.

'*Comment?*'

Angus continued, struggling with his halting French. 'The driver had no idea we were hidden in the back.' Angus told her how they had paid ten francs for their night's accommodation in the van and a very deaf garage worker had driven off without realising there were two English hitchhikers asleep in the back.

'Ahah, she said, finally beginning to understand Angus's twisted narrative. You were lucky, the driver might have robbed you,' said Françoise, laughing.

Where are you going?' Asked Angus.

'Aix-en-Provence.'

'Holiday?'

'To visit my parents. I needed to get out of Paris, too many riots.'

'And you two.'

'Marrakesh.'

'Wow.'

'Do you want come with us,' said Pete, in English.

Angus translated.

'Only as far as Aix,' she replied.

The boys did not take her comment seriously. Pete handed around the Gitanes, wanting to break into the two way conversation with Angus.

'Do you come from Liverpool?' Said Françoise, as she approached Angus, and gently gave his long, curly, black hair a tug. The same question had been frequently asked on their trip. Long hair was synonymous with pop, and pop meant Liverpool to the French.

'Do you play?' Françoise imitated strumming a guitar.

'The piano,' said Angus.

'Pop, classical?'

'Classical,' said Angus. Françoise nodded her head and smiled in approval. Angus wanted to kiss her there and then.

Meanwhile, Pete's frustration got the better of him. Angus was clearly making a good impression with this gorgeous girl and he was not getting a look in. 'Look, we all want to go south... yes?' said Pete.

'*Oui*,' replied Françoise, understanding this much of Pete's English.

'So why don't we all hitch together?' he said, putting his arm around Françoise's shoulder and sticking out his thumb out in a mock hitchhiking gesture. Angus felt an immediate pang of jealousy at Pete's intervention and Françoise's acceptance of being touched by him. 'You'll bring us luck?' said Pete, looking directly at Françoise with a big smile across his cheeky face. She understood enough of Pete's suggestion, and they all started to laugh.

"*Oui, oui, d'accord?*" she said.

Angus tried to dismiss his proprietorial thoughts about a girl he had only met ten minutes before. They walked a short distance away from the petrol station to find a suitable hiding place before Françoise started to hitch a lift.

Having an attractive female companion transformed their fortunes, and while Angus and Pete remained out of sight, Françoise stuck out her thumb and smiled at oncoming vehicle drivers. It was not long before a light wagon screeched to a halt. It was only after the vehicle had stopped that the hapless driver discovered he had two extra passengers. The two young men sprang into view from behind trees, dragging their heavy rucksacks with them.

Françoise kept her bargain, if a driver complained, she explained it was three or nothing. They all accepted. Angus and Pete were happy to be travelling south, but their sense of care for their female companion played on their minds. As Françoise endured the company of the garlic smelling, wagon drivers, the boys bounced around in the back of the lorries and took in the sunshine. Angus and Pete had no need to worry as Françoise was adept at looking after herself. She employed her persuasive charms to ensure drivers dropped them at the most advantageous locations for their next lift.

For the next two days they were constantly on the move. They had lifts in tiny vans, limousines and long-distance trucks. If they were sitting in the cab with the drivers, Pete passed around the Gitanes with a friendly, '*Bonjour*,' and then disappeared back into his own world. Meanwhile Françoise and Angus made small talk. Their journeys never lacked conversation, from, '*La révolution*' in Paris, football, Johnny Halliday and General de Gaulle's dislike of everything American.

At nighttime Françoise shared their small tent. The boys remained scrupulously chivalrous, making no midnight moves despite her being crammed in between the two of them. Angus offered her his sleeping bag but she refused and donned a sweater to keep warm. They both kissed her lightly on each cheek to say, '*Bon nuit*,' before they enveloped themselves in their sleeping bags.

Angus lay on his back staring at the frayed canvas tent awning and thought about Françoise. She was so near, but so far. Pete fell asleep and snored.

In the night, Françoise's hand strayed and lay on top of Angus, but sleep robbed him of the knowledge of this unintentional intimacy.

~

The closer the travellers came to Aix, Françoise's mind turned to her cantankerous father and world-weary, mother. Her father had not approved of her studying design in Paris. He would have preferred she had enrolled at Marseilles, where he could keep a closer eye on his precious daughter. Eventually, he came around to the logical argument that her Parisian course carried much more prestige, and the opportunity of better future employment prospects.

After their first day of hitching together, Françoise began to tune in to her new companions. She enjoyed their anarchic, amusing company, forever bantering among themselves although she could only understand some of their conversation. Angus did his best to translate for her. She also felt safer having two chaperones. Before they had met up, she had a bad experience of a man who tried to put his hand under her T-shirt and she had to dive out of the car when it stopped at traffic lights. Here anxiety melted at every kilometre south was a kilometre further way from the suffocating Jean.

'I'm going to ask my Papa if you can stay in one of his warehouses,' she said. 'It can be your home until you get your ship to Africa.'

'That would be groovy,' said Angus.

'What's your father's business?' said Pete.

'He's a painter.'

'An artist, like Picasso.'

Françoise, laughed. 'He paints houses.'

'Do you think he'll like having two English hippies sleeping in his building?'

'Probably not. My father doesn't have much time for Americans or Brits. He has a bit of a temper.'

'Doesn't sound very promising,' said Pete.

'Don't worry, I have my ways.'

You bet, thought Pete, a proper Daddy's girl.

'Do you have any brothers or sisters?' asked Angus.

'I wish I had. My parents wouldn't be so possessive.'

'Even your mother.'

'She's not so bad, but very Catholic. The church rules her life. My parents both love General de Gaulle. He *is* France to them.

'The students in Paris don't seem to agree.'

'Young people want to change the world, to be modern, like you.'

'Same at home, but we didn't rip up our streets and set fire to buses,' said Angus.

'I had other reasons for leaving Paris,' said Françoise.

'What was that?'

'I had an annoying boyfriend who wouldn't leave me alone. Coming here was a way of getting rid of him.'

'Didn't you tell him you were leaving?'

'No, I didn't want him following me.'

'Why?'

'Because he had became obsessive. I told him our relationship was finished, but he didn't take any notice. It was frightening, he used to follow me everywhere.'

'Sounds like a weird guy.'

'I don't know what I am going to do if he pesters me when I return to Paris in the autumn to start my new fashion course.'

'He'll probably have found a new girl by then.'

'I'm not so sure. He was like a limpet.'

'To look at,' said Pete trying to lighten the conversation that was getting a bit heavy.

Françoise laughed. 'More like a frog. He was studying to be a lawyer, he kept boasting about becoming one of France's leading advocates. He hated the student rioting, he would have had them all guillotined if he had his way.'

'You still don't do that in France do you? I hope he never becomes a lawyer, he sounds like a judge from the Revolution,' said Pete.

'Were his right wing views another reason why you get fed up with him? said Angus.

'I'm not political. I just love my fashion design work. I think he had a difficult relationship with his mother and stepfather. He was always complaining about them, I don't think they bothered about him much. He felt left out and ignored. I think he thought his mother had been stolen from him by his stepfather.'

'That could have been that root of his problems and his obsessive behaviour. An attention seeker, just like Pete, eh?'

'Very funny, Angus. And you're the crazy son of a firebrand preacher.'

'Shut up you two,' said Françoise.

'He's out of your life now, forget about him, you'll never see him again,' said Angus.

Chapter 12

At the end of the second day of hitching they arrived in the busy university city of Aix-en-Provence. Angus was excited as he knew that Aix was the home of Paul Cezanne, his favourite impressionist artist. 'Please, please take me to his atelier,' said Angus. Françoise nodded in agreement, 'Of course.'

'Cez who?' Pete asked.

'Philistine,' said Angus.

'Hebrew, actually.'

'Are you Jewish?'

'Better not mention that to my mother. But first I must persuade my Papa to let you camp out in one of his warehouses.' Françoise removed her belt from her jeans. 'Keep this for me, while I see my father.'

'Why on earth…,' said Pete.

'My dear Papa sent me an unnecessarily large amount of money for the train fare home. I spent his cash on cigarettes and this beautiful snakeskin belt from *Au Printemps* on the *Boulevard Haussmann*. Have you heard of it?'

'A very posh fashion store, a bit like Harvey Nicholls in London,' said Angus.

'Naughty, naughty,' said Pete.

Françoise took them to a café in the old part of the city and told them to wait. She disappeared into a phone booth at the rear of the café.

'What are the odds?' said Pete.

'Evens, I reckon.' Françoise had been gone for fifteen minutes. 'I think we have lost,' said Angus.

'Françoise said it might be difficult.'

Initially, her father's s reaction to Françoise's suggestion was predictable. Why should two English hitchhikers she had just met in Aix stay in one of his warehouses. Why hadn't she come home first instead of going into Aix to socialise. 'Are we less important than your friends?'

'Of course not Papa. The train station is in the centre of town and I just went to have a coffee.'

'Why can't these English stay in a camp site. There's plenty of them on the coast?'

'They did me a big favour. They got rid of a man pestering me in the café,' she lied.

'What man, where is he? I'll…'

'Calm down Papa. I have no idea where the man lives, he soon left after the boys had a quiet word with him.'

'How many times have I told you to be careful, my angel. Thank God you are home safe. Your mother will be relieved, she's been worried you might get mixed up with all the troubles in Paris.'

'It was a bit frightening, they threw cobbles at the police in the next street to mine and they even set fire to a bus.'

'The world has gone mad, come home quick, and you'd better bring the two English with you. It's only for a night.'

'Probably. They plan to catch a ship to Africa very soon.'

'Why are they going there, are they joining the Foreign Legion?'

Françoise laughed. 'They are going to Marrakesh.'

~

Françoise related the fabricated story to the boys, so they knew the chivalrous roles they had been cast. 'Not a word to my parents about hitching, they think I came home by train.'

'Our lips are sealed,' said Pete, putting his fingers on Françoise's lips. Françoise frowned, not understanding Pete's remark.

'It means we'll say nothing,' said Angus in French.

Henri Delores embraced Françoise for at least thirty seconds, kissing her on both cheeks and muttering tearful endearments. Angus and Pete looked on in embarrassment at this emotional greeting. Eventually, Françoise managed to disentangle herself from her father's embrace. Henri looked warily at the two long haired Englishmen and spoke in French to them thanking them for saving the virtue of his daughter. Pete got the gist of his language, but he could tell it was spoken through gritted teeth.

It was not long before they were dossing down in one of Henri's paint storage depots. Angus and Pete rigged up some rudimentary beds using old wooden packing cases that stood about a foot off the stone floor, out of reach of the scurrying rats that they had been warned inhabited the place.

'They need some cats in here,' said Pete, as they listened to scrabbling noises during the night. The make-shift beds were very uncomfortable and fell apart as they turned over in their sleeping bags, depositing them on the hard depot floor. The following night they tied them together with twine which worked better until the flimsy timber planks gave way under their weight, leaving them vulnerable to the nocturnal animal population.

The pair dashed off some cards home and spent a few days recuperating in the warm sunshine at the local lido. Angus made some tentative enquiries about passages to North Africa that sailed from Marseilles, their nearest port.

Françoise took Angus to see the Cezanne paintings. It was the first time he had spent time with her without Pete in tow. He was impressed by her knowledge of the great man and he relished having her all to himself. His French was improving and he was proud to be accompanying this beautiful girl who frequently received admiring glances from other men. The French were different, direct eye contact between men and women was much more overt than at home. He would just have to live with it.

At breakfast time on the third morning after their arrival, Françoise mentioned to her father the two itinerant Englishmen were likely to move on in the next few days as Angus had identified a ferry that was sailing from Marseilles to Tangier.

Much to Françoise's surprise her father asked whether they might be interested in staying to doing some painting work as he was very short of labour and had a lot of work on his books.

'You had better ask them, Papa. But be quick they are about to book a passage to North Africa,' she said, smiling at the thought she might have her trendy English companions a while longer.

Henri, put aside his reservations about Anglo-Saxons, and approached Angus with a proposition: 'You English, have you ever painted houses?' he enquired in broken, but understandable, English. He tried his best to smile encouragingly at Angus, but it was not a spontaneous reaction. In his few dealings with the two young Englishmen, he had been cool and Angus guessed he wasn't impressed that his precious daughter had befriended two hippy types.

'Some of my damn workers have walked out on me,' he said. 'I need help to finish a painting job for an important customer.'

Angus was not surprised of the fickle nature of Henri's employees if he treated them in the same abrupt manner he had experienced. He couldn't imagine that Henri bothered about good relations with his employees. 'Painting, oh yes,' said Angus, showing a conviction that even impressed himself. 'As students, we painted houses during our holidays.' Angus lied through his teeth.

It was all Monsieur Delores needed to hear.

'I'll pay you in cash, sixty francs a week.'

Angus paused, looked skywards as if contemplating a life and death decision.

'Sixty-five francs is my top price,' said Henri. It was about six pounds in English money. It should enable each of them to get by if they fancied hanging around Aix a bit longer. .

'Maybe,' said Angus. 'I'll have to talk to my friend, we were planning to leave in the next few days.'

'Let me know by midday, or I get someone else,' said Henri, returning to his usual curmudgeonly self.

By now Angus was enraptured by Françoise. He had been considering ways to delay their departure and this had all the makings of the perfect diversion. He had to speak to Pete. He knew Pete was being seduced by the warm sunny days of the south of France and the abundance of bronzed girls parading around at the lido.

The pair realised Françoise had become fascinated by her two long-haired travellers as she liked to parade them to her friends in the local bars and cafés, like exotic animals in a zoo. They burnished Françoise's new persona as a cool Parisian art student, importing her modern, new friends to provincial Aix. Angus and Pete enjoyed their new status, however bogus. They opted into the game of personifying the new hip, youth counter culture that was prevailing in the UK and US. They were both in thrall to Françoise, and if it made her happy, why not?

Pete's gregarious nature attracted girls, Angus posed as a more mysterious, ethereal figure, a man of deep thoughts, mostly about Françoise. She was never short of admirers but neither Angus nor Pete, could work out if she was serious about any of them. In company, she preferred to stick to her new English proteges.

Pete was returning from buying some cigarettes at a nearby *tabac* when Angus greeted him with the news of Henri's proposition 'You'll never believe this,' he said. 'Henri has offered us work painting villas for a few weeks.'

'What did you say to Monsieur Angry?'

'I told him we could be interested, but I had to ask you. It would mean postponing our trip for a few weeks.'

'Sounds interesting.'

'I think old Henri might be a bit desperate. Oh, by the way, I've told him we are both expert house painters and painted houses back home during the hols.'

'I've never lifted a brush in my life, except to paint aeroplane models,' said Pete, giggling.

'You'll be more than qualified. You can be our expert on the detail stuff, like drainpipes and guttering. What do you think?'

'What's he paying?'

'Sixty-five francs a week.'

'Offer him seventy-five if he's that keen,' said Pete.

'Okay, I'll have a word.'

Henri scowled at Angus's revised offer.

'Seventy francs,' he said, 'and if you're no good, you're *finis*!'

'Great! I could always do with a bit of extra cash,' said Pete, after Angus returned to tell him the news. 'We can continue on when the job's done. The money will pay for our sailing. And it *is* nice here.'

'Oh, another surprise. Monsieur Delores spoke to me in broken, but understandable English. God knows where he's learned that. We'd better be more careful what we say when he's around.'

Monsieur Delores swallowed the boy's story about their student painting. After a week's trial, he spoke to Angus. 'I'll keep you on but you are using too much paint. And tell your friend to hurry up, his work is good, but too slow.

'He's not Cézanne,' he said.

Chapter 13

Angus and Pete enjoyed their mindless painting work but tired of their uncomfortable, rat-infested, sleeping quarters in Henri's workshop. The last straw was when Henri demanded they pay a rent for the accommodation by knocking off some of their wages.

'Let's ask Françoise if she can find us somewhere more civilised. I had a rat crawl over my legs last night,' said Angus.

'Having to wash at the local piscine is an arse,' said Pete.

It was not long before they were inspecting a tiny, one room apartment for rent above a café. Françoise had received a tip from a friend and the three of them went to look around the proposed new digs. It was so small, it only took a couple of minutes to inspect. It consisted of two beds, a tiny hot ring, in a corner hung a grubby curtain behind which lurked a small, dirty-looking sink with a cold tap.

Down a dimly lit hallway there was a filthy shower and a smelly lavatory consisting of a hole in a stone slab which they would have to share with three Algerian itinerant workers, and an ancient French lady, called Odette.

Compared with Henri Delores's warehouse floor it was the Ritz.

It did not take them long to settle in and they quickly became accustomed to living over the café. It was their canteen, French style, and the centre of their social life. The Algerian workers were monosyllabic and exuded a threatening air about them that did not invite dialogue.

Odette was more approachable. When she emerged from her room she would squeeze past them on the narrow corridor and would give each of the boys a lascivious wink. Angus averted his eyes in deep embarrassment, while Pete revelled in the outrageous flirtation and would reply in his dreadful French, '*Bonjour ma belle*,' which Odette would return with a throaty cackle of laughter.

She wore a flimsy white, diaphanous cotton garment that revealed her wrinkled, semi-naked figure beneath. She never went anywhere without her tiny white poodle called, "*Fifi*," which she cradled in her skinny arms. They discovered the little dog was in the habit of crapping in the shower tray when Odette was either too drunk, or could not be bothered, to put the animal into the narrow street to complete its ablutions.

Over time, the boys got in the habit of talking to her in the bar and they discovered she was a rich source of racy stories. At some stage in her long career, on the edges of the demimonde, she worked at the famous *Folies Bergère* in Paris as a dancer *risqué*. The remnants of her once good looks were still visible under her sun-damaged complexion and the ravages of cigarettes and booze. She told them she'd once been married to an Austrian Count (*il était cruel*). Her second and last husband was a member of the French Government who turned out to be a cross-dresser.

'I came home one evening find him wearing one of my best evening gowns, plastered in make up and smothered in my expensive Guerlain perfume. Odette took a particular shine to Pete who liked to put his arm around her and gently squeeze her withered, dangling breasts. She giggled like a schoolgirl at this antic, but Pete had to be careful when *Fifi* was sitting on her lap as the dog was apt to nip his straying hands.

Odette never confessed to being a courtesan, but it was clear she had encountered many of the stars of France's literary and film world before the war. Whether these entanglements were social or in a "professional capacity," she never let on.

'Albert Camus, he was *tellement sérieux* ...I met Jean-Paul Sartre and his muse Simone de Beauvoir, Maurice Chevalier, and of course Ernest Hemingway, he always came to our parties, *il aimait les femmes*.'

She related how she had remained in Paris during the war and boasted unashamedly about her associations with many members of the German High Command based at the *Hôtel de Crillion*.

'Those Germans, always clicking their heels and bowing, with their big shiny boots, so self-important. But they were all the same in bed. They wanted their mothers and were afraid of dying just like the rest of us.'

'If you spent so much time with the Nazis, weren't you seen as a collaborator after the war?' said Angus.

'I was working for the Résistance, pillow talk can give you plenty of information. Those stupid *boches* never suspected anything. I was so good at it, I should have been an actress. The Government gave me a Croix de Guerre after the war,' she said.

'That must have been very dangerous work.'

'They had invaded my country and ruined Paris. It was so grey with their uniforms, checking on your papers and gothic signs everywhere in German. It was a bad time. But I drank plenty of champagne, that was my reward.'

After work, Pete got in the habit of knocking on Odette's door and inviting her for a drink in the bar. 'You've got the hots for Odette,' said Angus. 'She's old enough to be your granny.'

'Button it,' said Pete. 'She's a minefield of fascinating stories. I've never met anyone like her, she's amazing.'

After being plied with Pernod and water, Pete extracted more outrageous anecdotes from her colourful past. Her English was good enough for Pete to understand. How much was true, and how much fiction, he was never certain, for she was an accomplished storyteller.

'You should write a memoir,' said Pete.

Odette had moved from Paris to work as a croupier in the casino in Monte Carlo. 'You can triple your wages with tips from gamblers when they had a big win, they would slip you a few chips when they left the tables,' she said. She gave Pete a wan smile as she remembered happier, more affluent times. 'Men who gamble are often not interested in sex, playing the tables is their substitute,' she said. 'Who knows why, I don't know, but they like to see a pretty face dealing at the tables, turning the roulette wheel or taking the cards from the baccarat shoe.'

'Remind me never to take up gambling,' said Pete, nudging her arm.

Odette blamed her reduced circumstances on her last lover who said he was *Les Grand Chefs Arabes*, an Algerian aristocrat, called Maghreb. He stole her savings and vanished. Whenever his name was mentioned, she spat on the floor until the café patron shouted at her to behave. Invariably, this would ignite a furious shouting match between the pair.

Odette's exciting narratives did not offset the inconvenience of avoiding the dog faeces-stained shower tray. The boys went back to using the *douche* at the local *piscine* for their ablutions or plunging into the azure Mediterranean. But the salt water was no substitute for soap and warm water.

What they would do when winter came had yet to be figured out.

Chapter 14

Angus and Pete's decorating work frequently involved them staying away for several nights rather than trekking back to Aix. They kept their lodgings allowances and got in the habit of dossing down in the company's Citroen 2CV van, sleeping among spent brushes and decorators' paraphernalia. On very warm nights, when the paint fumes became dangerously intoxicating, they reverted to sleeping on beaches or where they could find a patch of grass. If the weather was poor, they booked into cheap rooms.

The two become experts at seeking out back street dives for entertainment and avoided the fashionable, expensive, bars of the Côte d'Azure. They developed a well-rehearsed routine posing as rock stars to crash clubs and woo girls. Pete was the most convincing, but one night they had a close call when a club manager, sensed the English pair were con artists invited them on the stage to jam alongside the resident band. Angus managed to play a "Whiter Shade of Pale" on an electric keyboard, but Pete feigned a 'sore throat' that prevented him from singing and he suddenly disappeared.

'You can stay for the rest of the season if you wish,' said Henri, one morning, before they set out for a day's painting. 'I will pay you eighty francs a week.' This was a surprise as Henri's unaccountable coolness towards them had not got any warmer over the weeks they had been working.

'His Algerians painters are unreliable, have you noticed how quickly they keep changing. I've not worked with the same guys more than once,' said Angus.

'He's prepared to pay us a bit more because he really needs us,' said Pete. 'We should ask him for more.'

'Let's not push our luck, he might take the huff and tell us to get lost. You know how unpredictable his is, ' said Angus.

'Isn't staying on for the whole summer an admission of giving up on our original plans. It was you that wanted to go to Marrakesh?'

'I know, but I am rather enjoying our careless life of freedom. It was what I *wanted* when I left home.'

The pair had slipped into a routine which was so far distant from their previous incarnations as could be imagined. But secretly, Angus wondered how long this Arcadian existence would last. He was still achingly hankering after Françoise but still dared not make the move in case he was rejected. He realised that painting houses and partying would become as boring as studying medieval literature, but if Françoise was in his life it would be tolerable. If the planets did not align with her it would be time to move on. Unless, God forbid, Pete beat him to it. He never gave up trying it on with her, but she never took him seriously. But did anyone ever take Pete seriously?

'What do think, Angus?' said Pete, as they trundled down the Corniche in their little grey van onto their next painting assignment.

'Shall we give it until the end of the summer when we'll *have* to go elsewhere to find work.'

'Okay, I am cool with that. What's the weather like in Marrakesh during the winter?'

'It's quite warm, the nights tend to be cool, so my research told me in the university library.'

'You did *some* work then.'

'We could probably get a job on a farm. They grow a lot of fruit, and we could team up with other travellers once we are there, and there's plenty of cheap weed to keep us happy.'

'Sounds like a plan.'

'I'll tell Henri and see if I can get him to smile for once in his life.'

~

It had not taken Angus and Pete long to become acclimatised to life in the south of France and now the decision to stay until the end of the summer had been made, they embraced French living. They enjoyed their simple diets of salads, seafood, copious French cigarettes and cheap wine. They even began to take for granted day after day of warm sunshine. They both became unrecognisably tanned from working out of doors and discarded their heavy English clothing and adopted shorts and T-shirts.

'I don't know how Henri attracts all these wealthy customers. There must be other painting contractors around here. Do you think he is in some secret club?'

'He can't be a Mason. Catholics in France are forbidden from joining, the dark arts and all that,' said Angus.

The boys were intrigued with the money that exuded from the fabric of many of the villas they worked on. They were located in one of the most sought-after stretches of coastline anywhere in the world.

'Perhaps Henri has mafia connections?' said Pete.

'More likely old war time networks, some back scratching from building contractors and other trades people,' said Angus.

The pair remained invisible to the rich and famous that inhabited this oasis of hedonism and beauty. Their little 2CV painter's van trundled anonymously down the boulevards and narrow streets. They were happy being one of the many tiny cogs of the local economy, busy drones to service the needs of those that have plenty.

Angus found his new existence liberating being away from the *realpolitik* of normal life. It was an enjoyable alternative reality. In this environment original thought no longer weighed him down. He drifted from one day to the next, dreaming of Françoise. The largest villas they painted were reminiscent of F. Scott Fitzgerald's, *Tender is the Night*. He marvelled at the impossibly glamorous lifestyles of the very rich Americans who had frequented the Côte d'Azure during the decadent summers of the 1920s. Sometimes, he had to pinch himself that he was really on the real-life set of those vanished days.

In contrast, Pete was fascinated with the wealth associated with the grand villas. He gazed longingly at the manicured lawns, exotic plants, and expensive statuary and wondered how he could own such a place one day. Occasionally, they glimpsed a beautiful Italian sports car or an expensively dressed occupant but they had strict orders not to speak to owners unless spoken to.

During their evenings away from Aix, carousing in bars and clubs, Angus always attracted more girls than Pete. This sometimes caused friction. But Angus's interest was only peripheral, he soon got bored, none were a match for Françoise. Pete, despite his dark good looks, was too pushy and obvious. One evening Pete got very angry with Angus about a girl that had taken his fancy. She was a petite blond that only had eyes for Angus, perhaps it was Angus's indifference that attracted her. Pete had tried his best to ingratiate himself with her by spinning some implausible line about training with NASA to be the first Brit in space. He had even procured cards bearing the NASA logo to back up his tale which he liberally dished out to disbelieving female admirers. His paint-stained hands were always the giveaway.

Angus saw no reason why he should give way to Pete and his carnal ambitions, and he quietly enjoyed riling him. His friend made the bumptious assumption that he should have first choice from any of the many females they encountered on their nighttime excursions. It never occurred to Pete that some girls might not succumb to his ridiculous blandishments, he seemed to forget that it was the girl who would do the choosing. Pete's fantasy stories rarely worked beyond a couple of dates until he was rumbled for being a charlatan. But Pete was thick-skinned enough to take these set backs in his stride. There was always another bar, another girl to charm.

One night Angus had some success with an attractive blond girl that Pete had failed to woo. Unusually, they had a furious argument on the way back to their digs and each slunk into their respective beds in angry silence. They had been living together and working on top of one another for too long, thought Angus. Although he didn't want to admit it, he knew their relationship was fraying. Marrakesh was now only a mirage.

To add to the disharmony, Angus was irritated by Pete continually trying it on with Françoise. It heightened his worries about losing her. Pete knew Angus pined for Françoise and he enjoyed flirting with her in front of Angus. As the summer wore on Angus's confidence of making a move wore thin, he could not bring himself to take the leap for fear of outright rejection. He was also riven by a sense of misplaced loyalty to Pete about abandoning Marrakesh. He knew if the tables were reversed, Pete would have no such qualms.

Unbeknown to Angus, Françoise was frustrated at Angus's perceived lack of initiative, *sans souci*. She lay in bed wondering if he didn't like her after all. Was her hair too long, was her blasted mole putting him off, were her breasts too small? Self-doubt stared her in the mirror. Perhaps he was gay? God no, he couldn't be, she'd seen the way he looked at other girls. Pete relished regaling her of their exploits on their overnight painting excursions which made her jealous. She was not sure if Pete was trying to drive a wedge for his own ends.

Then one evening it happened. Pete was away playing cards. Angus and Françoise were outside a bar sitting on an old stone wall, her long bare legs were nearly touching his cut down faded jeans. Angus was talking quietly to her in French about his wasted university studies. Françoise, unable to hold back her emotions any longer, put her hand on the top of Angus's bare leg and turned towards him. She brushed his cheek with her hand, and said: 'Angus, why don't you ever kiss me?'

Chapter 15

War Time France 1944

The destruction of the troop and armament train had been an unprecedented success. How many Germans had been killed and the amount of disruption caused would only be known in time. They would have an inkling of their effectiveness by the level of German reprisals on the local population that were bound to occur in the coming hours and days.

The far-reaching implications of the boy's involvement haunted him as he made his way back to his home farm. The images of the carnage and the charge through Rognac forest with the Agent suffused his mind. The memories were both terrifying and erotic in equal measure.

During his danger fraught return to his farmhouse his heart thumped and he felt unable to breathe. He had irrational worries that the Agent had fallen into Gestapo hands. His hand moved to his face where the brush of her lips had unexpectedly touched his cheek. He placed his fingers under his nose to detect her odour, but the only smell was the rank secretions of his own fear.

To reach the sanctuary of home he had to traverse seven kilometres of countryside, which included crossing a busy road frequently used by German patrols. *Les boches* would be scouring the area once the news of the train attack spread and they would be desperate to root out the culprits. There would be hell to pay in the local towns and villages. Nobody would be safe; innocent or guilty.

He calculated he had time to reach his farm in darkness provided he did not run into any patrols, but he had to hurry. He was finding it difficult to concentrate, his head was spinning at the thought of the Agent's unflappable courage, the softness of her gloved hand, and the kiss...

As he half-ran, half-walked over the fields his ears still rang with the grinding noise of the lumpen locomotive derailing, and the sound of splintering trees and screams of the trapped soldiers. On his journey he sometimes disturbed a grazing cow and frightened himself as much as the beast. He crept behind low walls and weaved through thickets of trees to avoid detection. He thought of his compatriots and if they were safe; their faces flashed through his mind, farmers like his parents, shop keepers, bandits, and professionals of all ages, comrades with common cause. And how long it would be before he saw *her* again.

His partisan group would have to hunker down after such a big raid. It would be a while before he saw the yellow Aix flag flying on the church tower, the signal for a meeting of the *Maquisards*.

Some outer fringe members of the *Maquis* lived in woods as self-contained guerrilla groups. In many ways those that lived in the community were more vulnerable as they were in plain sight of the Germans and informers. Every clandestine briefing meeting held was fraught with danger. They had to be doubly diligent after a successful mission, overconfidence could creep in, leading to sloppy security. The *Maquis's* spirits were running high, the Allied invasion was anticipated soon and they were receiving more ordnance and arms by RAF airdrops. Gradually their ancient rifles were being replaced with Sten guns, sophisticated explosives and grenades.

The Agent's orders to get home without detection rang in his head. The night's actions had forged a special bond between the boy and the Agent. For the first time he had experienced an adult feeling of belonging that made him feel alive, invincible. As he edged closer to his farm, a surge of excitement engulfed him. He was desperate to share the success of the evening's mission, he needed a third party's affirmation that his murderous actions had struck a blow for France.

He pushed on quickening his pace but before he could reach home he had to navigate the dangerous main road used by German patrols. As he crept through tall reeds close to the road's edge, he heard the roar of a lorry engine in the distance as it headed towards him. He waited hidden among the spiky foliage, crouched low, silent. The heavy vehicle slowed to a halt at the junction of the lane that led to the farm. The boy cocked his rifle and held his breath, he could hear German voices arguing in the cab, the wagon continued to idle, the lorry door opened and he heard the sound of heavy boots landing on tarmac. It was quickly followed by the rasp of a match, the boy could see the silhouette of a soldier and smelt the aroma of caporal tobacco. The infantryman stared in the direction of the farmhouse as he drew on his cigarette. The boy was less than twenty feet from the German, he dared not move an inch. After a moment, the boy saw a lighted cigarette butt arc through the air and land on the roadside close to his hiding place, it glowed in the darkness before it went out. The soldier stood listening for a moment longer and then turned and climbed back into the cab, the engine revved and the lorry jerked forward. As it disappeared in the direction of the town, the boy caught a brief glimpse of troops under the canvas in the rear. His stomach fluttered with relief, his feelings were tempered by the thought of what awaited the town's inhabitants. Doors would soon be hammered with rifle butts, followed by arrests and beatings.

He stayed hidden in the reeds until the only noise he could hear was the croaking of frogs. Then he slowly edged towards the road and sprinted across the tarmac into a vineyard, where he ducked down behind a row of neglected vines.. There was still no sound, so he ran towards the edge of the vineyard and scrambled over a low stone wall into the farmyard of his home.

He hastily buried his rifle in a heap of straw in the second of two barns, and tip toed across the yard and quietly lifted the farmhouse latch door and stepped into the darkened kitchen.

'Where've you been?' said a voice out of the darkness. The boy was shocked to find his father, partially hidden, in the larder doorway, waiting for him.

He was briefly transfixed with fear that his father knew of his clandestine activities. Manhood may have knocked at the boy's door that evening but he had not lost the childhood fear, that through some strange parental alchemy, they always divined when you had done wrong. He resisted the temptation to boast of his achievements.

'I've been with a girl,' he said. That was not a lie.

'You idiot! Don't you know there's a curfew. If *les boches* had spotted you could have been shot?'

'I know Papa.'

'If you're mixed up with those damn partisans, you'll get us all killed. Have you thought of that, it's just not you, it will be all of us who will face a bullet.'

'I know,' he said. The boy couldn't erase the image of the carnage he had created a few hours ago. It made him shake with fear.

'If I suspect you're up to something I'll have a word with your brother, Philippe. You know he's in with the *Milice*, it's his job to find Resisters.'

'But Papa, Philippe's a damn traitor.'

'Enough of your language.'

The boy was deeply ashamed of his collaborator sibling, he hated the arrogant way he strutted about in his blue uniform and cap. 'How can you bear the fact that he's doing the Germans dirty work for them.'

His father ignored the jibe. 'Who's the girl you were seeing? You're too young to be getting involved with women.'

The boy did not answer but made for the staircase to his bedroom.

'Who is she, dammit?'

The boy turned in the direction of his father across the gloomy kitchen. 'That's my business,' he said, and disappeared up the stairs.

'Remember what I said about your brother,' said his father after him. 'I'll not tell your mother of your exploits this time, but if you come home in the middle of the night again you'll have her to deal with.'

~

The following morning after the boy had left for work his mother had just removed a garlic bulb hanging from a hook on a kitchen beam. She planned to peel the bulb and put in a salad for her husband's lunch when a German kubelwagen with three soldiers in it roared into the farmyard. She dropped the bulb onto the kitchen floor in terror as she watched the vehicle carelessly come to a skidding halt half-way across her vegetable patch, crushing precious salad leaves, leeks and onions. Three soldiers piled out shouting loudly in German and waving their rifles about. The group was led by a fat sergeant who barged into the kitchen without knocking and barked loudly at the boy's mother in broken French: 'Where's you husband?'

'He'll be in the cow shed, milking, she said, pointing across the yard. The sergeant shouted an order to the soldiers and a couple of moments later one of the soldiers marched the boy's father into the kitchen. He was trembling with fear. Meanwhile, two shots were heard from outside as the remaining soldier shot a pair of chickens to take back to the barracks. The captain shouted through the window to stop it and get searching the barns.

'Where were you last night?' He demanded of the boy's father.

'At home, of course. There's a curfew.'

'Don't be clever, you'll regret it.'

'It's the truth, he was here,' said the boy's mother, on the point of tears.

'Keep quiet, old woman.'

The captain barked more orders and the other soldier started his search of the farm banging open cupboard doors and draws and throwing the contents onto the floor. Plates and jugs got smashed while the sergeant ordered the boy's parents to sit down poking them with his rifle as the ransacking continued.

'Try to move and I'll shoot you,' he said.

The sergeant took out a large hunting knife from his belt and ripped open the few threadbare cushions in the couple's possession. Then the soldier went up stairs where there was more loud banging as their measly contents were scattered about, beds turned upside down, mattresses and pillows opened, disgorging straw and feathers which drifted down the stairs to where the couple were frozen to their seats, rigid with fear.

Suddenly, there was shout from outside and the third soldier came into the kitchen brandishing a rifle in his hand and handed it to the sergeant. The sergeant snatched the weapon and studied it carefully. 'Ahah, a Lee Enfield.' Triumphant, he turned to the boy's father with a cruel smirk across his face.

'Monsieur, this is a *British* rifle. What's it doing here?'

The boy's father looked horrified. 'I've no idea, I have never seen it before,' he said, his voice cracking with emotion.

'Pig!' shouted the sergeant and drove the rifle butt into the boy's father's face. The farmer fell off his chair onto the stone floor, his nose gushing blood. His wife made to help him but was pushed roughly back into her seat by the fat sergeant with the rifle barrel. Then he shouted in German to the two soldiers. 'Take him away.' They dragged the whimpering, blood-stained man out of the cottage and threw him into the back of the kubelwagen. One of the soldiers dumped the two dead chickens onto his lap and sat down next to him to make sure he didn't try to escape.

'Perhaps you'll remember where you got your English gun when we've finished questioning you at headquarters,' said the sergeant as he got into the driver's seat.

The boy's mother howled in grief as the Germans drove over the remainder of the vegetable bed before driving out onto the lane in a cloud of dust.

Chapter 16

'Is Mademoiselle Françoise at home,' said the small, neat young man who arrived unannounced at Françoise's parents' cottage.

'No, she's in town today,' replied Madame Delores. 'May I ask who is calling?' she said, replying in the same formal tones of the dapper youth who stood meekly at the doorway.

'I am a friend of Françoise from Paris. I happened to be passing, my name is Jean Fabron, I met your daughter in Paris.' They shook hands. He had small, rather clammy fingers, thought Madame Delores, a bit girl-like. 'If you wish to see her you could come back later today when she has returned from town.'

'What time do you suggest, Madame?'

'Sometime after six o'clock would be best. I cannot guarantee she will be here, she has a busy social life.'

'Oh, I see,' he said. He appeared disappointed at Madame Delores remark about, "busy social life."'

Despite the handshake, Madame Delores was favourably impressed by the polite and well-presented, young man. 'So much better than those long-haired English youths she spends all her time with,' she said to her husband. Henri had returned home from work and appeared disinterested in his wife's remarks and had grunted an inaudible reply.

His English painters had got him out of a jam but he did not much care for them, especially the tall, quiet one, who Françoise seemed besotted with. In Henri's opinion he was totally unsuitable company for his beautiful daughter. But he was in a quandary, their work was satisfactory and at least they were consistent. If he gave them the boot, he would be short of reliable labour, and he had orders stacking up. His greed overcame his reticence. Anyhow, his daughter would be leaving for Paris in late September which should put paid to any relationship.

'You never say anything to your daughter, Henri,' said Madame Delores. 'She's mixed up with those English hippy types. I didn't think you liked English people anyway. It will all end badly. What's wrong with French boys, she has plenty of admirers? Someone like that nice young man that who called here today. He would be a more suitable companion.'

'Don't worry, she'll be back in Paris soon with a different crowd, intelligent people, and *French*.'

When Françoise returned that evening her mother could not wait to tell her about the visitor.

'Who?' said Françoise.

'Jean Fabron, a very nice young man, smart, and so polite.'

'Oh hell! What do you say to him?'

'He's calling back tonight.'

'Oh no.'

'Why do say that, dear?'

'Because he's an old boyfriend, but we split up ages ago.'

'He seemed very pleasant.'

'He's not.'

'Why?'

'Because he won't leave me alone. I have no idea how he managed to track me down here. What a pain!'

'He must be very keen on you.'

'He's a creep, mother.'

'Don't say things like that, it's not nice.'

'I can't be here when he comes back. Please tell him I am out, not available, *anything* to get rid of him.'

'You can't do that, it's rude.'

'I don't want to see him, can't you understand, Maman?'

'What shall I say?'

'Tell him, I've gone away.'

'I can't do that, I told him that you'd be home tonight.'

Just then Madame Delores spotted the diminutive, neatly dressed figure walking carefully across the broken concrete courtyard towards the beaded entrance into the kitchen. 'Too late, he's here now.'

'Tell him to get lost,' said Françoise. She raced upstairs to her bedroom and slammed the door shut. From her room she detected muffled conversation. Then she heard her father shouting at the foot of stairs to come down. She took no notice.

'Do sit down, Jean,' said Madame Delores. 'Tell me, where are you from?'

'Poitiers.'

'You travelled to Aix today, it's a long way?'

'Yes, in truth, I wanted to see Françoise very much.'

'Is she expecting you?'

'No, I wanted to surprise her.'

'Oh, I see, how nice…you are a student in Paris, are you involved in the design course with Françoise?'

'Oh no, nothing so trivial. I'm studying to become an advocate.'

'Admirable, a proper profession.'

'There's nothing trivial about my daughter's design course young man,' said Henri. 'Someone has to design the clothes that you so obviously like wearing,' he continued, annoyed at the impertinence of the young visitor.

'Of course you are correct Monsieur, it's just different from law,' said Jean. There was an embarrassed silence.

'Would you care for some wine?' asked Madame Delores.

'That would be very nice, thank you Madame. I'm a little tired after my long drive.'

'I'm sure Françoise will be down soon. She's only just back from her classes at the art school and is probably getting changed.' Madame Delores turned to her husband, 'Henri, can you pour Jean a glass of our good wine and I'll join him too,' she said. 'Jean is studying law.' As if this qualified him to be served her husband's expensive wine. There was an exasperated grunt from Henri.

Madame Delores led Jean into the adjacent dining room where he sat down on a small upright chair. Henri was annoyed at having his evening disturbed by this bumptious, uninvited guest. It was the last thing he wanted, and he didn't like dishing out his good wine to strangers. He banged about pouring wine into a decanter and placed four of his smallest glasses on the table.

Jean looked around the sparsely decorated room like an estate agent calculating its value. He noted the large crucifix on the sideboard. 'The church is so important in today's fast-changing world,' he said.

'I do so agree,' said Madame Delores, as she removed her apron and sat down next to him. 'So, you met Françoise in Paris?'

'Yes, we've known one another for the last seven months. We are very close.'

'It's strange, she's never mentioned you before.'

'You'll remember I am sure when Françoise came home Paris was in chaos. Riots were occurring all over the *rive gauche*, it was dangerous to venture out, and it was then we somehow lost touch.'

'Yes, we were very worried about her safety and ordered Françoise to come home straight away,' said Monsieur Delores, making it clear by his manner that he was in control of his daughter.

'You have other friends here in Aix?' said Madame Delores.

'Not really... as I said earlier, I came here especially to see Françoise.' He gulped a little as if he were going to cry. He ceased talking for a moment as he got his feelings under control.

'You were saying' said Henri, embarrassed at the young man's show of emotion.

'You see, I would like to speak to you Monsieur, on a very personal matter.'

'Whatever you wish to say, you can say in front of my wife?'

Jean hesitated. 'I love Françoise from the depths of my heart and I know that secretly she loves me too.' There was another pause as the parents absorbed this revelation.

'Jean, how can you be so sure the love you profess for Françoise is reciprocated,' said Madame Delores. 'I hate to dash your hopes but she seems infatuated with some young Englishmen, she spends all her free time with them in Aix.'

'Oh, really.'

'She's never mentioned you in the past, except...' Madame Delores, paused for a moment thinking how to put it tactfully. 'You see when I told her you had visited earlier today, she told me she had finished going out with you in Paris?'

Jean's gaze didn't falter. 'I know she is in love with me, I have known it since we first met. The reason for my visit today is to ask for her hand in marriage.'

Henri was pouring the wine, his hand momentarily paused and spilt some of his precious wine on the fruitwood surface of the table. 'Damn,' he said. He turned to look at the foppish young man in case he had misheard his remark. He put down the wine decanter. 'You want to marry my daughter?' he said.

'Yes, that was my intention, with your permission of course,' Jean said, his voice quavering.

'I'm sorry but she's far too young to think of marriage,' said Madame Delores, intervening before her husband exploded. Henri remained rooted to the spot, aghast at what he was hearing.

'I love her,' said Jean.

'Have you asked her?'

'Not formally, but we talked about it in Paris.'

'Talked about it, but you've not actually proposed to her?' Henri's relief was palpable, his daughter had not committed herself to this ridiculous *poseur*.

'This is all a bit of a shock, we've never heard of you until you arrived this afternoon. Marriage is not something you can just jump into on a whim,' said Madame Delores.

'Well, you know how secretive Françoise can be?' Jean said with a knowing smile.

Madame Delores and Henri looked at one another in tacit understanding.

'Firstly, I think you'd better ask my daughter if she wants to go along with your idea. We could not contemplate you marrying our daughter until we know more about you and your family background. Tell me how you will support a wife when you are both studying, said Henri. He was barely containing his ire at the impertinence of this jumped-up dandy sipping his expensive Rhone wine.

'I have money,' said Jean. He spoke in a dismissive tone, regaining his former composure.

'Money doesn't make a marriage, young man.'

There was an awkward silence as Jean and Madame Delores took a sip of wine, Henri gulped down half a glass.

Upstairs, Françoise had ignored her father's calls to join the party. She could hear muffled fragments of Jean and her parents conversation, that was enough. She opened her bedroom window and shimmied down the drainpipe into the cottage backyard. Then she quietly freewheeled her Solex Sioux bike out of the gate on to the road and kick started the motor and tore off towards Aix in search of Angus.

Henri endured a couple more minutes of intermittent conversation with Jean, then left the room to search for Françoise. He suspected she had bolted. To be certain he slowly opened her bedroom door and found the room empty with the window wide open. His suspicion was confirmed. It was a familiar escape method used by Françoise when she was much younger. He was relieved to avoid the confrontation with her in front of the unwanted visitor. He needed to hear the truth from her as all the signs indicated Jean was a troublesome imposter. Henri came back into the room with a half-smile on his face. 'I am afraid Françoise is unable to see you as she is not feeling well, she has a terrible migraine.'

'Oh, poor thing, may I see her for a moment.'

'No chance,' said Henri. 'She was insistent, no visitors, she has to be kept in the dark until it passes.'

'Are you staying locally? Do you have an address in Aix where she can contact you,' said Madame Delores.

Jean gave them the address of a fashionable hotel in the centre of the city. Madame Delores hastily scribbled the details on a piece of paper and before he could finish his wine Henri placed a large hand on Jean's thin shoulder and escorted the suitor to his car.

Jean clambered into the little Renault and realised what an utter fool he had made of himself. Henri did not wait for the car to leave but turned his back and strode back into the cottage. By the time Françoise returned home that night her parents were in bed and in no mind to discuss their daughter's tangled love life.

The following morning, Henri waited at home to speak to his daughter. He was fuming with suppressed anger and wanted an explanation. Françoise emerged, behaving as if nothing out of the ordinary had happened. 'Good morning Papa, why aren't you at work, this morning?' Françoise knew only too well what was coming and waited for the inquisition which would undoubtedly ruin her breakfast coffee. Her mother was riding shotgun at her husband's shoulder.

'Sit down,' said Henri, gesturing to the same chair where her would-be fiancée had been nervously perched only twelve hours before.

'What are you playing at Françoise?'

'What do you mean Papa?'

'He moved forward as if to strike her.' She instinctively ducked, she has been on the receiving end of his rages since childhood. Madame Delores grabbed Henri's arm and pulled him back.

'Henri, leave her, the girl's an adult. Give her a chance to explain.'

'I've already told Maman yesterday, I finished with Jean in Paris, and never want to see him again. Ever. He's like a limpet, he won't let me go. He's obsessive, I think he's a bit crazy.'

'What's he doing coming here?'

'I have no idea how he found me, I never gave him my address. His turning up is as big a surprise to me as it is to you. I left him in May.'

'Have you any idea what he asked me last night, sitting on the chair where you are now?' Said Henri, pointing at the chair, as if the innocent piece of country furniture was somehow to blame.

'I've no idea, Papa.'

'He asked for my permission to marry you.'

'What? You have to be joking, Papa!' Françoise roared with laughter and covered her face with her hands.

'It was no joke. He told us that he'd as good as asked you when you were in Paris together.'

'Never, never, he's deranged, Papa. He never hinted at such a thing, nor did I encourage him. In the beginning we were friends, then he became clinging, after that he started following me around. He even broke into my apartment.'

'Did you call the police?'

'No, I just threw him out and threatened to report him.'

'Where *do you* find these boys?'

'At least he's better than those long-haired English clowns you hang about with,' said Madame Delores.

'Be quiet woman.'

'*Henri!*'

'So why did you run away last night? Did you know I had to put up with him drinking my best wine while he sat there smirking, with a superior expression on his face. '

'I told Maman to send him away. He's a pest, now he's discovered where I live and he'll start following me around again.'

'You'll have to ask him to go away,' said Madame Delores.

'I *have* done on countless times. He doesn't take any notice of me.'

'I'll make him take notice.'

''We'll have none of your summary justice, Henri, the war's over,' said Madame Delores.

'She's my daughter.'

'What did he say when he left,' said Françoise.

'He left an address of a posh hotel where he's staying in Aix.'

'Let me speak to him.'

'I'll threaten him with the police,' said Henri.

'Leave it me, Papa. He's my problem, I'll deal with him.'

'Are you sure that's wise?'

Chapter 17

Jean returned to his hotel. He was shaking with a mixture of suppressed rage, humiliation and fear that he had ruined his chances of ever reigniting his relationship with Françoise.

He went up to his bedroom and threw open the shutters, unlocked the balcony double doors, and stepped outside and breathed in the cool evening air. His room was on the third floor and he looked down at the busy street below, people going about their lives, care-free, unfettered with heartaches. He could see young people sitting at a fashionable café, chatting, smoking and drinking. Their happiness stung him. He fought back a tear as he contemplated throwing himself over the low balcony rail. That would show Françoise how much he loved her. Before his grief overwhelmed him he turned back into the room and shivered with fright at his own black thoughts. He must not give up, he thought, that was the coward's way, not worthy of a leading advocate.

He suddenly felt hungry. He had not eaten since leaving his parent's house, he took the lift to the ground floor and drifted into the restaurant in a daze. When he sat down, he felt nauseous with stress, and his earlier hunger diminished. The maitre d' took his simple order of an omelette with undisguised disdain. He drank a carafe of expensive, poor quality dry white wine. It was not a patch on the wine Henri Delores had served him earlier. He was surprised, he had taken Françoise's father as a man with no taste, an artisan. As he finished his *omelette jambon*, Jean mulled over his next move. Then he remembered Françoise's mother had mentioned some English boyfriends. He decided to seek his rivals out.

~

Françoise had enrolled at a local art school and was undertaking a summer portraiture course. Her evenings were mostly spent with Angus now they were together. She had commenced a series of pencil portraits of Angus with the intention of completing a finished watercolour at a later date. He would pose on a chair in the little room above the café while she sketched him. But somehow, they always ended up in bed, and the picture remained unfinished.

Pete and Angus's nights out together came to an abrupt halt. Even when they were away on jobs, Angus's enthusiasm for clubbing was muted. He returned to Aix as soon as possible to be with Françoise. Pete became more and more and frustrated that his partner had dumped him for Françoise, a girl he would have dearly liked to date himself. To add to Pete's alienation, now he was often allocated different assignments with other French decorators, so their time together was prised further apart.

Pete was effectively cancelled. He ventured out to play cards in the café with the locals. The shine of his relationship with Angus had become tarnished as Françoise took over his friend's spare time. As the summer months were coming to an end he considered pressing on to the Marrakesh, but he was not certain what he would do if he got there. Suddenly the whole concept of North Africa looked unappealing and out of reach. It was Angus's idea from the start. His options were to stay in Aix or go home. Departure at this stage would be an admission of failure after only a few months of their planned adventure. The thought of his father gloating and chiding him on his return made the prospect even more unappetising.

~

After his sparse dinner, Jean had returned to his room where he slept restlessly. In the morning, he picked at his breakfast half-heartedly which he had served in his room. Jean was determined to identify, and if necessary, confront his rivals. That would require surveillance. He discarded his half-finished breakfast and cleared the tray from the small desk in his hotel bedroom. He picked up a hotel biro and notepaper and started to write. Despite creeping doubts, he needed to convince himself that Françoise really did still love him. The reason she had left Paris so abruptly was the fear of the violence coupled with the stern demands from her bad-tempered father. He wrote on the paper in large childish rounded letters:

Françoise loves me
Demanding father (a bit weird)
Ashamed of her family (low class)
Fear of Paris violence

His eyes filled with tears of fallacious pity at the thought of her being afraid while living in Paris alone. He agonised he had been unable to provide her with the love and protection when she needed it most.

Jean thought Françoise's parents were peculiar, southern types, parochial, and unsophisticated. Their reaction to him arriving so unexpectedly was predictable. He should have thought about that before arriving on their doorstep unannounced. It was a stupid, crass, mistake.

He convinced himself that Françoise wanted to keep their relationship secret so he could be shielded from their humble ways. The more he mulled this reasoning over, the more convinced he became this was the real reason why she wanted to end their affair. He loved her all the more for it. He added 'social divide' to his list.

It was whilst Jean was looking over his notes that the 'phone rang on his bedside table. 'A Monsieur Delores is calling,' said the hotel receptionist. 'May I connect him?'

Chapter 18

Pete's disillusionment with his lot was not helped by jealousy that Angus had captured Françoise's heart. He had secretly held designs on her from the day they first met at the petrol station. For a man who liked to win he had resolutely failed, the problem was she had never taken him seriously.

Now he had to suppress his feelings and remain loyal to Angus. He was annoyed with himself for not being assertive enough, but now it was too late. The tables may have been turned if he could have spoken French. But he recognised that Angus's serious outlook on life and his kindness, had charmed her into his bed. And he had to admit Angus and Françoise were probably better suited, his own devil-may-care attitude did not have a universal following. He also suspected that Angus had no inkling of the feelings he secretly harboured for Françoise.

He had been spending more time with Françoise when Angus was away on separate painting assignments, and this had drawn them closer. She had done some pencil portraits of him while in the café bar and had successfully captured his smiley, happy-go-lucky nature.

'Hello Pete,' said Françoise, as she came into the café in search of Angus. Pete stopped playing cards and got up and bought her a drink.

'I do hate it when Angus is away,' she said.

'He'll be back later this morning,' said Pete. 'I'm sorry if I am a poor stand-in.'

'Of course not,' she said, and squeezed his hand before she took a sip of citron-pressé. 'I enjoy our chats about my portraiture course. I have a very good teacher, I think I am his favourite.'

'You are everybody's favourite.'

'It fills my time while you and Angus are away painting Papa's villas,' she said, ignoring Pete's remark.'

'I'm sorry we have never got it together before you took up with Angus.'

'Are you jealous?'

'A bit.'

'I will do another portrait of you to make up. In watercolours this time. So you can keep it to remind yourself of your missed love,' she said, with a giggle.

'I would love that. Thanks.'

'You have an interesting face, Pete. It's full of humour.'

'I'm not handsome like Angus.'

'You don't look like a typical European.'

'My parents are Polish.'

'Of course, it is the Slav connection.'

'I had forgotten, your parents were Jewish.'

'Does it bother you, me having a Jewish background?

'Of course not.'

'I am not a practising Jew, I'm an atheist, if truth be known.'

'Bad luck, it's good to have a belief in something.'

'Where was God when all my relations were murdered by the Nazis?'

There was a pause, as Françoise hesitated before she spoke. 'The Vichy government were not kind to the Jews here. People never talk about it these days.'

'Are they ashamed?'

'Yes, but they would never admit it. We are still a strong Catholic country.'

'I thought the church was loosening its grip on French life.'

'Up to a point. The older generation is still devout. My Maman is ruled by her faith. But enough of all this talk about religion. You are getting like Angus, too serious.'

'I'll never be like him. His problem is he thinks too much.'

'Pete, why haven't you got a nice French girlfriend? Your French is getting better.'

'I've dated a few but they never want to go out with me more than a few times. I think their parents warn them off.'

'Rubbish. You have to stop telling so many silly lies. You don't need to impress them. Just be yourself.'

'I wish I was dating you. I might be a bit more serious.'

'Oh shut up about me. Think about Angus. Anyhow, you couldn't cope with me. You'd soon get fed up with my untidiness and moods. I need to be allowed space and time to concentrate on my art and design. Angus gets that. And my parents are a nightmare. They think I attract the wrong sort of boyfriends.'

'Is Angus the wrong sort in your parents eyes?'

'Yes, he's English for a start. My father doesn't like the British for some unfathomable reason.'

'But he's employed two Englishmen.'

'Only because he was desperate for labour.'

'Hypocrite.'

'I love Angus. He's very kind, although he can be a bit heavy at times.'

'You're not kidding.'

'How come you two are friends? You're both quite different.'

'I don't know. We met at school. Although we appear to be opposites, it was his idea to go to Marrakesh.'

'That's a surprise. I thought it would be you.'

'He got fed up of university and being hounded by his over ambitious father. He wanted Angus to achieve ever higher academic successes. Did he tell you his father was a priest and the head of the school we both attended.'

'No, I didn't know that, he has never mentioned his parents.'

'He wanted to put them to the back of his mind on this trip. For both of us it was an escape from reality.'

'Talking of parents, do you remember me mentioning I had an old boyfriend in Paris.'

'You said something about a guy who kept following you?'

'That's the creep. Well, he turned up at my parents yesterday, despite me finishing with him months ago.'

'You have this effect on people, Françoise.'

'Don't tell Angus. He'll go mad. But listen to this, he asked my father if he could marry me.'

'Angus did?'

'No, the ex-boyfriend from Paris.'

'Bloody hell, what did your father say?'

'He was furious and threw him out.'

'Did you see him?'

'I escaped from the house and avoided him.'

'Unfortunately, I will have to face him again and tell him to get lost.'

'Why are you bothering. Can I help in some way? I could pose as your boyfriend and give him the hard word?'

''That's very sweet, Pete. I have to see him off, once and for all.'

'If Angus does find out he would as likely hit him.'

'That doesn't sound like Angus.'

'He's very passionate. Probably better to say nothing.'

'Okay.

'Are you sure I can't help with this nutter?'

'I have to face him and not hide behind my parents all the time. I got involved with him. It was my stupid choice. I never even slept with the guy.'

'Maybe that was what has been driving him mad, he is filled with crazy unfulfilled lust,' said Pete, giggling.

'Don't say that, it makes him sound even more frightening.'

'Sorry.'

Don't forget, I want to do a proper portrait of you. That is if I can get you to sit still for an hour.'

'No chance.'

Chapter 19

As Angus entered the café he noticed Pete and Françoise were sitting close together in conversation, she had her hand on Pete's forearm. She removed it quickly when he approached the table and Angus felt a seam of jealousy. He had never fully trusted his old pal when it came to matters of the heart, he had the habit of moving in when he was chatting up girls during their club adventures.

'Hey you two love-birds,' said Angus, in an effort to be cheerful. Pete looked embarrassed. He had been so engaged talking to Françoise that he had not noticed Angus come into the café.

'Finished the Antibes job?'

'It took bloody ages. The wife of the owner made me go over one of the outer walls facing the sea. It was completely unnecessary. I think it was an excuse to keep us there.'

'Haven't we been there before? If I remember the woman was really hot, she looked like a movie star,' said Pete.

'She was a fashion model and married a rich guy from Lyon. He never seems to be there.'

'How do you know all this? I thought you weren't meant to talk to the owners,' said Françoise.

'She brought me a beer. She told me she liked Englishmen.'

'I'm not the only one then.'

'I think she fancied me, it was a bit disconcerting. She likes parading around topless.'

Pete roared with laughter. 'Just your luck, lover boy,' said Pete. Françoise scowled at him.

'Don't worry, darling. I didn't lay a hand on her.'

'Are you sure Angus, you sly old dog. Still waters and all that.'

'What do you mean,' said Françoise.

'It's an English expression,' said Pete. 'It means quiet people have hidden depths.'

'Do you mean secrets.'

'Leave it Pete, stop stirring things.'

'Angus?'

'Don't be silly, darling. Pete is just winding you up.' Françoise vigorously stubbed out her cigarette in the ashtray as if she was squashing a fly and gave Angus a long look.

That was a change, making Françoise jealous, Angus thought.

~

Jean's heart raced, as he waited to be put through to Henri. Françoise's father must have thought matters over after had talked to Françoise. Now he wanted to give his blessing to the union.

'*Bonjour, Monsieur*,' said Jean, as he tried to contain his excitement.

'I have been speaking to my daughter this morning,' said Henri, but before he could continue, Jean interrupted him.

'Yes, of course Monsieur, she'll have explained everything.'

'Yes, she has, in no uncertain terms' said Henri. His tone was stern, business like. Of course he would be serious if he was about to offer his daughter's hand in marriage, thought Jean.

'Excellent news, I knew you'd understand once Françoise told you of our love for one another. I am sorry to have arrived at your little house without warning. It was wrong of me to spill out my intentions in such a peremptory manner. It was unforgivably rude, please accept my apologies.'

'Will you listen to me, Monsieur Fabron, and please stop interrupting.', said Henri.

God, he is being formal now, "Monsieur Fabron." He has seen sense at last, thought Jean.

''My daughter has confirmed to me very clearly that she wishes to terminate, with immediate effect, whatever friendship you enjoyed in Paris. Do you understand the words: "terminate," "finish." In simple terms your relationship is at an end.'

It took a while for Jean to take in what he had heard. There was silence on the line.

'Are you still there?' said Henri. 'Do you understand what I have just told you, Monsieur Fabron? My daughter does not want to see you again.'

Jean paused before replying. 'I can't believe that's true Monsieur,' he said. 'You make it sound as if she is ending a contract. I really must talk to her face to face. There has been a dreadful misunderstanding.'

'You don't seem to be understanding me.'

'I know that your daughter loves me. Perhaps she's a little young. I'm prepared to wait, say, until she's twenty-one. Would that be more agreeable to you?'

'This is the final time I will say this Monsieur Fabron. My daughter's relationship with you is over as far as she's concerned.' Henri waited to see if this had finally registered. 'However, against my wishes, she has agreed to speak to you. I suppose she owes you some form of explanation. I am sorry if you have been misled and have had a wasted journey to Aix,' said Henri, in a more conciliatory tone.

'Oh, that is wonderful news, Monsieur, thank you,' said Jean. 'I'm certain when we meet, you'll see that she is still serious about me. I'll be a model son-in-law for you. I plan to be a leading lawyer.'

'I don't give a damn if you want to be President of the Republic,' said Henri, returning to his belligerent tone. 'I only want what's best for my daughter and she doesn't believe that includes you. And neither do I.'

Jean wanted to respond to this devastating summary but decided to hold his tongue. Henri Delores was not a man worth getting into a slanging match.

'Do you know when she will be in touch?' said Jean.

'Some time tomorrow. That is if you can be bothered to stay in Aix for what will be a pointless meeting. I can't be more specific, it's up to my daughter.'

'Thank you, Monsieur.'

'Don't thank me. But mark my words, if you don't do as she asks and go back to Poitiers, you'll have me to answer to.'

'Are you threatening me Monsieur?'

'No, I'm telling you. Don't go near my daughter once she has spoken to you, or there will be trouble. And I mean *trouble* Fabron. For starters, I'll have you for breaking and entering my daughter's apartment in Paris. Trust me, I am a man of my word.'

The phone went brrr…Jean stared down helplessly at his little feet encompassed neatly in the brown leather loafers. He noticed a small stain on the beige carpet and he got up and stamped on the stain as if it was Henri Delores's head.

He walked around the room taking deep breaths and then threw himself full length onto his bed and beat his legs up and down so ferociously his loafers were thrown across the room. He looked like a child in a frustrated rage.

The pompous old fool, he thought, I'm not giving up my beloved Françoise just because he said so. The sound of screeching swifts swooping around the buildings irritated him and he got up and banged the shutters closed. He went back and lay on his bed again, and studied the ornate ceiling cornices and wondered how he could spend the next twenty-four hours until Françoise contacted him.

He felt exhausted after yesterday's long drive, his botched meeting with Françoise's parents, and the terrible telephone call with his future father-in-law. He put his head onto the pillow, stuck his thumb into his mouth, and eventually dropped into an uneasy sleep.

Chapter 20

After two hours Jean woke up. He had to work out how he was going to spend his day. He went down to reception and asked for a map of the city. He had remembered that Madame Delores had mentioned that Françoise was attending a class at an art school.

He got in his car and following his map found the art school after an hour of searching. He located a tall old building with deep windows, there was a car park with bike and scooter parking at the rear of the building. It could only be accessed via a narrow stone archway. He couldn't park his car there, he would be too visible He needed to find a place on an adjacent street. His plan was to follow Françoise after her classes ended which should lead him to her English boyfriends.

He returned to the hotel pleased with his afternoon's work. He bought a newspaper and went into the sumptuous bar and ordered a Campari and soda. He relaxed with his paper and read about the simmering aftermath of the riots and the febrile peace in Paris. He noticed his hands were shaking and the paper rattled in his grasp as he tried to control it. After a while, a middle age man came and sat at an adjacent table. He was expensively dressed in a silk suit and wore a brightly coloured bow tie, he was drinking cognac. Jean wondered if he was a homosexual.

'Are you visiting Aix on holiday or business?' The man asked after a few minutes.

'I'm here on personal business,' said Jean, not wishing to engage with the stranger.

'I'm sorry to disturb you but you seem rather agitated,' said the hirsute man.

Jean hesitated a moment before answering. 'I'm here to meet my fiancee but she…' his voice trailed off as he fought back tears. Jean fumbled in his pocket and got out a handkerchief and blew his nose, then dabbed his eyes. "Excuse me, I have a cold,' he said.

The stranger was not fooled by Jean's excuse. 'I am a professional psychiatrist, can I be of any help? It is sometimes helpful to unburden your worries to a third party.'

'It's complicated.'

'Matters often appear that way. On the surface unsolvable. But they can be eased by talking. We call it a type of therapy.' The man's voice was sympathetic and soothing. 'If you would like to talk tell me why are things not going right for you?'

Jean put down his newspaper and took a gulp of his Campari. His instinct was to tell the man to mind his own business, but despite his garish bow tie he had a kind face. It might be helpful to get his advice. 'It's quite simple really,' he said.

'Problems are often simple but somehow intractable,' said the sympathetic man, as he drew his chair closer to Jean.

'I love this girl very much and I think she loves me, but her parents…'

'Are they against your relationship?'

'Exactly. Her father has threatened me, I believe he's preventing her from seeing me.'

'But you say you're engaged.'

'Well, not exactly. I asked the father, but he turned me down.'

'What did your girlfriend say?'

'I haven't asked her yet. I wanted to get the parents approval first. But her father sent me away.'

'Why did the father think you were an unsuitable to marry his daughter?'

'Because I come from a wealthy family and he is lower class.'

'Are you sure that's correct? Could there be another reason you have not considered. Is she too young to marry, does her father have another person in mind that would be more agreeable to the family? I suspect your potential father-in-law is very protective of her. Is she an only child?'

'Well, yes. You have a point there.'

'Is your bride in total agreement to your plans? You say you have not actually asked her yet.'

'Of course. She's just embarrassed about her family's circumstances.'

'Has she told you this?'

'Not in so many words. But it's obvious.'

'You said earlier that you thought she loved you, so there is some doubt. Perhaps she has conveyed these feelings to her parents and can't face telling you about her doubts.'

'But I am going to be a top lawyer, when I have qualified I plan to be a leading figure in France's judiciary. I will be a fantastic husband, she will have a wonderful life, money and the prestige and being married to a famous advocate.'

'I would have thought that your girlfriend's father would be pleased if his daughter was marrying a man with professional ambitions.'

'So would I.'

'What do your own parents think about your proposed marriage?'

'My father is dead and my mother doesn't give a damn what I do. She's remarried the most dreadful man and has had lots of children by him. They are all awful.'

'You don't get on with any of them, I guess.'

'Correct.'

'Are you telling me you have not spoken to them about your plans to marry.'

'No, it's nothing to do with them.'

'I think you need to have a good heart-to-heart with your girl to see if you can resolve these problems.'

'I am hoping to see her very soon.'

'May I advise you keep a cool head and let her explain herself in full. You have to recognise her personal and family barriers that are perhaps holding back your relationship progressing. Trying to force your opinions upon her will drive her away.'

'I think she has another boyfriend, an Englishman.'

'That could explain a lot.'

'Don't worry, I will sort him out. Now stop asking me these bloody stupid questions. It's got nothing to do with you.' Jean downed his drink and slammed his glass onto the table with such force it shattered the stem. Fragments of splintered glass showered across the floor to where the psychiatrist was sitting.

'Shit, shit, shit,' said Jean. 'Look what you've made me do.' Jean got up and threw his crumpled newspaper at the kindly man. 'If you want something to do, read this, instead of interrogating strangers.' Jean stomped off across the bar towards the foyer, his leather loafers crunching on the broken glass.

The psychiatrist got out his notebook and scribbled in it: "Classic behaviour: paranoid schizophrenic."

Jean went to his bedroom and ordered a bottle of whisky be brought to his room. He drank himself to sleep.

~

The sound of the bedside telephone ringing burst into Jean's consciousness. He sat up and saw sunshine filtering through the closed shutters. He looked at his watch and saw it was nine thirty. He had been asleep for ten hours and his head throbbed. The half empty whisky bottle was on the floor.

He grasped the phone: 'There's a lady in reception to see you, Mademoiselle Delores.' Jean's heart went bang, bang in his chest. God, she's here, everything was going to be okay. 'Ask her to come to room 26.'

'I'm sorry, single young ladies are not allowed to visit gentlemen in the bedrooms unaccompanied,' said the receptionist. 'These are the hotel's house rules.'

He sat on the bed edge and tried to compose himself. 'Okay, tell her I'll be down in five minutes,' he said. He jumped off the bed, ran into the bathroom and splashed cold water on his face. No time to shave or shower, he ran a comb through his dishevelled hair and splashed cologne over his face and body. He picked his clothing off the floor and found a clean shirt. He grabbed his wallet and car keys and dashed out.

While in the lift, Jean took some deep breaths to calm himself before he entered the hotel lobby. Françoise was sitting in a low chair pretending to read a tourist magazine. She was aware of Jean as he emerged from the lift but she did not look up until she saw his scuffed, tasseled loafers in front of her. Jean appeared stressed and smelt strongly of some ghastly cologne. He looked like he had a bad night out on the town, his normal tailor's dummy demeanour was absent.

'Hello stranger,' he said and bent down to kiss her cheek, but she moved her head to avoid his embrace.

She stood up. 'We need to talk. I know a café near here where we can be private,' she said.

'I thought we could take the car and maybe go somewhere?'

'No need.'

'It's no trouble,' he said, dangling the Renault keys. At that moment the psychiatrist with whom he had been speaking to the previous evening walked past the pair and gave Jean a cheery wave as he went out the front door. Jean ignored him.

'Who was that?'

He said nothing.

'I know a café just around the corner, five minutes' walk, said Françoise, brusquely. The idea of getting into his car horrified her. He could abduct her and she remembered Pete's jokey remark about his pent-up sexual frustration. Françoise led the way down a narrow street jammed with market stalls. Jean tried to grab her hand but she pushed him away. The café was small and dark, and they took a table in an alcove at the rear. Françoise knew the café well from her school days, it was a secret rendezvous for meeting boys. They ordered two coffees and Françoise lit up a cigarette.

'They're bad for you,' said Jean.

'Stop trying to control me,' she said, blowing a long stream of exhaled tobacco across the table at him.

'For Christ's sake, Françoise.'

'Jean, just what are you doing here? I told you in Paris that our relationship was over. That was over four months ago.'

'It took some finding you.'

'You've spent all this time looking for me?'

'I love you.'

'I'm sorry, I have met another man and I am in love, with him.'

Jean's face collapsed in despair. It was what he has been dreading. 'But I want to marry you.'

'So my parents informed me. It was good of you to consult me about your plans.'

'I didn't know at the time. It was only after you ran away, and I felt so lonely.'

'That's not a reason for getting married. What got into your head that I wanted to marry you?'

'I'm sorry, it was stupid of me to say anything to your parents. I sort of blurted it out. I was nervous, your father was very intimidating.'

Françoise smiled, sometimes having a grumpy father could be a help. 'He was only protecting my interests. Isn't that what girls' fathers are for?

'I don't know, my father died when I was five.'

There was a silence, and Françoise felt momentary sympathy for this pathetic figure. He really was just a little boy. She should never have encouraged him, she had been equally naïve. Françoise underestimated the effects her beauty could have on vulnerable men. Her great aunt had been correct when she told her to be careful. What a mess! She leaned across the table and took his hand, it was trembling and clammy with sweat. 'Jean, get this into your head, we had a few months of fun, but I am sorry, I don't love you and I never will. I may sound cruel, but you have to accept the reality and forget you ever met me.'

'But…' He looked like he might burst into tears. 'I nearly killed myself last night when I thought I could never be with you again.'

'Jean, you'll meet someone much better suited to you than me, I promise you. Look, you are wealthy and attractive, and one day you'll be a leading advocate, a magistrate...you need a nice girl from a good family. Someone who will truly love you.'

'Oh come away with me now. Let's start again Françoise,' he grabbed her hand.

'Jean, for the final time, please understand that our relationship is over. It was finished when we were in Paris months ago. I don't love you. I never have.'

'You did love me. I know you did,' said Jean, his voice getting high pitched.

'You're deluded.'

People in adjoining tables started to look around at the attractive auburn haired girl and the pathetic sounding young man. Jean was grappling with her arm.

'Let go of me. You heard what my father said. You must go back to Poitiers and get out of my life.'

'I want YOU, no-one else. At which point he attempted to man-handle Françoise out of her seat.

'Let go of me Jean. Let GO!'

The beefy café owner, who had been witnessing the escalating row, stepped from behind his counter. He came forward and got hold of Jean by the shoulders and made him release Françoise's arm. 'Leave her alone, Monsieur. The Mademoiselle wants to leave now, without you.' He gesticulated with his head for Françoise to leave.

'Get off me, you lout,' said Jean, but he was helpless in the man's iron grip. He could only watch as Françoise freed herself. She turned to face the pinioned Jean. 'This is the final straw, Jean. Our relationship is over. Do you understand? OVER!' If you try and lay another hand on me, you'll have my father to contend with.

'But...'

Thank you, Monsieur,' she said to the café owner.

'Do you want me to call the police?'

'No, no. Just hold him until I've gone. And thank you again.'

Françoise bolted out of the café feeling very frightened by Jean's manic behaviour. She hurried back to where she had parked her Solex and headed for home at top speed.

The café proprietor held onto Jean for a few moments longer so he could not give chase. 'Now pay up,' he said.

Chapter 21

Even after his outright rejection in the café Jean's obsession was not dampened. If anything his paranoia was heightened as he had now concluded that Françoise was under the control of her new boyfriend. After all, that is how he would behave if the tables had been turned.

The only way he had any chance of resolving the issue was to meet his nemesis, face-to-face. He returned to his hotel and checked in for a further three days. He called his mother in Poitiers.

'Hello mother, it's Jean.'

'Who?'

'Jean, your son.'

'Of course, dear. Where are you? You seem to have been away a long time.'

'I'm in Aix en Provence.'

'You never said you were going south.'

'You never asked.'

'Well, what do you want, I'm in a hurry I am taking your brother and sister to the cinema this afternoon.'

'I'm staying in Aix for a few more days, I am seeing my girlfriend.'

'Who is that?'

'Someone I met in Paris.'

'Very well Jean, you must do as you wish. Do let me know when you are coming back, you know Jacques gets annoyed if anyone turns up unexpectedly.'

'It is my home too, mother, I'm hardly "anyone."'

'Of course dear, now have a nice time with your friend, and please don't get so agitated. I don't know what's wrong with you these days, Jacques says you ought to see a psychiatrist. We can arrange an appointment when you get home?'

'Jacques should mind his own business.'

'Goodbye dear,' said his mother, as if she had just enjoyed the most heart-warming conversation with her son. She put down the telephone and sighed in relief. Jean was just like his late father, arrogant and mentally unstable. She hoped he would not follow in his father's footsteps and commit suicide. She really must try and arrange some counselling for the poor boy. She would speak to Jacques about arranging an appointment.

~

The little Renault was parked on a side street close to the art college with a clear view of the car park entrance. Jean watched Françoise leave on her moped. On the first day she went straight home, but on the following day she zipped into a labyrinth of narrow streets in the older part of the city. He managed to keep her in sight at a discreet distance until she pulled up outside a scruffy-looking café. She took off her helmet and shook out her hair. Jean watched it cascade behind her back and his mind was flooded with the memory of running his hands through her thick mane. He felt a bitter pang of longing.

After hiding his car in a tiny courtyard, Jean waited at the corner of the street watching the café. It was not long before he saw Françoise emerge with her arm around a tall young man with long dark curly hair. He looked like a hippy and was wearing a tie-dyed T-shirt, cut off denims and espadrilles. She couldn't be in love with that thing surely? His mood immediately lifted and he followed the pair at a safe distance and saw them enter a fashionable fish restaurant. He decided to return to the café from which they had emerged.

He went in, it was a small, dingy place, certainly not the sort of establishment he would normally be seen dead in. He ordered a coffee at the bar and noticed another long-haired young man sitting at a table with an old tart. She was wearing a flimsy white dress that looked in need of a wash. The hag had a poodle on her knee which she was feeding pieces of bread dipped in her wine. She was having an animated conversation with the young man who was speaking in broken French. He looked German, and Jean wondered if he was friends with Françoise's new boyfriend. After a while, the pair left the bar and disappeared upstairs.

Jean decided to come back the following day to see if could find Françoise's boyfriend and tackle his adversary head on.

~

Over lunch Françoise decided to tell Angus about the surprise reappearance of Jean.

'I remember him now, you told us about a pestering guy in Paris. Why didn't you tell me he'd turned up again?'

'I was trying to avoid upsetting you. I just wanted to get rid of him without any fuss. I thought you might want to harm him. Pete said that you might go a bit crazy.'

'Pete knows about this guy but you didn't care to tell me.' Angus had become angry that this confidence had been shared without his knowledge.

'That's why I'm telling you now. I think he's a bit unhinged.'

'The fact he has come from Poitiers shows how fanatical he is about you,' said Angus, as he cracked open a langoustine claw.

Angus listened with astonishment to the account of Jean's visit to the farmhouse, his proposal of marriage, and his outburst of irrational anger in the café.

'He tried to drag me out, I was only saved by the proprietor who stepped in.'

'Sounds like the man's off his head.'

'He's a frightening guy. He had a funny look on his face, as if he was possessed.'

'Are you sure you're not exaggerating his paranoia…he's just mad jealous, and you are beautiful enough to drive men insane.'

'Oh Angus, you're so sweet.'

'Look, you have to be careful, men get jealous too, it's not just women. You must not lead them on.'

'I never led him on.'

'You do, I've seen you flirting with Pete.'

'He's harmless. Are you jealous?'

'About Jean? No, I just feel sorry for him. About you, of course, it's only natural. You won't ever leave me will you?'

'I promise. But please don't get like my Papa, he wants to know about everything I do. It's very claustrophobic.'

'He's only doing what most caring fathers do.'

'Oh please don't be patronising Angus, it's not in your nature.'

'Let's hope Jean's got the message by now and he'll slope off to Poitiers.'

'What if he turns up in Paris?'

'Don't worry, I'll be with you by then.'

'Are you coming to Paris with me? That's fab, Angus! But what about your trip to Marrakesh with Pete?'

'I've decided I must start doing something more academic than painting villas. Anyhow, I can't face being without you.'

'Oh darling,' and she leaned over and kissed him on the cheek. 'Will you come and live with me in my little apartment?'

'If I can find a job.'

'What will you do?'

'I don't know yet, I'm thinking about teaching English.'

'Sounds too romantic for words.'

'I don't think your parents will approve, particularly as your father is paying the rent.'

'I don't care what Papa says. Anyhow, how will he know? We are in Paris, and he's in Aix!'

'You make it all sound so simple Françoise. You know life is never like that.'

'Oh, you're such a cynic Angus. How will I ever cure you of your Anglo-Saxon melancholy?'

Chapter 22

The mind of a love-sick person works in mysterious ways. What is obvious to a casual onlooker is that Jean's relationship with Françoise was dead in the water. In Jean's troubled mind he believed it would be possible, by some alchemy, to rescue Françoise and fulfil his destiny of happiness with her at his side. The more his inner voice spoke to him, the greater the conviction that Françoise and the hippy were a temporary fantasy.

Jean believed Françoise had succumbed to the influence of the hippy's drug habits. It was the reason her father said she was unwell when he had visited her home. She didn't have a migraine, but was out of her beautiful head on some mind altering substances. Why had it not occurred to him before when he recalled her excessive smoking? He had read how nicotine was a precursor to marijuana or perhaps even worse. Once she spent time in his company he could make her clean again.

Monsieur and Madame Delores would be forever in his debt, his foresight had spotted the subtle changes in their daughter's behaviour. It was his exceptional skill of observance that assured him of becoming a leading advocate. He would show his mother and stepfather how they had misjudged him. All that was required was for him to claim his beautiful wife, and then everything would fall into place.

~

Françoise set out from her parents' cottage at a little after ten o'clock for the centre of Aix. Jean followed the moped in his car, keeping a cautious distance behind. It did not take long for Françoise to spot the little Renault in the moped's mirrors. Once in the city centre, she suddenly veered up a narrow pedestrian alleyway not wide enough for vehicles. As soon as she had shaken him off, Françoise pulled up at a phone kiosk, and called Angus at the café. There was a sigh of frustration at the end of the phone, *Le patron* hated taking messages. She heard him shout for Angus. Thankfully, he was already drinking coffee in the café waiting for her. They were going to have a day at the beach.

'He's following me in his car,' she said.

'Who?'

'Jean.'

'Where are you now?'

'I have given him the slip. I'm in a phone kiosk in the *Place de Boulangerie*.'

'Can you get here by using side-streets?'

'I'll try.'

'How far away are you?'

'About ten minutes,' she said, sobbing in fright.

'If you see him again, stop your bike and go into a shop or café and telephone me immediately. I'll come and fetch you from there. And don't panic, he can't harm you.'

After about fifteen minutes Angus started to get anxious. Then Françoise burst into the café and threw herself into Angus's arms.

'Come and sit here and calm down,' said Angus. He pulled back a chair and the patron brought over coffee and glass of water. She gulped down the water before tackling the strong coffee. Françoise felt safe now she was in Angus's company and they began to discuss their plans for the day. But she still remained on edge and kept glancing over her shoulder towards the café door. 'Angus can we get out of here? I have a bad feeling he might turn up, he's been following me around Aix for days and probably knows this is our meeting place.'

'Don't panic, I'm here to protect you. Just let me finish this *pain au chocolat* before we go.'

Angus was wiping his lips with a paper napkin when Jean entered the café. Françoise had not seen him as her back was to the door. Angus noticed the short, dapper young man and watched him as he scanned the small café. As soon as he spotted Françoise he strode towards their table. His face was pale and unhealthy, as if had not slept, his jaw was set rigid. He had one hand held behind his back. Angus soon guessed this was the infamous Jean, and he sensed trouble. The man's eyes were bulging and menacing. Before Angus could stand up from the table the young man grasped Françoise's shoulders. Françoise screamed in fright. 'She's coming with me,' Jean said. The voice was boy-like, petulant.

Françoise looked around terrified. 'Jean, get your hands off me.' He put one arm around her neck and Françoise glimpsed in his other hand a flick-knife blade, it flashed in the sunlight.

'Don't be silly,' said Angus, calmly.

'You won't succeed in turning her into a drugged up hippy, she needs a good French husband. Someone who will look after her and give her the life she deserves. She's going to be the wife of a famous advocate.'

'You're mad. How will you become an advocate if go around kidnapping people at knife point?' said Angus.

'Shut up, Kraut.'

'Do you believe Françoise can't make up her own mind with whom she wants to spend her life.' Angus's tone of measured reasonableness disarmed Jean.

'I know her best. She needs me to make her life complete,' said Jean. He could not understand how his demands were being batted off in such an off-hand manner.

'I think you are deluded Monsieur, I am neither a drug addict nor a German. I would suggest you put the knife down before someone gets hurt.'

'Jean, stop behaving like a lunatic,' sobbed Françoise. 'Have you lost your mind? You don't want to hurt me or my friend here, for God's sake drop the knife before…'

Jean grabbed Françoise's halter top and pulled her up from the chair to her feet with one hand, with the other he pointed the knife tip into her back. Françoise could feel Jean's skinny, hairless arm trembling around her neck. Jean felt the knife blade touch Françoise's bare, sun-browned flesh, and he felt a surge of power. 'We are leaving now, don't try and stop us. Françoise will soon realise it will be better this way. If you try and follow us she'll only get hurt.' Françoise was shaking with fear as she felt the point of the blade on her skin. Jean started to shuffle backwards towards the café's doorway. Angus looked on, powerless to intervene.

While this drama had been unfolding, Pete had come down the stairway from his room and entered the café unnoticed behind Jean's back. As Jean continued edging towards the doorway, his one arm pulling Françoise by her flimsy top, the other still pointing the knife into her back. Jean was unaware that Pete had picked up a café chair and lifted it high above his head before he brought it crashing down onto the assailant's skull. The wooden chair and knife clattered to the floor followed by Jean who collapsed sideways, upturning one of the café tables in the process. Angus pushed the stunned Françoise to one side and leapt on top of the semi-conscious Jean, who was sprawled on his back, his head bleeding. Once Angus was on top of him, he pinned his shoulders to the floor with both knees and drew back his fist and drove it into Jean's face with a mighty smack. The blow broke

Jean's nose and showered blood down his crisp linen shirt and his tight-fitting trousers. The force knocked him unconscious.

'Someone call the police,' shouted Angus, as he relaxed the pressure on Jean's limp body. It was clear Jean was going nowhere. Pete comforted a hysterical Françoise, while *Le patron*, and the three other café customers burst into spontaneous clapping, and shouted 'Bravo, Bravo.' Angus was stunned by his own ferocity and its effectiveness. He could not remember ever hitting anybody before.

'Do you know who this mad man is…or was,' said Pete.

'One of Françoise's exes,' said Angus, as he slapped Jean's face in an effort to bring him around.

'Well, that's one way of getting rid of your rivals,' said Pete, always ready with a quip to lighten the drama. 'Is this Jean the Paris boyfriend, the nutter that Françoise talked about?'

'The same one.'

'He must have been keen.'

'He was trying to abduct her. But thanks to your action with the chair, you stopped him scarpering with Françoise. Well bloody done, Pete.'

'All part of the service, that's what mates are for. But it will cost you a few beers.'

'The least I can do. I might need to buy *Le patron* a new chair too.'

'It's on the house,' said *Le patron*.

Angus felt unexpectedly liberated by his act of violence towards Jean who lay bleeding on the floor. The idea of anyone violating Françoise overwhelmed his normal passive senses and had unleashed a fury he'd no idea he possessed.

'I told you he was passionate,' said Pete, to Françoise, who was still shaking with fear.

It was not long before they heard the wailing klaxons and three gendarmes burst into the café with guns drawn. Everyone instinctively raised their hands, except Jean who was now awake, moaning on the café floor, his face covered in blood. *Le patron* told the police what had happened and he handed them as evidence the knife. He persuaded them not to cuff Angus, who they immediately suspected was the culprit. Angus, Françoise, Pete and Jean were all bundled off to the police station for questioning. Jean, who had come around was nursing his bleeding head and swollen nose. He was crying like a child and was placed in the front of the police van, handcuffed to a gendarme. 'It's not fair, it's not fair, I'm going to be lawyer,' he muttered, between his sobs. The other three were shoved unceremoniously into the back of the Black Maria together with a third officer. They set off at an unnecessarily high speed with sirens blaring.

Jean was held in police custody for twenty-four hours until his mother could find the time to come and pay the bail money. The court judge wanted to place him under *garde a vue*, but his stepfather grudgingly, following his wife's instructions, hired a top lawyer who pleaded his case for release. He would appear at a *cour d'assises* some months later. In the meantime, Jean was banned from being within a twenty-five-kilometre radius of Aix-en-Provence. Until his case was heard, Jean's parents booked him into a secure, private psychiatric hospital for examination and treatment.

'Hello, we meet again,' said the man with the bow tie, on Jean's first session with a psychiatrist. It did not take him long to determine that Jean should remain under secure, close supervision until he stood trial. Under no circumstances should he be let out.

Chapter 23

Two months had elapsed since Jean's attempted abduction of Françoise. When the case was heard Angus and Pete were called as witnesses. Françoise's testimony was read in court as she could not bear to face Jean across the court room. She was still traumatised by the attack. Henri was in the public gallery glowering at the pathetic figure of Jean. Given the opportunity he would have been back in court himself for unspeakable violence towards the broken young man.

Stupidly, Jean insisted on handling his own case without a defence lawyer. He argued that his promising career in the law was in jeopardy because of his obsession with a beautiful young woman. He pleaded that this was an understandable hazard for a young, impressionable Frenchman. The female judge looked at him in amazement and quickly concluded the young man was seriously deranged. The psychiatrist confirmed the judge's suspicions with his damning testimony: 'He poses a threat to the public and requires lengthy therapy before he should be considered for release.'

To the horror of his mother and stepfather, Jean also pleaded his alienation from his family which he believed was a contributory factor to his mental breakdown. Jean received a six year sentence for attempted abduction and endangering life. He was ordered to receive psychiatric treatment during his period of incarceration and would only be released when he was deemed to be no longer a danger to the public. He was lead away shouting Françoise's name. 'You know you love me,' were his final, pathetic words before he disappeared from view, cuffed to a large male nurse. Françoise wept when she learned of the carnage she had unintentionally inflicted on the poor man.

Jean's trial was a catalyst for Angus. He secretly started to make enquiries into part time teaching English at *lycées* in Aix. He thought some experience would help his chances of securing a teaching position in Paris at the end of the year.

Despite Pete's heroic rescue of Françoise, he had become increasingly huffy about Angus's all-absorbing relationship with Françoise. In turn, Françoise was increasingly demanding of Angus's spare time and had started to get impatient with him when work pressures got in the way of their social plans.

'Why are you working on Saturday, you know we have arranged to meet Charlotte, Pierre and the whole gang at the *Le Bar Renard*,' it was agreed weeks ago,' she said.

'Your Papa needs this job finishing before the owners arrive on Monday. I can hardly refuse him because I'm taking his daughter to a party. You know his attitude towards me is ambivalent at the best of times.'

'I think he makes you work on weekends to just to keep us apart. He doesn't like the fact that we are dating. Anyhow, why can't Pete finish this blasted job?'

'Because he trusts me to do a better job.'

'He takes advantage of your good nature, you're too easy-going with him. I've been looking forward to this party for weeks, it's Pascal's birthday.'

'I'll be back by seven and then we can go out?'

'I know your "*sevens*". It'll be nine, and anyhow, the day will be ruined. The party is at lunchtime.'

'I'll ask Pete to come along to keep you company.'

'It's not Pete I want,' said Françoise, her bottom lip wobbling in frustrated anger.

~

Angus was angry about missing the gathering at *Bar Renard*, he hated letting Françoise down and he cursed Henri under his breath. Françoise was probably right about Henri's none too subtle ways of messing up with their social lives. The only benefit was overtime pay which he had been saving up for his planned move to Paris. Angus mentioned the party to Pete and suggested he looked in at *Bar Renard*. He floated the idea there would be a surplus of Françoise's attractive girlfriends so he should try and make it.

On the day of the party, Pete was feeling particularly pleased with himself as he has just struck a lucrative side deal selling Henri's surplus paint from jobs, to a one-man decorator with whom he played cards. Pete had just trousered a hundred francs and was feeling flush as he hurried to *Bar Renard*. Pete was on the hunt for a regular female companion as he had all but given up on Françoise, she seemed completely loved-up with Angus. Pete had made an effort to learn French as Angus was no longer always on hand to act as translator. He was still a long way from being fluent but he could hold a conversation of sorts.

Bar Renard was buzzing and he had high hopes as the girls heavily outnumbered the men. The odds looked favourable for a fun afternoon, and there was no Angus to look disapprovingly at him when he went over the top. As he was anxious to create a favourable impression he bought the group an expensive round of drinks. Pete had his eye on a kinky-looking, dark-haired girl, with a page-boy haircut who he had clocked previously in an old town bar. This afternoon looked like the opportunity to get better acquainted but she was wedged in at the opposite end of a long table with a boy on either side. If he'd had got there earlier he could have been better positioned.

For some reason the party never really got going and several people drifted off after they had eaten. 'I thought we were going to hit the clubs later on,' said Pete.

'Doesn't look like as this is going to happen,' said Françoise.

Just as Pete edged close to the dark-haired girl she got up to leave. 'Do you fancy coming dancing later,' he asked.

'Sorry, we are off to the cinema,' she said. And much to Pete's annoyance, his possible date departed, hand-in-hand, with one of the young men who had been sitting next to her. He didn't even get a farewell kiss. So much for the round of drinks, he thought.

By four o'clock everybody had left, leaving him at the table with Françoise.

'Looks like we are going to have to party on our own,' said Pete.

Françoise was still bristling with annoyance about Angus's no-show and she was about to get up and go.

'C'mon on, let's have a final drink,' said Pete.

Françoise hesitated for a moment. 'Oh, well, why not?'

'I'll order a bottle of Chablis, you look as if you need cheering up.'

'Pete, I've already had several drinks, you'll be getting me drunk. Angus will not be pleased to find his girlfriend inebriated when he gets back.'

Pete just smiled. He returned from the bar with two glasses, the frosted wine bottle chinked enticingly in an ice bucket. They moved from their large table to an intimate booth where they could chat privately without being overheard. During the next hour they giggled over vacuous gossip, and said all the stupid things they never dared to say to one another when sober.

'I've decided now is the perfect time to do your portrait, Pete. I did promise, remember.'

'How could I forget?'

'It's the least I can do after saving my life from poor mad Jean,' said Françoise. She scrabbled in her large bag and fished out a pencil and drawing pad. 'I'll add the some colour later, I think I'm a bit too drunk to do more than the preliminary sketches.'

'Let's go back to the apartment, it will be quiet and easier to draw there,' said Pete.

By the time the pair sneaked up the café back stairs and out of view of *Le patron*, Françoise was quite drunk.

'Hello,' said Odette, as she passed them in the narrow corridor. 'Got a new girl, Pierre? Naughty boy,' she cackled with her throaty laugh.

Chapter 24

Although it was early September the weather was still warm enough to feel like a hot mid-summer day in England. Angus had anticipated that by late October, as autumn started to turn to winter, their exterior painting work would be tailing off. Then would be the time to sever their arrangements with Henri Delores.

He had no intention of following other itinerant summer workers and go north to ski resorts to work in bars during the winter months. Being stuck up an alp in cold weather held no appeal, and anyhow, he couldn't ski. Angus was keen to fulfil his embryonic plan to go and teach in Paris and, more importantly, join Françoise. It would not be long before she started her fashion course and the idea of giving up painting villas was a welcome relief. The novelty had become the mundane, it had been fun in the early days, but now it was a slog. His mind had atrophied enough, it was time to exercise his brain muscles again. And he certainly would not miss being ordered about by irascible Henri.

He had to face up to Pete and tell him his plans. The idea of being away from Françoise until Christmas was unthinkable.

Three weeks after the lunchtime party at *Bar Bernard* Françoise was packed and ready to start her design course in Paris.

The day after her drunken portraiture session with Pete she had been racked with guilt about what had occurred. She was furious with herself for allowing Pete to take advantage of her when she was drunk. At the time it had seemed the natural thing to do. If nothing else, it had laid the ghost of Pete's constant flirting. She could not even remember if it was any good. But her guilt was so great she could no longer face sleeping with Angus. She excused herself with period pains and stress about the new course. She stopped coming to the café and avoided seeing Pete.

Angus said a sad farewell to Françoise at Aix railway station. Angus's good nature prevented him from quizzing her about the fabricated stories of period pains and nerves about her new course, although he had an underlying suspicion about their veracity.

'Darling, please, please write loads,' said Angus.

'Of course, I will. Come to Paris soon.'

'As soon as I can get away. I love you.'

'I love you too, dear, Angus,' said Françoise, bursting into tears. She clung to him, her tears wet her cheeks and the strands of her long auburn hair. Angus gently brushed her hair aside and kissed her lightly on the lips.

'Don't worry darling, it won't be for long. Quickly, get on the train before it leaves without you.' As the train pulled out of the station Angus watched his beautiful, weeping girl, as she waved from the window. He was suddenly overwhelmed with a dreadful sense of gloom. He tried to contain his own feelings as the train disappeared out of the station. Station platform departures were such emotional clichés.

Angus wrote regular, lively letters, full of witty anecdotes of life in Aix. He talked about Henri, and her mother, and of course, Pete. Françoise's initial correspondence shone with her usual exuberance, her writing large and flowing, her stories spilled over with gossip about her design course, new friends, she even included rough sketches of her dress designs, asking for Angus's opinion. By the end of October, her correspondence wilted to infrequent cards hurriedly scribbled in pencil. Angus had hesitated and was still painting for Henri while Pete was keeping an uncharacteristically low profile. He had announced to Pete he was heading to Paris very soon. To Angus's surprise, Pete seemed indifferent to the news. 'What will you do when I've gone?'

'Henri has asked me to help in his office.'

'Good heavens, could you face dealing with him every day?'

'Might be worth a try for the winter months. I reckon his buying is inefficient and his stock control is non existent. I know because I have been selling his surplus paint on the quiet for months.'

'Bloody hell, Pete. Is there no end to your subterfuge?'

'They were going to waste anyway, he never cared. I am going to pitch him a deal on taking a percentage of what I save him on top of a wage.'

'Will he buy it?'

'You know Henri, he's greedy.'

~

In early November Françoise wrote to say she was coming home. She said she needed to "talk about things." Angus was at first overjoyed and then anxiety flooded his mind. Her note was ambiguous. Had she met someone else, or was she going to give up her course before the year had barely started? He sensed there was something badly wrong. Françoise would be back soon. He would have to wait.

Pete was no longer his exuberant self; Angus sensed he was avoiding him. He spent more time getting drunk with Odette in the bar below the apartment, accompanied by Fifi, the shower-crapping poodle. He wondered if he and Odette were…no, they couldn't be?

Françoise's return to Aix in mid-November was muted. She remained stand-offish, their meetings lacked any intimacy. She avoided seeing Pete who was noticeable by his absence. He had started taking interior painting assignments a long way from Aix and was often away for nights on end. Angus wondered if he was having an affair with a married woman. He had suddenly become secretive, normally he boasted about his conquests. Then unannounced, he had taken a two week holiday and disappeared.

It was clear that something was seriously amiss, his relationship with Françoise had stalled. Angus suggested a day's bus excursion to Marseilles where he hoped they could talk privately, away from Aix. He had planned to ask her to marry him when she returned from Paris at Christmas. He wondered if now would be the time to spring the question. But as the bus journey progressed the atmosphere did not lighten and he dismissed the idea.

He had made up his mind that he wanted to make a new life in France. He had fallen in love with the relaxed French lifestyle and found the person he wanted to be with for the rest of his life. But Angus had forgotten the fortune teller's unequivocal prediction that he would never live abroad.

The bus journey was undertaken in a depressing silence. Their lunch in a café was desultory, Françoise hardly ate anything, and disappeared mid-meal to the lavatory. She returned to the table, pale and drawn. 'Are you sure you're okay,' said Angus. Despite his probing, she would not be drawn on why she had returned to Aix before the end of her first term. Angus felt a hopeless melancholy sweep over him.

In the afternoon they walked to the seafront and sat side by side on the harbour wall in the Vieux-Port. The late November watery sun played on the white-hulled boats that bobbed gently in the harbour's oily water, the wintery light reflected off their paintwork. A cool wind was coming off the sea, Françoise wrapped her arms around herself, she was only wearing a flimsy waterproof, it was made for style, not warmth. She was trembling with cold and apprehension, this was the moment she has been dreading for the last few months.

'I'm pregnant,' she said.

Chapter 25

War Time France 1944

'This is your doing!' the boy's mother screamed at him.

The boy had just returned from his day at the paint factory. A day he had spent in a fearful state. His anxiety had only been relieved by thinking about the Agent's farewell kiss. During the day he had overheard his fellow workers talking in low voices about arrests in the nearby town. He tried his best to ignore their conversations and dispel the magnitude of his night's actions from his mind.

When he had opened the cottage door that evening, he discovered his mother sitting in an upright chair rocking back and forth, her head in her hands. The farm cottage looked like a hurricane had passed through it, cupboard doors hung open and the stone floor was littered with broken china, assorted paper and torn books. His mother could not summon the effort to clear the detritus, tears rolled down her sun-worn cheeks, she looked as old as his ancient grandmama.

'What have you done, what have you done, you stupid, stupid boy!' she wailed.

'What's wrong?' he said. Where's Papa?'

'After you left for work this morning, three Germans turned up and searched the place. They discovered a rifle in the barn. They've arrested your father and taken him away. God alone knows where? They suspect he's a Résistance member. For Jesus's sake what is a British gun doing in our barn?'

'My God,' he said, his face filled with guilty fear as the results of his carelessness was brought into sharp focus. His mother didn't need to be a mind-reader to know that her son was somehow implicated.

'I suppose the gun is yours?'

'Is it hell,' he said. 'Of course it's not mine. Why are you accusing me?'

'Because you're a damn liar, and always have been.' The boy had to think quickly.

'It was probably planted by one of the partisans. You know they hate us.'

'Why pick on us?'

'Because Philippe is in the *Milice*, why else?'

His mother remained silent while she thought about this possibility. It did worry her that Philippe was regarded as a collaborator. She knew that his actions would eventually rebound on the family. A lot of his customers had stopped going to his butcher's shop and she frequently received malicious remarks from people in the street. She had even been spat at.

'Where have they taken Papa?' said the boy, as he tried to steer the conversation away from the British Lee Enfield rifle he had so badly hidden in a pile of hay in the barn.

'The police station. Where else?' she said, and started to cry again.

'Have you been in touch with Philippe?'

'I took a bus to town to look for him, but the shop was closed.'

The boy left his mother weeping and disappeared up to his room to think things over. He removed his paint-stained overalls but struggled to pull up his clean trousers as he shook with fear as the implications of his carelessness with the rifle sank in. His father had been arrested and was most likely being tortured; he had compromised his fellow partisans, and worse still, he had let down the Agent. His mother was not easily fooled, she suspected he was the culprit.

The boy came downstairs, 'I'm going out to feed the pigs,' he said, as if nothing unusual had occurred. This was a chore his father normally undertook every evening and it did nothing for his mother's anguished state.

She let out another howl as he slipped out of the door into the farmyard. The boy spent a sleepless night wondering how long it would be before he was rounded up for questioning.

Chapter 26

'How? We've been so careful,' said Angus.

Françoise bowed her head. She could not look Angus in the eye. 'I don't know how to tell you this... but I can't lie to you.'

Angus paused, breathless. 'Well, it's okay, we'll get married.'

'But we can't.'

'I rather like the idea of you having our baby. Who will stop us?'

'I will.'

'Don't be ridiculous, the life inside you is as much my responsibility as yours.'

Angus, Angus...it's not *your* baby.'

Angus gasped, unable to take in Françoise's words. 'What do you mean it's *not mine?*'

'Because you're not the father.'

'I don't understand, how...?'

'Because...' Françoise's voice trailed off. She was unable to utter the words. She could not admit the shame of her adultery.

'Françoise, you're kidding me. Tell me, this is your idea of a terrible joke.'

'How could I joke about such a thing?'

'Who then? Who's the bloody father, a student in Paris?'

Françoise remained mute, her head lowered as she stared at her painted toenails that crept out from stylish sandals. All Angus could see was her tousled auburn hair. He watched in disbelief as her tears landed in large drops on the quayside's white stone paving. It was like the start of a thunderstorm. Angus turned towards her and tried to put his arms around her shoulders, but she shrugged him off.

'Don't touch me, Angus. I can't bear your sympathy, I'm not worthy of it.'

'You can't make these crazy statements and not tell me who is the father of your child.'

Her silence was only interrupted by sobs.

'Françoise, you *have* to tell me? Do you love the father?'

'No.'

'So what is stopping us marrying, just tell me for God's sake? I don't care who the father is, just *marry me*.'

Angus's mind was racing. He tried to fathom ways to rid them both from this nightmare of nightmares. He would do anything to hold on to her. *Anything*. 'Nobody would ever know. I can't bear the thought of being without you my darling.' His eyes filled with tears. 'Don't you still love me?'

'Angus, how can you still *love me* when I have been unfaithful to you?' She spat the words out, as if she was deliberately trying to punish herself.

'How many times?'

'Only once,' she whispered. '*Un moment de folie*.'

'*Folie, folie*...is this what French girls do to their boyfriends when their back is turned? I can't believe you could betray me like this.'

'Darling Angus, it was the most stupid thing. You have to believe me. I was very drunk ...the father is Pete.

'Pete, PETE, PETE!' he roared. Then Angus let out a loud howl of anguish. A man tying up his boat on the jetty looked up and saw a man with is head in his hands with a tall girl next to him weeping. He considered going over to investigate but thought better of it. Why get involved with other people's problems, he had enough of his own.

'We were both drunk. It was idiotic, foolish, I don't care about him, I only love you, Angus.'

'Pete of all people, Pete...the utterly selfish, self-serving bastard. Where is he? I'll wring his bloody neck.'

'Oh no Angus, don't make things worse than they already are.'

'Wait until I catch up with him, the cowardly, sod.'

'Don't say those things, it's all *my* fault.'

'He took advantage of you, and me. I'm supposed to be his oldest friend, the selfish bloody sod'

'Angus!'

'Are you sure he is the father, how can you be so certain?'

'He didn't use a condom. And the timing matches.'

'When did this happen?'

'Do you really need to know the details? What's the point in punishing yourself any more.'

'*I want to know when I was betrayed*.'

'It was the day of the party at Bar Renard in September. You were finishing a job for Papa. What does it matter anyway? *I'm to blame*. Don't blame Pete. I allowed it to happen, I was drunk.

'And I encouraged him to go to the party instead of me, just wait 'till I get hold of him...'

'No Angus, fighting will solve nothing.'

'How can I be angry with you? I know what Pete's like. Always out for his own ends. The complete, utter bastard. Screw your best mate's girl and make her pregnant, then leave her to pick up the pieces.'

Angus' acceptance of her innocence was like a knife skewering her soul. She didn't deserve his unwavering sympathy, it made her feel dizzy, sick to her core.

'He wants me to marry him,' she said.

'WHAT! He can't. Never, never, never, I won't allow it."

'He's insistent, he says his child has to have a proper father. And that father is him.'

'So, *he* is aware of his infamy. The conniving bastard. I knew he always fancied you, and this is his way of stealing you away from me. You've worked all this out between you. Well he bloody well *can't. I am going to marry you.*'

'He says he has to, it's his duty, he calls it, "The honourable thing."'

'What *honour* is there in that?'

'Oh Angus, how could you bring up a child as one of your own, if you knew the father was your oldest friend?'

'It wouldn't bother me as long as I had got you. We could have children of our own.'

'Oh, Angus.'

'Have you thought about...ending the pregnancy?'

'Don't even mention the subject of termination. You sound like Pete. You English have no morals. Abortions are illegal, remember, I am a Catholic. I would never *murder* my child under any circumstances, whoever the father was.'

Angus's indignation spilled over: 'English morals! That's a bit rich! I didn't think good Catholic girls go around sleeping with their boyfriend's mates. How could you Françoise? HOW COULD YOU?'

'I don't have any excuses. I have no alternative, I have to marry Pete.'

'But why for God's sake? You don't love him.'

'Because my child deserves to have his *real* father. And my parents have insisted, in spite of my father's dislike of Pete.'

'They already know all the sordid details?'

'Yes.'

'And I'm the last to be told. You've got it all stitched up between your parents and Pete, behind my back.'

'How long has this secret pact been hatched?'

'Since I came back.'

'But Pete knew you were pregnant weeks ago, didn't he, that's why he's been avoiding me?'

Françoise looked up at Angus, tears streamed down her cheeks, she bent forward and kissed his lips, and slipped off the jetty wall. He watched her as she ran, sobbing into the maze of the old town's cobbled streets.

The boat owner looked up as he saw the tall girl run along the jetty into the town. It reminded him of his own heartbreaks when he was a young man. He wished he could tell her she would survive it.

As the sun disappeared below the horizon, Angus remained riveted to the top of the wall, he was catatonic and unable to give chase. He stared in disbelief at the darkening sky as the harbour lights flickered into life. He was unable to fathom the implications of what he had just been told. Another elderly boat owner, wearing a captain's peaked hat, passed him as he took an evening stroll. He was a accompanied by a woman of a similar vintage who hung onto his arm, he turned and gave an embarrassed half-smile, she looked straight head.

The shattered looking young man perched on the jetty wall did not move.

Chapter 27

It was quite dark by the time Angus slipped down from the harbour wall. He felt utterly wretched. The enormity of the wrecking ball that had smashed into his life was only just registering.

Angus would have readily murdered Pete if he'd seen him that evening. He recalled the anger he had experienced when Jean had threatened Françoise, this time his rage was combined with righteous indignation and a dreadful sense of needless ruin.

After he left the quayside, Angus could not remember much about his random journey as he weaved aimlessly around the Marseilles streets. His mind span as he went over and over what Françoise had confessed. He tried to make sense of her brief, shattering sentences. He wandered into several street cafés where he chain-smoked and choked down pastis after pastis. He stared out into the bustling streets and wondered if Françoise had harboured a desire for Pete all along. Or had *he* had designs on her from the outset? Was Françoise the real reason for his readiness to stay in Aix and his ambivalence to continuing the Marrakesh journey?

Much later, bewildered and drunk, he wandered into a small hotel seeking sanctuary. An attractive girl was seated behind at a tiny reception desk. She looked at him curiously. 'Are you okay Monsieur? You look unwell,' she said. Angus pulled himself up straight and managed a grim smile, trying not to give away how far gone he was.

'No luggage?' She said, it was often a sign of guest trouble, men who tried to sneak mistresses into their rooms.

'Nah, I have none, I missed my bus to Aix,' said Angus. 'How much is your cheapest room…I'll pay now,' he said, trying to deflect the creeping doubt of the receptionist. He rummaged in his pocket and threw some notes on the desk top, at the same time he dropped a crushed cigarette packet and assorted coins on the floor. He bent down to retrieve the various items off the patterned tiles but felt very giddy as the hexagonal shapes of the terracotta flooring went in an out of focus. Eventually, he got into a semi-upright position by holding on to the reception's countertop. He retrieved his blue passport from his back pocket to prove his identity.

'Ah English?' said the receptionist, flicking through the passport pages. 'You speak good French,' she said, taking in Angus's long hair. 'Are you from Liverpool?' She looked closer at his passport and saw the place of birth was Leeds. Her face fell in disappointment. 'I am not a rock star, but I do know one very well, he's a robbing bastard.'

'What is his name?'

'Pete Jagoda from "The Betrayers.,"' he said, as he scribbled his name and address on the hotel entry form.

The receptionist looked blank. 'I've never heard of them.'

'You've missed nothing, he's very, very bad.'

The receptionist reluctantly handed him a room key. After a brief battle with the ancient concertina doors to the lift, he found his room on the third floor. Angus opened the window shutters to reveal a view of the adjacent property's rendered concrete wall. There was a narrow, cobbled alleyway below and he hung his head over the Juliet balcony and was violently sick. He staggered back into the room and threw himself onto the bed. As he looked up at the ceiling the room started to spin round and round, he laid out his hands to hold onto either side of the thin mattress to try and control the circling sensation. He closed his eyes to make it go away, and finally, he fell into a drunken coma.

He was awoken early the following morning as a rubbish truck negotiated its way down the narrow alley, the bin men were noisily emptying refuse containers into the back of the vehicle. Angus looked up at the cracked ceiling and watched an ordered army of ants traversing the chipped plaster cornice before they disappeared into a crevice. They don't have a care in the world, he thought, what a nice simple life they must enjoy, filled with purpose and order. His head throbbed and his mouth was as dry as a summer river bottom. He got up and ran some water into a tiny basin in the corner of the room. He splashed his face with the lukewarm, brackish water. He was tempted to drink some but decided not to risk it, he felt bad enough as it was. He would wait for a coffee later.

Angus sat on the edge of his bed and thought about what to do next. His life was in tatters. He could not face meeting Pete, that would have to come later. He had to see Françoise again. To question, to understand, to find answers. There had to be a way out of this nightmare. The night's drinking had done nothing to relieve his mental state, he put his head in his hands and wept uncontrollably.

~

'Where've you been? You should have been here three hours ago,' said Henri, his face a purple paroxysm.

'I'm quitting. Now,' said Angus.

'You can't, you have work to complete.'

'I'm telling you, I'm finished. *Comprenez-vous?*'

'Is this to do with Françoise? I suppose you've heard what your friend has done to my beautiful daughter? That swine, the son of a whore.' Henri started to froth, spittle appeared at the corner of his mouth, a large blue vein stood out on his bronzed forehead. 'The fornicator... now he has to marry my precious girl.' He approached Angus, his arms waved about incoherently. He was out of control and he needed somebody with whom he could vent his anger .

'Monsieur, you are forgetting, *c'est moi*,' said Angus jabbing his finger into his own chest. 'I'm the one who has been cheated. Your daughter has betrayed me, *how do you think I feel?*"

'Bah, you English!' he roared, throwing his arms up again in a gesture of hopelessness. 'You're all arrogant, morally corrupt, Godless, long-haired, heathens...' Henri's hysterical raving rendered him briefly speechless. 'Get out, out of my yard, I never want to see you again.'

'I am here to speak to Françoise,' said Angus, with quiet menace, barely managing to suppress his hatred of the crazed, little man. Angus felt his fists clench, he was ready to hit the ranting Frenchman if he got any closer.

'LEAVE THIS MINUTE, or I'll call the gendarmerie.'

Just as Angus was poised to plant one on the incandescent figure, Françoise emerged from her parents' cottage. She had heard her father shouting and saw the disheveled Angus. He was standing bolt-upright in front of her father and she knew Angus was poised to hit her father very hard. She had seen him do it before.

'Papa, Papa. Stop it, stop it!' she shouted from the cottage doorway. 'It's nothing to do with Angus.'

'Keep away from him. English scum, he's no better than your foreign lover-boy.'

'I'll do what I want,' she screamed, dry tears burning her eyes as she ran towards Angus.

Henri turned towards her. 'That's your problem, Françoise, you've always done what *you want*, see where it's got you.' He was about to strike his daughter to stop her reaching Angus.

Angus, who was easily a foot taller than Henri, grabbed his arm with a vice-like grip, his pent up fury surfacing. 'Leave her alone, you stupid bully. She's not one of your workers,' said Angus, holding his raised arm while with his other hand he pulled the little man closer to him. 'I am going to speak to Françoise whether you like it or not,' he said, looking directly into Henri's bulging eyes.

'If you're not off my premises in five minutes I am calling the police,' said Henri. Angus eased his hold, and Henri sensed Angus's menace and decided against taking on someone decades his junior. Angus pushed him out of the away to speak to Françoise and Henri scuttled off towards the cottage.

'Angus, I'm sorry about Papa. I told you they know the whole story…Pete, the baby.'

It already existed, a baby growing inside her, it has a form, a person with an identity a place in the world, it is already included in conversations, a living thing that Pete and Françoise have created. Angus had not anticipated the awful proof of their intimacy would be laid bare so soon.

'Angus, you look awful. I don't want to know what happened to you last night, I can only guess.'

'I went out to celebrate the ruination of our lives.'

Françoise's shoulders slump, 'Have you any idea what *my days have been like?* Papa went absolutely crazy, and my mother threatened to send me to a convent and have the baby adopted by a Catholic family.'

'Isn't that's what they do in Ireland. It's bloody medieval.'

'I have to see the priest this afternoon to confess my sins and start to arrange the wedding,' she said, ignoring Angus's bitter remark.

The abyss had opened, within just a few days of telling her parents, she was now consulting God's representative in Aix, and arranging a marriage to a man she doesn't love. It was only then that Angus realised the control Françoise's parents exacted over their daughter. She was incapable of disobeying them. In her parents' eyes, she was a child until she reached twenty-one, and until then she was under their ownership. It was like going back hundreds of years.

'So, you're going ahead with this ridiculous charade?'

'What options have I?'

'Marry me instead. I'll bring up the child as my own'

'Pete insists he wants to marry me. It's *his* child, he says he couldn't stand anyone else bringing it up. You know how proud he is.'

'What! Pete has suddenly found his moral compass? I can't believe you are going through with this. It's crazy.'

'Papa has already met Father Dominic to get permission to marry us. Priests are not keen on Catholics marrying anyone outside the Faith. It will cost him a big donation to the Church.'

'My heart bleeds for him. Why can't we just runaway together and forget all this Church nonsense. We could marry in England at a registry office.'

'Papa would set the gendarmerie on us and you could be locked up for abduction, I'm under twenty-one.'

'Françoise, you're throwing your life away. *For pity's sake don't do it.*'

'Angus my darling, my mind is made up, I have created this mess and I am going to have to live with the consequences,' she said. She started to cry.

Angus felt helpless, unable to touch her, even when red-eyed and weeping, Françoise was still the most beautiful girl he had ever known. He wanted to take her in his arms, but he was incapable of moving, torpid with grief and exhausted with desperate longing.

Suddenly Henri emerged at a trot from the cottage. He was carrying an old rifle over his arm and was accompanied by Madame Delores at his shoulder, dressed entirely in black. He looked like a cowboy sheriff with his deputy two steps behind. They both glowered at him with malice, Angus wondered if Madame Delores had a concealed meat-cleaver under her widow's weeds.

Françoise looked at Angus one last time, she hesitated as if to kiss him, but her gun toting father was approaching fast. She turned, and ran past her strutting parents, back into the cottage. Angus stood his ground, his arms hung loosely by his side. If it was not so serious it would have been a laugh, Henri waved his rifle around, fingering the safety catch as if he were in a spaghetti western. Madame Delores, recognised her husband's unpredictability, and decided it would be better if she did not witness him commit murder. She turned on her heel and hurried after her distraught daughter. As she closed the house door behind her, Angus heard Françoise's anguished cry.

Angus let out a bitter laugh and slowly walked out of the yard, leaving Henri alone, rooted in his Mexican stand-off pose.

Chapter 28

Angus returned to the apartment above the café with the dodgy Algerians, Odette and the crappy white poodle. He wondered if Pete would be there or if he had gone to work.

He immediately noticed all Pete's belongings had vanished. He'd done a runner, the coward's way out. There was an envelope with his name on it lying on the bed cover. He recognised Pete's writing and was in two minds whether to open it or rip it to shreds

Angus's hangover was reaching the melancholy stage but still the shock of the last eighteen hours of drama were somehow keeping him functioning. The farce of the raging Henri who had waved his ancient gun about like a demented gangster, Françoise's final howl, the scowling Madame Delores who kept crossing herself as if she was in the presence of the devil incarnate, and Henri's pudgy fingers playing around the safety catch of his rifle like Wyatt Earp. It was like a scene from a terrible movie in which he was lead actor. In a stroke, Angus's whole life had been turned upside down, all certainties ripped away, everything he had planned and hoped for shredded. It had all been destroyed by the people he trusted and loved the most.

He sat on the edge of his bed and picked up his discarded backpack and started to rummage around inside until he found what he was searching for: the tiny bible that his father had given him. He riffled through the wafer-thin pages until he came across the passage he wanted: Ephesians Chapter 4, Verses 31-32. It was a piece his father used in his sermons on forgiveness:

"Get rid of all bitterness, rage, anger, brawling and slander, along with every form of malice. Be kind and compassionate to one another, forgiving each other, just as in Christ God forgave you.'

He read the tiny manuscript and wept again, salty tears dropped onto the tissue-like paper of the little bible. He tossed the tiny black book across the room. Enough of this pathetic weeping he said to himself; he wiped his eyes with a towel and stood up and clutching Pete's unopened letter he went downstairs into the café.

The place was empty of customers. '*Bon jour,*' said *Le patron*, 'Are you having a day off, you're not normally here at this time. I have some *moules frite* if you'd like a late *déjeuener?*' he said. Angus nodded his agreement. And a carafe of the vin rouge, *s'il vous plaît.*' To Angus's surprise, *Le patron* came over and pulled up a chair and placed a bottle of 1962 Chateau Latour and two sparkling claret glasses on the table. He poured one out for Angus and another for himself. '*Santé*' he said, raising his glass.

'Now Angus, what's going on? Your friend left in a hell of a hurry this morning. He's paid your rent for two months' in advance. You've been here seven months and I thought you were going to be permanent fixtures. Pete ran out of here as if he'd committed a murder.'

'In a way he has,' said Angus, as he took a sip of the blackcurrant-coloured wine. 'This is a very fine wine, Monsieur.'

'On the house, it was a gift from someone for whom I once did a favour, it has been in my cellar for years,' said *Le Patron*, with a smile. 'You look terrible and need cheering up, so I thought now...' *Le Patron* shrugged with a typical Gallic gesture. 'Everything is better after a glass of good wine.'

'Thank you,' said Angus, with a faint smile. The wine lulled his delicate state, and unusually for a normally private person, he proceeded to unburden himself of his story of betrayal.

When Angus told him about Henri Delores threatening him with a gun, the café owner said, 'Monsieur Delores's family has a reputation for violence. During the war Henri Delores was in the *Maquis*, but his elder brother, a local butcher, was a *collaborator* and was murdered in 1944. Some say Henri killed his brother, nobody really knows the truth, but there was no love lost between them. Henri has many influential friends in this city, but he has many enemies too. His business has been successful because of his connections. In some ways you are better not being involved with that family, although his daughter is undeniably a great beauty.'

'It's interesting you say that because his attitude to Pete and myself has been one of subdued hostility from the outset. Most French people are okay with us Brits, but he has always been very guarded with us, cold...although he did give us both jobs.'

'Because it suited him. I'll bet he paid you well below average wages and probably in cash to avoid taxes.'

'Correct,' replied Angus.

'Now my friend, you've been badly wronged by Monsieur Pete. Do you want me to arrange for something bad to happen to him? I know people in Marseilles and he deserves a punishment... perhaps a broken arm or a good beating?' Angus looked up in surprise at the *Le patron*'s suggestion, then shook his head.

'It's a kind offer. It might make me feel better for a while, but it will solve nothing, and would only hurt Françoise.'

'You're a forgiving man, Monsieur Angus. Many men would want to kill him for what he's done to you.'

'If you'd asked me yesterday, I might have taken up your suggestion. Now, let me buy you bottle of good wine and perhaps now I'd better have the *moules*.'

Not long after, Odette tottered into the café looking for Pete. *Le patron* took her aside and whispered in her ear to give her the news. She came over and sat next to Angus as he was finishing his *moules*. She took his hand and gently kissed him on both cheeks. She smelt like one of his Scottish grannies, a mixture of carbolic and booze. Angus was moved by her gesture of kindness and he kissed the map of blue veins and age spots on the back of her bony hand.

'*Mon petit*, I weep for your loss, but you know your friend will never stay the course with the beautiful Françoise, mark my words. I know the sort of man Pete is, and I know Henri Delores. Monsieur Delores is a man with a grudge, and eventually he'll drive your friend away. In years to come you'll remember the words of wise old Odette. Take comfort from this at least,' she said. 'May I be permitted a glass of your delicious wine? I've not seen a bottle of Latour for many years, certainly not in here! I want to drink to your health and for happier times. You're a good man, Monsieur, and one day you'll find a good woman to be your companion and lover.'

Angus did not open Pete's letter until the following morning. Purposefully, he went into a café away from the apartment to take his morning coffee and smoke a Gitane.

Dear Old Friend

I know you will want to kill me, and you have every right to feel bitter about what has happened, but I want to explain. I never had long-term designs on Françoise Our once and only bedroom romp was a drunken, stupid, spur of the moment lark that we both regret. If I hadn't been so keen on "bare-back riding," Françoise would never have got pregnant and nobody would have been any the wiser.

I know you'll see this as a betrayal of trust and friendship and nothing I can say will stop you thinking that I'm the biggest bastard that ever walked this earth, and you're right. I am gutted about what has happened as it has damaged our very long dear friendship as well as putting the kybosh on our plans for Marrakesh, although I suspect you'd already given up on that idea?

However, irresponsible you think I am, I am very conscious of my obligations to Françoise and our, as yet, unborn child. It is for this reason that I am trying to make amends by 'doing the right thing' and marrying her as soon as possible. I don't want her to have to bear the stigma of being the mother of a bastard child. As you can imagine my father-in-law to be is not exactly brimming with goodwill about having me as his son-in-law. It will not be an easy ride.

I have paid two months' rent in advance on the apartment which might ease the burden as I presume, you'll stop the painting job. Whatever I say you'll still think me an absolute bugger and I have no excuses that I can trot out other than to say I am truly, very, very sorry.

If you'd like to meet up for a heart-to-heart, then come to the paint depot one evening.

As ever,

Pete

The self-serving twat thought Angus, as he tore up the letter into tiny pieces and stuffed them into an ashtray. "*Bedroom romp*," "*bare-back riding*." Some "old friend!" It's all one giant joke to him, a bit of a lark. Typical Pete. I hope his father-in-law makes his life hell. He'll be stuck down here painting houses for the rest of his life, silly sod. He had no intention of meeting up with him, and if he did, he would probably try and strangle him on the spot.

Angus went home to Leeds that Christmas and returned to Aix in early January after he secured a job at a *Lycée* teaching English to young students. When he returned in the new year to his little café apartment, he found an invitation from Françoise to the wedding later that month. He looked at it in disgust and wondered who she was trying to hurt most.

Chapter 29

However much Angus thought about the Ephesians bible passage, he could not reconcile Pete's actions to anything else but a monstrous betrayal of trust. Forgiveness did not register on his radar, his only companion was a self-tormenting sadness that pervaded his every day.

Despite his lamentations he surprised himself by deciding to attend Pete and Françoise's wedding. Why he was putting himself through this self-inflicted purgatory he was not sure. Perhaps he wanted to see Henri's face as he gave his precious daughter away to an imposter atheist. Maybe it was a perverse desire to punish himself by glimpsing what might have been?

No, *what should have been*.

He did not attend the civil ceremony at *La Mairie* which preceeded the Catholic wedding mass. The number of guests was very small and even they appeared cowed by the soaring space of the church, the humourless priest and the shame of Françoise's all too obvious pregnancy. Two key colleagues from Henri's business and their wives were in attendance along with Pete's father, Piotr Jagoda. Mrs Jagoda was surprisingly not in evidence and Angus wondered if they were aware of his own claim to Françoise.

The other attendees were Françoise's great aunt from Paris, two married couples who were Françoise's Godparents, plus a couple of close girlfriends of Françoise. Odette arrived uninvited. She wore a large white hat and a stylish, silk Dior suit of many years vintage. She sat next to Angus and squeezed his hand. 'What are *you* doing here?' she said. There was a strong smell of wine on her breath, Angus smiled and put his fingers to his lips.

Finally, an unidentified late middle-aged lady, dressed entirely in black with a small hat and veil, crept into the church just before the ceremony started. She would have looked more at home at a funeral service as she sat spectre-like, at the back of the church. When Odette turned around to look at the late comer the elderly lady responded with a withering stare. She crossed herself several times and ran her rosary beads through her gloved hands. Angus wondered if there has been some past form between the two women as they were probably a similar age.

The priest lit two large candles while two incense bearing acolytes stood to one side. It was plain for all to see that the priest was going through the motions of the marriage service and could not hide his distaste of having to marry a pregnant Catholic girl, to an unbeliever. He delivered his wedding address accordingly in a joyless monotone. From what Angus could glean of its echoing contents, there was plenty of loaded, moralising comments about bringing up children in the sight of God. There were no *enfants de honneur* with flower petals to add any light touches or innocent charm to the proceedings. Pete, stood at the altar, looking solemn, while Françoise' responses were all but inaudible. Pete smiled briefly as they exchanged rings.

The highlight of the service for Angus was when Odette wobbled forward from the back of the church with high heels clacking on the stone paving to take the sacrament at the altar. When she got up to go forward there was a loud tutting noise from the elderly lady at the back. Despite the cold weather, Odette was wearing no nylons and her age-spotted, spindly, blue-veined legs stood out against her blue silk skirt. She acknowledged Pete with a wink as she passed him, there was an audible gasp as her gesture was noticed by several guests, including the horrified priest.

Neither Angus, nor the mysterious lady in black, despite her outward signs of devoutness, went forward to take the wafer, and she slipped out of the church unnoticed by the other guests before the ceremony concluded. The solemnness of the service reminded Angus of his father's church gatherings in Scotland. As a child, he used to assiduously search for a sign of God's presence in the cold church. It finally dawned on young Angus that God was absent because of the discordant singing and the pious, pinched-mouthed congregation. He concluded that God had done a detour of his father's Kirk and was more likely to be found in the surrounding hills and picturesque woods, where the abundance of nature ably demonstrated the Almighty's good works.

As Angus left the vast church, and while Pete was distracted talking to his father, he turned briefly to greet Françoise. Despite her five-month bulge, she looked chaste behind her veil. As he parted the white lace and bent forward to place his lips on her cool cheeks, he could not fail to notice the overwhelming sadness in her large brown eyes. He briefly touched her hand that was holding a small bridal bouquet of white flowers. The posy was shaking lightly, the petals fell to her feet. Angus said nothing, no mention of luck or congratulations. Then he drifted away, he did not even acknowledge Pete or Mr Jagoda.

~

Teaching English at the small *Lycée* provided little respite from Angus's melancholy. He half-heartedly dated one of the teachers until she became possessive. She was older than Angus and talked of marriage. Eventually, Angus could no longer bear to be in Aix as everywhere he went there were memories of Françoise. He half-dreaded, half-wanted to bump into her to chat and laugh like old times. But he knew he could not utter a word if the occasion arose.

Fortunately, he found a lucrative position in Monaco tutoring a sixteen-year-old Greek girl, the daughter of a wealthy shipping-line owner. His new life could not be more different to the hard-core surroundings he had endured in the tiny slum room above the café in Aix. In his new post he was well paid and lived in a luxurious, self-contained flat, part of the family's expensive harbour-facing property. His new environment was glamorous but lonely. The bonus was he found time to indulge his passion for reading and study. The Principality was full of rich, self-satisfied people, and he tried his best to adapt to his new circumstances. He had his hair cut, bought new clothes and conformed

The main body of his work involved teaching English, but he also tutored the young girl on European literature, a subject Angus loved. His pupil, Alecta, lived up to her Greek name.

'You like me Mr Angus, no?'

'You are very nice Alecta, but your father has employed me to teach you English.'

'I know. My father very boring man. He wants me to love English. I love you. You English, no? You love me. I can tell way you look at me.'

'I don't look at you. Stop it Alecta. We have to work.'

'I come to your apartment tonight. Secret. You can kiss me.'

And so it went on. Her endless flirting brought back memories of Pete and Françoise. Alecta a dark haired, olive skinned version of Françoise, precocious and exuding a knowing, child-like innocence. Angus was embarrassed by Alecta's attentions, the trust of his employer and his own morality was challenged daily. She had taken to rubbing her smooth-skinned brown legs against his thigh when sitting next to him. When he asked her to move to a chair opposite him she became moody and uncooperative. She attempted to play footsie with him until he tucked his own legs under his chair .

Fortunately, Angus's feelings towards the temptress became diverted after he met an engaging English girl at a British expats reception.He was fortunate to be rescued from a potentially ruinous relationship with the alluring Alecta, the Greek shipping magnate's daughter. This serendipitous event saved his sanity and his job.

Angus was at Monaco's annual garden party for ex-pats hosted by the English consulate . This special celebration, was always held the day before the famous Grand Prix road race. It was an informal gathering of retired English racing drivers, and a smattering of famous, and not so famous Brits resident in the Principality. Angus was not one for social gatherings but his invitation had come from an English friend of his Greek employer, a man who claimed to be an Air Attaché based in the British embassy in Rome. 'You must come, it's the highlight of the season, although that's not saying much,' said the enigmatic man. Angus immediately suspected the man was a spy.

Angus had quickly learned that Monaco was populated by strange people like the embassy man. The Principality exuded expensively dressed stateless people, characters you could not pigeon hole, rich tax exiles with opaque jobs. The common denominator was wealth. He was trying his best to negotiate a monosyllabic but polite conversation with a small coterie of English residents and was wondering how he could make excuses to bow out early. He felt out of his comfort zone and had been obliged to buy, at some expense, an Italian pale blue lightweight linen suit and a new white shirt and tie for the occasion.

Suddenly he was aware of a large man in a white jacket at his shoulder, his jacket cuffs sported naval-style gold rings and he was accompanied by a tall, slender girl with shoulder length hair, in her early twenties. 'Good afternoon,' he boomed, prizing Angus away from the group, 'I'm Valentine Principle, may I introduce you to my niece, Priscilla.' The girl held out her hand and smiled at Angus giving him direct eye contact. Angus noticed her clear blue eyes and the softness of her hand to touch but the hand shake was surprisingly firm, he wondered if she was a tennis player. 'For my sins I'm supposed to be Priscilla's chaperone in Monaco,' said the large man. He laughed loudly inferring he did not take this role too seriously. The girl looked flustered at her uncle's introduction, her rose petal cheeks flushed with embarrassment at his levity. Valentine Principle's hand shake nearly crushed his fingers.

Angus was immediately attracted to the English rose and decided to stay a little longer at the party. Later on when Priscilla had shed her chaperoning-uncle, she cornered Angus while he was gazing over the beautiful harbour, the tranquility shattered by the roar of racing car engines as they undertook practice laps on the city circuit.

'Do you like motor racing?' she said.

'Not really. I probably shouldn't say so in the present company,' he said, looking around at the gathering on the open air terrace.

'I'm not much of a fan either, but it is exciting to watch, particularly as we are so close to the action.'

They exchanged polite pleasantries for a few more moments. It was clear to Angus that Priscilla wanted to move the conversation from Surrey cocktail party pleasantries to something more interesting.

'What on earth brings you here,' she said.

'It was suggested by a friend of my employer. They said it might be good diplomacy to show my face. And what's your excuse, you look nearly as bored as me.'

'My uncle runs a private boatyard down the coast. He builds expensive yachts for very rich people from all over the world. He likes to "network," as he calls it. Evidently, it's good for business and he has dragged me along as his female escort.'

'Boat building in Monaco, that doesn't sound like a normal profession for an Englishman.'

'He's a bit of a character, our Uncle V, as he's known in the family. He came here sometime in the 1950's and never went home. He's my mother's younger brother, the black sheep of the family. Two wives and assorted other affairs. Any money he makes boat building he quickly loses at the casino, he's an inveterate gambler.'

'So much for being your chaperone, he does not seemed to have led an exemplary life.'

'He's fun and very kind, it was he who encouraged me to come to France when my parents were set against it. He's supposed to be keeping an eye on me to make certain I don't elope with a Monaco arms dealer,' she said with a giggle. They both laughed.

'That sounds far too outrageous for a sensible English girl.'

'I'm not always sensible, still waters and all that,' she said, then regretted the remark and blushed again for the second time that afternoon. She hoped this handsome man didn't think she'd pop into his bed at the drop of a hat. Although she wouldn't mind that. Angus smiled at Priscilla's very English embarrassment.

'Uncle Valentine lives well here,' she said quickly, brushing the remains of a foie gras canapé from her lips with an embroidered handkerchief. 'Monte Carlo is a beautiful place to have a home and run a business. There's so much tax-free dosh slushing around the Principality, it makes it an attractive place for investors.'

'I can't quite figure out what people do here?'

'Sit on their money and enjoy themselves.'

'Somewhat vacuous.'

'Hedonistic more likely. I suspect that Uncle V relieves many of his clients of their dodgy money in exchange for a smart new yacht, and no questions asked. He's terribly well connected; he's on first name terms with the Grimaldis. He will be in their private box at the Grand Prix tomorrow.'

'Oh my,' said Angus. 'The high life indeed.'

It did not take long for Angus to discover that Priscilla's roots sprung from solid Home Counties virtues: ambitious, loving, and with an honest desire to recreate a way of life for herself that partially mirrored her middle- class upbringing, but with several twentieth century additions of her own. Priscilla told Angus how she first broke with conformity by calling off her engagement to Nigel, a successful, but dull, stockbroker from Haywards Heath.

'Do you know what my mother said when I told her that I didn't love Nigel? What's love got to do with it dear, you will never have to worry about money again. And when I told them I was going to leave home and work abroad they thought I had gone completely bonkers. So my supposed madness has brought me here to this beautiful place on this lovely day to talk to you.'

'Lucky me,' said Angus.

'I think you make your own luck.'

Angus learned that Priscilla worked as a secretary in a real estate firm in Monaco. She was quite different to Françoise, and she quickly recognised that Angus was damaged goods but it did not divert her attentions. She had spotted Angus at the reception and encouraged her Uncle to make the introduction. She was singular and determined to get her own way once her mind was made up. She knew from their first meeting that Angus was the one.

Over the coming months, Priscilla gently eased Angus out of his trough of despair and helped him recover his self-belief. She quickly discovered Angus's underlying kindness, but it took her much longer to get him to lower his emotional drawbridge. She was prepared to put in the time until her handsome, intelligent man, allowed her in.

The June sunshine that bathed Angus and Priscilla's first meeting at the Consulate's party was a portent of better times ahead. Priscilla turned out to be a refreshing breath of English common sense, and offered Angus uncomplicated love, sympathy and companionship. Without realising it, Priscilla's normality was the perfect healing balm.

Priscilla's final act of rebellion was to fall in love with a handsome academic from Yorkshire. Where exactly is Leeds?' she said, 'I've never been further north than Peterborough,' she confessed.

Their engagement was published in the *Daily Telegraph*. It was not a newspaper Pete ever read.

Chapter 30

Felicja Jagoda was horrified when she heard the news of her son's infamy. 'The shame of it,' she said, 'my boy getting a nineteen-year-old Catholic girl pregnant.' She wrote him a long letter haranguing him for his selfish behaviour spelling out the reasons why she would NOT attend his wedding. She had a ferocious row with Piotr, her husband, who insisted he was going to attend, with or without her. 'Such disloyalty is beyond belief,' she said. 'Your son is a disgrace to the family.'

But Pete's mother had other reasons why she was reluctant to travel to the Côte d'Azur. Reluctantly, she came around to the idea and helped her husband apply for a passport. He purchased a Kodak Instamatic camera to capture the occasion. Mr. Jagoda ventured to a travel agent in central Leeds who arranged his train and ferry bookings; he ordered travellers cheques and French francs from the Yorkshire Bank on Park Row.

He would be away eight days, most of it taken up with travelling, it would be the longest period he had been apart from his wife since their marriage. He made himself a new lightweight wool and silk suit and ordered a new trilby hat from Brills. His wife fussed about, endlessly checking he had his passport, money and tickets and packed his newly-purchased suitcase with his new suit, clean shirts, ties, socks, highly polished shoes, underwear and cufflinks. Finally, he was on his way and she waved him off in the taxi to the railway station. Secretly, she regretted her decision not to go with him.

Piotr was nervous about his various train connections and hoped the French he'd been taught as a young man would return once he heard the language spoken again. He had sensibly purchased a French phrase book from Austicks University Bookshop and was surprised how much of the language he remembered. When he reached France, it became clear his phraseology was very old fashioned, the language he had been taught in the early 1930s had since become sloppy and modernised. However, he could make himself understood, despite the occasional strange looks he received.

The travel agent had booked him into a small, central hotel not far from the *La Mairie*. He had arranged to meet his son and future daughter-in-law on the steps of the *La Mairie* on the morning of the civil ceremony. He arrived fifteen minutes early and paced around the cobbled square to keep warm. At last he spotted Peter and his bride-to-be among a gaggle of guests hurrying towards the entrance to *La Mairie*. A chill January breeze was blowing accompanied by light rain and his new lightweight suit did not provide much protection from the unexpected cold. He stepped inside the impressive, stone-built *Place de l'Hôtel de Ville* out of the rain and was introduced to Françoise. She kissed him lightly on each cheek and he was immediately impressed by her beauty and a haunting melancholy that emanated from her. His son looked drawn and embarrassed. He had lost weight and was not his usual ebullient self. Mr. Jagoda was struck by the tense atmosphere between the couple and the other guests. He was pleased that his wife had not made the journey. Françoise's parents had yet to arrive.

'Hello Father, thanks for coming all this way to our little marriage.'

'How could I miss it?'

'I'm sorry the weather is so foul, I hope you're not getting cold, haven't you brought a coat.'

'I thought it would be warmer.'

'I like your suit.'

'I know a good tailor,' he said with a smile. 'Your mother was sorry she could not come, she worried about the long journey.'

'No need to make excuses Father, she sent me a nice letter explaining everything.'

'She never mentioned it to me.'

'Well, you know how secretive she can be.'

'I presume Angus is coming?'

There was a moments silence. 'I'm not sure, he has a new job teaching at a local *lycée*. He was not certain if he could get the time off.'

'I thought he would be top of your list, your best man?'

'French schools are not as lax as back at home about taking time off mid-week.'

Mr Jagoda thought this was odd and he noticed a reticence in Françoise when Angus was mentioned.

Henri and Madame Delores finally shuffled in with a small group of other guests. Momentarily, he thought he was going to be ignored. His velvet Kippah stood out at this Jesuit family gathering. Eventually, Peter introduced him. The handshakes and greetings were as warm as the Baltic Sea. He studied the small, self-important little man, Françoise's father reminded him of some of his worst customers in Leeds. The Frenchman's wife was taller than him, slim and severe looking, her hair pulled back in a bun. She was dressed expensively, but the dark grey colours of her fitted suit appeared sober for a wedding. He wondered how they produced such a beautiful daughter.

Whilst he understood the circumstances of the marriage, Piotr was saddened that his son was joining such an openly hostile family. The absence of cordiality continued throughout the civil proceedings at *La Mairie* and later during the church service. Nobody had the courtesy to exchange more than an occasional frosty smile, he felt like an unwanted bystander. The feeling of alienation was something he had not experienced since he was a boy in Poland. As he watched the humourless Priest conduct the marriage he seethed with anger about his son's foolhardy behaviour. Why couldn't his son have found himself a nice *baleboste*, from Leeds, not some *shiksa!* What right do they have to be so rude. *Where is their God?*

On the church steps, Piotr was pleased to catch a glimpse of Angus, so he had made it after all, he noticed him kiss Françoise and he sensed an intimacy between them. He quickly lost sight of him in the small crowd and disappeared. He was disappointed he had not spoken to him, he would have been a friendly face to talk to.

At the wedding breakfast, Piotr was pleasantly surprised to find himself sitting at the top table with Françoise. During the meal the atmosphere lifted and Françoise chatted to him in French. He warmed to this charming young woman, she was quite different to her uncommunicative parents.

'Tell me about Peter when he was younger, he tells me nothing,' said Françoise.

'He was very naughty but clever at school. He was a good mathematician and he gave up a good job in England as an accountant before he came to France.'

'Impetuous?'

'That is a good description of your husband. Hard working, but only when it suited him.'

They talked amiably and for the first time that day his spirits rose. He caught his son's eye and smiled.

On his return to England, he telephoned the Macintyre family to tell them that he had been to the wedding. Marjorie Macintyre answered the 'phone:

'I sensed there was a rift between Angus and Pete,' he said.

'You are right Piotr, I am afraid they have had an awful bust up over the girl.'

'You mean Françoise?'

'Yes, that's her, Angus was very cut up about the whole affair. He said Peter stole the love of his life. Well, that's how he put it to us,' she said. 'He wouldn't go into all the details but he wanted to marry her. We didn't want him to go back to France after Christmas, but he was insistent. He said he wanted to face his demons.'

'That is very courageous of him. I'm very sorry to hear of this Marjorie. I know your son is a kind young man and I'm embarrassed and hurt by Peter's selfish behaviour. Perhaps we'll never get to the bottom of what happened, nevertheless it is unforgivable, they are such old friends too.'

'Yes, it's a tragedy, I cannot see them ever being reconciled. My husband says it is God's way of punishing Angus for leaving his studies. Whilst I know God moves in mysterious ways, I'm certain He has bigger things to worry about than Angus and your son.'

'Hopefully he is young enough to get over the break up. I am certain he'll meet another girl in time.'

'Let's hope so, it's all we can do.'

'Indeed, it is part of the twists and turns of life and sometimes we can never work out why things happen. I believe that one day there will be forgiveness between the two of them.'

'I do hope you are right, Piotr.'

~

Pete was having to adjust to his new life, one of his own making. The marital bed was off-limits until after the baby arrived. Like Priscilla, Pete patiently bided his time. Once his son Charles was born the baby became the bond that helped glue their relationship. Pete tried his hardest to make Françoise love him for what he was, not because he was the father of their child.

He devoted his energies to working diligently in his father-in-law's office where he quickly proved to be a shrewd buyer and negotiator. Madame Delores slowly warmed up once her lively grandson arrived. She removed her black clothing and returned to wearing normal attire. Pete and Françoise made a home for themselves in a converted gardener's cottage in the Delores's garden. Whilst this proved to be a convenient short-term solution, Pete found it oppressive being under the constant scrutiny of his new in-laws. Henri, despite developing a private admiration for Pete's business acumen, and a love for his grandson, maintained a civil but guarded relationship with his son in-law.

'Long term, I would like for us to live in England,' said Pete, one evening while he and Françoise lay in bed. Charles's cot was at the other side of the room and he spoke quietly not to wake the baby.

' I want Charles to brought up in France.'

'I would like to pass my accountancy examinations and start a new career. I don't want to spend my life running a painting business, watched over by your father.'

'Don't raise your voice, you'll wake Charles,' she said. 'My parents would hate it if we moved.'

'I'm not married to your parents.'

'Where would we live? We have a nice little cottage here, and Papa pays you well enough. We want for nothing.'

'I want to forge my own way in life, Françoise. I don't want to be always indebted to Henri. It's humiliating, I feel like a kept man.'

'Maybe you should have thought about that before marrying me.'

'I don't recall having too many options.'

'Angus would have married me. But you didn't want him bringing up your child.'

'At least think about what I want for a change. Not what your parents want.'

'Why? You know what my answer will be.'

Pete turned out the light and turned against the wall.

~

A little over a year after the birth of Charles, Angus bumped into Françoise and Pete at a Cezanne exhibition in Marseilles. It was one of those encounters where it was impossible to avoid one another in the confines of a small gallery space. Angus was accompanied by his attractive English girlfriend. When Pete spotted them, he thought they looked an ideal match. She was pretty and intelligent looking, not quite a blue stocking. Pete was relieved that his thoughtful old friend looked happy in his new relationship.

To the casual observer, Françoise and Pete look like a regular handsome married couple as they admired and commented on the paintings. Since when had Pete been interested in impressionist art, Angus thought to himself? Françoise must be trying to educate the philistine.

Françoise froze in horror when she first saw Angus but they could not avoid speaking. Angus remained remote and disinterested. He treated Pete and Françoise as if they had briefly met before on a holiday years ago. 'So what's it like being a father?' asked Angus, with as much interest as if he was asking about the weather.

'Absorbing,' Pete replied.

'When you are not working for Papa,' said Françoise.

Priscilla stood to one side of the three of them in bored silence, it was clear she had no interest in Angus's old acquaintances. As Françoise took in the encounter she tried to work out if Priscilla was aware she and Angus were past lovers and the circumstances of her marriage. Although she did not want to engage she was mortified by Angus's cool indifference towards her. It was if she had never been part of his life. She should not have been surprised that Angus had constructed an impenetrable barrier to protect himself; she tried to catch his eye but all she saw was Priscilla glaring at her. It was clear that Angus was Priscilla's property now, she was his sentinel, and no one else was going to get near him. The encounter had reawakened in Françoise a hidden yearning for Angus she thought she had lost, and coupled with a vanity she could still exercise a hold over him after all that had passed, crushed her self esteem.

Angus maintained a bland cordiality throughout their brief meeting. He refused to acknowledge that under two years ago they had lived as passionate lovers never out of one another's company. Angus's redeeming quality of kindness was no longer on display, even his sense of humour seemed to have evaporated. What have I done to that nice man thought Françoise as she inwardly wept?

They parted politely, briefly parrying about meeting again, both couples knew this was a charade of English manners.

On the car journey back to Aix, Pete remained uncharacteristically silent. In the strained atmosphere of regret, Françoise started another row about Christening their son. Pete was a non-believer and thought it a waste of time, but the conditions of their Roman Catholic marriage was the child must be brought up in the Faith. Eventually, he knew he would have to cave in to pressure from church, family, and his wife. For Pete it was just one of his childish games he liked to play to wind Françoise up.

As the car stalked its way through night, Françoise thought about Angus and what might have been. Seeing him again reminded her of all the reasons why she had fallen in love with him and she cursed they had ever visited the gallery. His outright rejection of her after so short a time undermined the precarious relationship she was trying to build with Pete. Perversely, and in secret through friends, she managed to keep a track of Angus's whereabouts since their break up. She had heard he had a new amour but knowing that he was still in touching distance in Monaco was like a comfort blanket. Even if it was a cold one. She realised it was unhealthy trying to keep tabs on him, she had to rid her mind of Angus for the sake of Pete, Charles and her own sanity.

When the Christening was finally arranged a few months later, she had obtained Angus's address in Monaco and posted him an invitation to the Christening.

He never replied.

Chapter 31

War Time France 1944

After the German's had discovered the boy's poorly hidden rifle and arrested his father, his mother had eventually made contact with her other son, Philippe.

'Where is Papa, do you know where he is? Is he still alive? The Germans hit him with a rifle and cut his face and nose when they arrested him, poor man.'

'He's been taken to Marseilles for questioning.' Her son did not mention his father would be interrogated by the notorious, Ernst Dunker Delage, the man responsible for Résistance repression in the region. Philippe was livid that a British army rifle had been found at his own family's farm. It threw into question his own loyalty with his German masters. He worried that they might think he was a double agent for the British and he could find himself in the same cellar as his father at 45 Rue de Paradis, the Marseilles Gestapo HQ.

His mother gave no inkling of her suspicions about Phillipe's younger brother. There had never been any love lost between the two of them. His father had told him that outside his job at the paint factory, the boy led a secret life. Philippe decided to speak to him privately before the Gestapo got their hands on him. Despite their past differences, the thought he might have to arrest his own brother filled him with dread.

It took all of Philippe's persuasion to extract his father from his incarceration in Marseilles. The old man emerged heavily beaten after his spell at the hands of Ernst Dunker and his stooges. Philippe sowed the seeds of a story that the rifle may have been planted by a Résistance cell on his father's farm out of revenge for his *Milice* membership. It was quite a plausible theory, but nonetheless the Gestapo would eventually want to question his younger brother. In the meantime, the Gestapo were concentrating rounding up other members of the boy's *Maquis* group. They would know soon enough the true ownership of the rifle as one of them would be bound to break down under torture.

When the news that some of his compatriots had been rounded up for questioning the boy wondered if it was his uncovered rifle that had blown their cover. He knew he had to disappear and fast. He racked his brains for a suitable place where he could hide, but the fear that gripped him had emptied his mind. He considered making his way to the Spanish border with the idea of walking over the Pyrenees.

The next day at the paint works he learned of his brother's murder when he overheard the gory details of how a butcher had been strangled with piano wire and strung up on a meat hook in his shop window.

'Serves the bastard collaborator right,' said one of the workmen to his mate.

'What do you think of that young comrade?' Said the workman, looking at the white-faced boy.

'He deserved everything he got.'

'Correct answer.'

It was fortunate his workmates had no idea the murdered butcher was the boy's brother. The boy felt the world was closing in around him. Had his brother been responsible for his partisan comrades who had been arrested? The idea that they could have been betrayed by his own brother was difficult to comprehend. The conflict of loyalties this war had thrown up had confused his young mind. The boy returned to his mixing paint duties without another word. He couldn't bear the conversation any longer.

The boy was finding it nearly impossible to act normally. Wagons that arrived at the paint factory yard startled him as he imagined there were detachments of soldiers coming to pick him up; an unexpected order from his boss made him jump. The boy's nightmare was amplified as later in the afternoon a wagon driver had told them two mayors in neighbouring towns and many local inhabitants, had been corralled and shot out of hand. The Occupiers were no longer bothering to find out if the individuals were guilty. The reprisals demonstrated that any trust the Germans may have had with the French population was exhausted. The punishment executions did little to cow the local population into submission, but rather it served to harden their resolve. Although the boy did not know it, the French revenge would not be long in coming.

~

The boy was relieved when it was time to cycle home. As he pedalled, he made up his mind that if he was approached by the Germans, he would make a run for it, with any luck he would be shot, it would be a quick end to his misery.

As he slowly pedalled he half expected a German patrol to arrive at any moment and he scanned the countryside to work out how far he would reach before a bullet ended it all. He breathed in the sweet smell of the fields' springtime renewal as if they were his last breaths. Then his mind was filled with imagined images of his treacherous brother's gruesome demise. He wondered if his assassination would steer the Gestapo's suspicion away from him. Although his brother's death had been a grisly business, he could not summon up feelings of remorse. They had never got on while growing up, their childhood was characterised by scrapping and arguing and it was no surprise that they should hold diametrically opposing views on the German occupation.

A girl wearing a black beret and a green coat with the collar pulled up, overtook his cycle, the rider was pedalling fast. 'Follow me,' the rider hissed, as she sped past. It took him a moment to recognise the Agent. The boy immediately followed her down the country road before she made a ninety degree turn down another lane away from the farm. He was excited by this unplanned rendezvous and had to pedal hard to keep pace. Eventually, they arrived at a dense wood and the Agent veered off down a woodland track. She cycled at breakneck speed for about two kilometres, bumping over tree roots into the heart of the forest, she stopped and dismounted. The boy wondered if this was the start of another mission.

'Hide the bike in there,' she said, pointing to a tangle of brambles. 'Make certain it can't be seen.'

'Where are we going?' said the boy, as he picked bramble thorns out of his hands.

'We have a long walk ahead of us. You're to go to a safe house. First, we must double back in case anyone spotted us. Your group cover has been blown. Unless you come with me now, you'll be arrested and most likely shot tomorrow.'

The boy gasped in horror at her blunt statement of fact. He could scarcely believe he had been taken under the wing of the Agent, he felt euphoric at his unbelievable deliverance.

'We need to get going straightaway, it's over twenty kilometres and we must reach the house before dawn,' said the Agent. The boy snapped out of his reverie and they both started walking before darkness descended on the wood.

Chapter 32

Early Summer England 1988

No-one was more surprised than Angus to receive a large, expensive-looking invitation printed on paper so stiff it felt like cardboard. It read:

Mr & Mrs Peter Jagoda
Requests the pleasure of
Angus and Priscilla Macintyre
To a Reception and Dinner
To celebrate Pete's 40th Birthday
Friday May 24th

Black Tie — *At Home*
Carriages at 3pm — *RSVP*

Raisford Hall, Raisford, Sussex

Their names had been hand-crafted in copperplate script by a skilled calligrapher, Angus turned the card over and on the back there was a scribbled note in a cruder hand: '*Hope you can make it. It would be good to catch up. It's been too long. Your old mate, Pete.*'

Old mate? I guess we were once, thought Angus. It had been over eighteen years since he'd last seen Pete in the art gallery in Marseilles. There had been times when he thought about making contact with him again particularly after hearing his marriage to Françoise, had predictably, fallen apart. That was a terrible irony after all they had been through.

Angus had considered contacting Françoise, but to what purpose? He was married and Priscilla was expecting their first child. That painful time was best forgotten and since their divergent careers progressed, the threads that had once bound them had become untied. Angus had given up hating Pete and in a way he felt sorry for the mess he had created for himself, his son, and especially Françoise.

Over the past twenty years, his life with Priscilla had followed a predictable trajectory: contentment in the early years with the fulfilment of two children. Only latterly, as the children had grown older, had Priscilla become more impatient with him. Lack of money was the recurring theme. Meanwhile, he had disappeared deeper into his life of academia, an absorption that could air-brush over the fault-lines that had started to appear in his marriage. And, of course, there were his children, with whom he exercised his boundless kindness.

Since Pete returned to England in 1972 he had succeeded in systematically building himself a fortress of money and possessions. They went some of the way to compensate for his failed marriage and repair his battered ego.

Over the years Angus and Pete exchanged Christmas cards. As Pete's business success gained momentum the cards had the facile addition of a 'round robin' letter marking the many achievements of his business career, his illustrious new wife and gifted son. Like all of these missives, it was what was not included that was more interesting.

So why this olive branch now? Angus was still pondering this as his car approached a pair of enormous stone gate posts marking the entrance to Raisford Hall. Large, wrought iron gates swung open on their electric motors and a beribboned security guard checked their names on a list before they were allowed entry into the hallowed grounds. Winged griffin-like objects in stone adorned the top of each pillar. They peered querulously down at the lesser mortals who dared enter. 'Looks like we are entering the Greek underworld,' said Angus.

'They're completely over-the top, ostentation does not do them justice,' said Priscilla, tutting. 'This is Sussex, not Athens.' Priscilla was rattled that Angus had accepted the invitation after the mental damage that Pete had caused her husband many years ago. If it had been her she would have never spoken to her adversary again. But Angus was different, his kindness meant he could not hold grudges. Live and let live was his attitude.

The fairy lit avenue of trees lining the hall's driveway and all the other paraphernalia of celebration was what Angus had anticipated. However, once the grand house hove into full view, even he was impressed.

Reaching forty was supposed to be some sort of watershed, although Angus has no plans to recognise his own birthday in a few months' time. He planned to ignore the whole tedious occasion. He must remind Priscilla not to waste the money, but not tonight. He did not want to start a row.

'Pete was always the showman, I think it was an insecurity thing, probably something to do with his parental background,' said Angus, as if this explained the vast house and very visible trappings.

'That's enough of your "Brains Trust"analysis, it looks to me like he's trying to prove a point,' said Priscilla, as she absorbed the surrounding rolling parkland that stretched into the distance.

Angus had read about Pete's palatial country house in one of Priscilla's celebrity gossip magazines. The article appeared soon after Pete had married his second wife, Suzy Barclay-Harrington. Obtaining media exposure was just one element of Pete's unrelenting self-aggrandisement. 'I hope the Duke is ready to receive us,' said Angus.

'Your old friend *must* be seriously wealthy to afford a place like this, it's like a stately home.'

'No doubt all on the back of his student housing empire.'

'His wife has money,' said Priscilla, as if this explained everything and Pete's own accomplishments were a trifle. 'Her father is Sir Humphrey Barclay-Harrington, he builds ships.' Angus remained tight-lipped as he peered through the car windscreen at the Hall's beautiful Palladian frontage. The floodlighting highlighted some incongruous modern sculptures dotted around the drive perimeter, there was an underlying flashiness about the place that suggested a private golf course was hidden away somewhere.

'Nervous darling?'

'Of course not,' said Angus, annoyed that his wife had noticed his look of astonishment. He would never have admitted it to Priscilla, but he had considered turning his little car around and making a bolt for home.

Priscilla wound down the VW Beetle's window to get a better look of the property as they approached the front. 'The facade is very typical of the Burlington style of architecture,' she said. 'I would reckon it was built around 1725.'

Priscilla, who was always seeking ways to supplement, what she deemed to be her husband's inadequate income, had taken a part-time secretarial job at an exclusive firm of estate agents, Carstairs-Palmer. She had become a bore about large country houses, particularly since she had been promoted to show prospective buyers around properties. Much to Angus's annoyance, Priscilla had begun to adopt some of the airs and graces of her employers and had become adept at sucking up to wealthy prospective clients. She had started to study the history and architecture of interesting properties in the county. This assiduousness had yet to catch the eye of the firm's senior partner, Max Bulstrode-Palmer.

'Carstairs-Palmer would love to sell this place, it must be worth a million,' she said. Secretly, Priscilla bristled that an alleged old friend of her impoverished husband has accumulated so much wealth. 'I can't wait to tell Max that I've been inside Raisford Hall,' she said, sensing indefinable opportunities.

A lackey in a uniform, far too tight for his muscular frame, approached the car. He looked more like a club bouncer than a parking attendant.

'Park your motor out the back, Sir,' he said in a strong Essex accent. His forced obsequious manner failed to obscure his normal job as an enforcer. It was clear he was not used to calling anyone 'Sir.'

Angus steered his car towards the rear of the house where the less flashy vehicles were parked. The cobbled square at the back of the property was bordered by stables and what looked like an old laundry. It was clear that Angus's shabby VW was being deliberately shunted away from the Bentleys, Jaguars and Aston Martins that lined the gravel sweep to the left and right of the front entrance. Angus manoeuvred the small car in between two refrigerated catering vans painted in a Harrods's green colour emblazoned with gold lettering proclaiming: *'Horatio Horsley, Purveyor of Fine Foods & Exceptional Wines to the Gentry and Nobility.'*

It was a warm, scented early summer evening and as Priscilla and Angus negotiated their way across the fine pea-gravel drive towards the elegant, curved steps leading to the front door, they heard a blackbird and a song thrush compete with one another in a nearby copse. The two songbirds were oblivious to the melodious music that emanated from a string quartet playing a piece of Bach chamber music inside the wide entrance hallway. Angus had to admit it was a bucolic setting and the contrast from Pete's family home in Leeds was astonishing.

On entering the wide black and white tiled hallway, he could not fail to notice a large hand drawn banner strung across an oak panelled wall proclaiming, "Happy 40th B'day Pete." It was soon apparent that this party was more about impressing Pete's business acquaintances and hangers-on, than welcoming his old friends. As soon as they crossed the threshold Angus and Priscilla had glasses of Pol Roger thrust into their hands by a liveried flunky. Angus looked around to see if he could recognise anybody he knew. He managed to spot an old accountancy colleague of Pete's who he used to go drinking with.

For a moment, Priscilla was rooted to the spot by the extravagant floral decorations that were draped around the bannisters of a beautiful oak staircase which rose from one end of the entrance hall. She was still admiring the lilies and assorted flowers protruding through the balustrades when Angus grabbed her hand and pulled her towards the only familiar face in the hall.

'Angus, how nice to see you, it's been a long time. Join us in the humble guest corner,' said the accountant. He quickly introduced two other couples whose names Angus immediately forgot. They appeared equally cowed by the lavish hospitality and scale of their surroundings. A group of incongruously tarty-looking, young women were sitting on the staircase chatting excitedly among themselves. They were consuming champagne and puffing away on cigarettes. Priscilla gasped in disbelief as she saw one of the girls crush out a cigarette butt on the oak staircase with her stiletto heel.

'Well, Pete has done well for himself,' said the accountant.

'I said to Priscilla earlier that I presume this place must have been purchased with the fruits from his letting property empire,' said Angus. 'He buys and converts houses for student accommodation all over the country, wherever there are universities and colleges of further education.'

'Only some of it,' said the accountant.

'He has night clubs,' said one of the women. She nodded towards the staircase where the decorous young girls were gathered. '"*Customer Service Hostesses*," is what Pete called them,' she said. 'They're supposed to be serving drinks but it looks like they are just helping themselves.'

'He's been diversifying in recent years, commercial property, fashion boutiques, fast food franchises and driving schools all stuff he can sell to his student tenants, very shrewd,' said the accountant.

'You seem to know a lot about him,' said Angus.

'We are his accountants.'

'What are all those young girls doing here?' said Priscilla.

'They maybe friends with his son.'

'I didn't know he had a boy,' said the accountant's wife.

'He lives in France with his first wife, Françoise,' said Angus. 'He will be grown up now, so they could be his friends, but somehow they don't look the type.'

'Pete never talked about his time in France when he came back to the office,' said the accountant. 'I think he missed his son, he would go to France to visit him for special occasions. He looked shattered when he rejoined the old firm. He once told me that his French father-in-law had tried his best to destroy his marriage; he wanted his wife to come and live in England with his son, but she'd refused. I think that was one of the causes of their break up.'

'I met his French father-in-law a long time ago, to say he was not easy would be an understatement,' said Angus. 'He had a peculiar antipathy towards the English; neither Pete or I could ever understand it. He had an awful temper and once threatened me with a rifle.'

'Really, but why?'

'I told him I didn't want to paint his villas any more,' said Angus, skirting the real reason. 'I think his French pride had been hurt, but I don't believe he would have used it.'

'Once Pete returned to England,' said the accountant, 'he worked really hard to pass all his exams. He knew he had some catching up to do to but eventually he became a very gifted accountant, if a little unorthodox.'

'Is that a polite way of saying sharp practice?' said Priscilla.

'No, you could call it creative accounting. He was red hot on tax and was sought-out by our clients. I think that is how he came into contact with Mr. Barclay-Harrington. It was then he realised how wealthy he was. Pete always claimed that marriage to his daughter was true love, but you never quite know with Pete.

'Meow,' said Priscilla.

'Have you met Suzy?' Asked the accountant's wife.

'Not yet,' said Angus.

'She's lovely and keeps Pete in order by all accounts, I heard on the grapevine that she was not very keen about this lavish party. Her family don't think it is the "done thing" to be seen squandering one's money. "*Esse quam viderei*" is their family motto, "*To be, rather than to seem.*"'

'This bash seems a bit at odds with that sentiment,' says Angus.

'You're not kidding,' said Priscilla, gulping down her champagne.

Just at that moment there was a loud cry: 'Angus, you old rogue, how the devil are you.' A red-faced and plump looking Pete strode towards the group with a champagne glass waving in one hand and a half-empty bottle of Pol Roger in the other.

'Congratulations on becoming a quadragenarian,' said Angus. He lightly tapped the back of Pete's crushed-velvet smoking jacket. For a moment Pete looked slightly baffled.

'Oh, making forty you mean…top up? So glad you could make it,' he said, filling up Priscilla's empty glass. Pete looked much like his old self except that he had added some pounds along the way and his hair was greying at the temples with tell-tale signs of a receding hair line. In another decade he'll probably be bald or wearing a toupee.

He wouldn't put that vanity past him, thought Angus. 'Your good lady wife, I presume?' said Pete, bowing theatrically. He placed the half-empty champagne bottle on the exquisitely tiled floor while he grasped Priscilla's hand and kissed it. Priscilla was in two minds how to respond to this over-the-top introduction, but she remembered the value of Raisford Hall and decided there was no point in being rude to a possible future client. Priscilla responded in kind, and gave Pete a good humoured mock curtsy.

'Glad to see that you have a good sense of humour, just like my old pal, Angus,' said Pete.

'Where would we be without it,' said Angus, mentally grinding his teeth at the "old pal" reference.

'Do you know that I have known this man for bloody years,' said Pete, as he stared at Priscilla, as if he was eying up someone's ability to afford one of his rents. It was clear that Pete was overwhelmed by the splendidness of his own self-created celebrations. 'How long has it been Angus?'

'Must be thirty or more years since we first met at school,' said Angus.

'At least, and when did we last see one another?' There was an awkward silence as Angus thought to himself, fuck you, as if you can't remember.

'Maybe it was at the wedding of your first wife?' said Priscilla. 'If what Angus has told me of your past histories is correct.'

Pete ignored Priscilla's barbed remark and looked up into the air as if trying to recall a long lost date. After a moment's pause, he said, 'bloody hell is it that long, I could have sworn I've seen you since then?'

'I think it was at the Cezanne exhibition in Marseilles when you were still married to Françoise,' said Angus, diplomatically rescuing the situation.

At that moment, a tall, beautifully dressed woman in a knee length sapphire blue cocktail dress walked up to Pete's side and slipped her arm into his. 'Well aren't you going to introduce me to your nice-looking friends?'

'Of course, darling, this is my oldest chum from school days and his wife,' he hesitated briefly trying to remember Priscilla's name...

'Priscilla,' said Angus.

'Er...this is Angus, terribly brainy fellow, he's a university lecturer.'

'A professor, actually,' said Priscilla.

'Oh, we are honoured,' said Pete.

'Oh, *be quiet*, Peter. Hello, I am Susan, but do call me Suzy, everyone else does. It's my burden to be married to this oaf,' said Suzy, beaming at the assembled group.

Everyone shook hands as the introductions were made, Angus noticed Suzy's long slim fingers and he wondered if she was a pianist. She appeared to be a cultured woman, an interesting contrast to Pete's rampant commercialism, and Angus wondered how Pete had managed to snare her. She couldn't have been short of suitors.

'Now tell me Angus, in which faculty do you work?' said Suzy, looking Angus straight in the eye. She exuded perfect social ease that accompanied a good education and generations of old money. Angus was aware she was a respected barrister and he warmed to her immediately. She looked to be in her late thirties but he suspected she was older than Pete. Despite her lineage she was not an old-world snob, but part of the new generation of university-educated, highly intelligent, career women. He imagined her politics were Liberal which would annoy the hell out of Pete. Angus pondered why Suzy was attracted to Pete, perhaps when they first met he was more measured, before his metamorphosis into "Toad of Toad Hall." Angus smiled to himself at his own witty analogy.

'What are you smiling at Angus,' said Suzy, with an infectious giggle.

'Oh, it's nothing. I was thinking back to when Pete and I were young, he's come a long way.... but to answer your question: English is my life's work.'

'How interesting, any particular period?'

'Medieval mainly, but I also have a fascination for European literature, particularly Spanish and Italian,' he said, trying to banish the Mr Toad image from his mind.

'It's a shame none of your academic interests ever rubbed off on Pete. But Pete's boy, Charles, is surprisingly studious.'

'Is he here tonight, I would love to meet him?'

'I don't think so. Pete has a rather fractious relationship with him. It's a pity, he's a nice boy and he'll go far. He is very French, you would hardly know he had an English father.'

There was some more small talk and Suzy bowled questions at Priscilla about juggling working in an estate agent's office and bringing up children. Pete had briefed her well. Angus suspected Suzy was even better informed about Pete's important clients' wives.

'Please excuse me, but I had better be a good host and circulate. It has been a real pleasure to meet you, Angus,' said Suzy. 'Pete often talked about you and the fun you had together in your younger years.

I would love to know more, I suspect that he never tells me the whole truth about anything,' she said, turning to give her husband a knowing look.

Too bloody right, thought Angus.

'Absolute rot. What you see is what you get,' he said, shrugging off the remark with an embarrassed smile. 'Time for us to mingle with the great unwashed, I'll catch up with you all later.' He turned and clapped the shoulder of a fat man in a cheap dinner jacket who came shuffling past. The man had a young "customer services hostess" clamped to his arm. He looked out of place among Pete's wealthy, professional business colleagues.

Angus overheard Pete as he drifted off: 'Ah, Councillor Jenkins, just the man, a word in your ear,' before Pete disappeared into the crowd, deep in conversation with the incongruous figure. I wonder what he's doing here, thought Angus. Meanwhile, Suzy elegantly glided away to join a group of women that look as if they'd stepped off the set of "*Dallas*."

'Look at that herd of shoulder pads,' said Priscilla in Angus's ear. As he leaned forward to listen to Priscilla's aside, he noticed a striking looking woman with auburn hair across the hallway. She was in conversation with a small cluster of guests. She looked up in his direction and then opened a small clutch bag and put on some stylish spectacles.

Angus was reminded of a pair of sunglasses at a French petrol station forecourt.

Chapter 33

Pete steered Councillor Jenkins into a quiet corner of the library. 'Sylvie, make yourself scarce for a while,' said Pete to the Councillor's female companion. 'I need a private word with Mr Jenkins, he'll join you later.' The girl disengaged herself from the fat man and gave him a nudge before she disappeared to rejoin her decorative friends on the Hall's stairs.

When it came to matters of business, Pete soon focussed on the issues whatever the circumstances. 'I'm sorry to press you Councillor, tonight of all nights, but can you bring me up-to-date on the Stead Mills deal?'

The sweating man shifted uneasily on his feet, his cheap leather substitute shoes looked as if they were pinching him. 'Now look, don't hassle me Jagoda. I'm doing all I can,' he said. His flat northern vowels were defensive.

'The university is asking me questions and I've promised to have the place converted and fitted-out for the start of the new year. It's already May, and time is getting very short,' said Pete.

'There's a finance committee meeting next week. It's top of the agenda and I've made certain your bid is the best one. But don't count your chickens. There's a chance it could get referred to the Secretary of State, there's been some discussion whether the building should be listed.

'Listed! That building is derelict, it's a bleedin' health hazard.'

'Some of our lot regard it as part of the city's architectural heritage. You know the crap they come up with?'

'Councillor, I thought you'd got this ironed out. You said there'd be no problems.'

'I'd not anticipated our heritage officer and the local preservation society sticking their oars in,' said the Councillor, his forehead breaking out in beads of sweat.

'Your Council will get the blame if there's not enough accommodation for students attending the new law faculty. The press will have a field day and we'll have to erect temporary portable cabins,' said Pete, mentally thinking of one of his own subsidiary companies and a tasty margin. 'If this does happen, there is going to be a load of brown stuff flying about with your name on it,' said Pete.

'Don't tell me... don't I bloody know it,' said the Councillor, sitting down heavily on an antique Sheraton chair. For a moment, Pete wondered if his expensive antique would hold the obese Councillor's bulk. Pete, decided he had said enough and changed the subject. He was worried that the fat man might keel over at any minute, his breathing had become very laboured.

'Are you okay?'

'Just let me get my breath.'

Pete pulled up a chair alongside the Councillor. 'How was the holiday in the States?'

'The Mrs loved it, she took to the American grub like a duck to water,' said the Councillor, still looking uncomfortable, as he was reminded who had paid for the trip.

I bet she did, she's another fatty, just like him, thought Pete, as he mentally envisaged the pair tucking into surf and turf dinners. He wondered if the Councillor was holding out for another sweetener. Maybe their cooperative architect could fix it with the Council Leader if things start to go pear- shaped. We might even get a quicker result.

'Oh, by the way, what's the name of the Heritage officer that's kicking off?'

'Ronnie...Ronnie Stafforth.'

'I might need to speak to him, do you know where he lives?'

'No, but I can get you a phone number. But be careful of him, he's a religious nut and might get funny about any inducements.'

'I'll pray for him,' said Pete. 'Let me have the number next week, and please keep me posted on your meeting. Now, you'd better get back to see your Sylvia, she'll be missing you. Have you checked into your room at the Woodman yet?'

'Sorted. Thanks.'

Sorted indeed, thought Pete.

~

As the fat Councillor waddled off to find his young companion, Pete tried to put the implications of what he has just been told to the back of his mind. As he looked around his library, stuffed with ancient volumes of erudite unread books, his thoughts returned to his chat with his old pal, Angus, and his frosty wife.

He had lied purposefully about not remembering their meeting at the art gallery in Marseilles. He recalled it clearly, their meeting had precipitated a row with Françoise later that evening, precisely about what, was lost in the mists of similar altercations. He recalled Priscilla to be an attractive, demure, well educated, English girl, straight from the Surrey Hills. It was obvious she was besotted with Angus and couldn't keep her eyes off him, the only time she lifted her gaze was to glare at Françoise. She must have known about the saga of Angus's broken relationship.

Eighteen years on, Priscilla's good looks was still in evidence, she was surprisingly trim considering the onset of middle-age and the effects of childbirth, but he could not help noticing a marked tension between the pair. He wondered if Françoise still held Angus in the same thrall after all these years. At the time, he'd been a complete bastard and robbed Angus of his life's love. It was odd, that now of all times, the guilt of his treachery resurfaced more frequently. He'd been in two minds whether to invite Angus and his wife and was surprised they'd accepted. He would like to rekindle his friendship, old friends were so few and now his life was full of acquaintances, people who just wanted to know him because he was a rainmaker in business circles.

Pete had not much truck with academics, they rarely touched his sphere of interests. Perhaps their lives had drifted so far apart to make a reconciliation beyond reach? Pete's prejudices were grounded in ignorance; he incorrectly imagined Angus was surrounded by coteries of self-obsessed Guardian readers who considered themselves to be above the oily rags of commerce. Pete never spent much time thinking of the past as there was always so much to absorb him in the present. But as he had reached the landmark age of forty he had become more reflective. His parents had become fragile, they were here at his party but he didn't know where. It was typical that his evening had been absorbed glad-handing his business connections and forgetting his family.

Now, here he was today with a big house, a beautiful, clever wife and a successful business. But the failure of his relationship with his seventeen-year-old son hung over him. His party invitation had been declined, despite sending him first class airline tickets. He sensed the boy's tennis tournament excuse was a ruse. It had all the hallmarks of his grandfather's work preventing him coming to England. Henri still tried to control Françoise and Charles's lives, despite all the cash he shovelled their way every month. If only Françoise had remarried, Charles would have had a stepfather to guide him and dilute his grandfather's influence.

It had been a mischievous ploy to invite Françoise but he hoped the surprise might cheer up Angus's evening. He hoped that after all their years of marriage, Priscilla would have parked her past resentments. But now he had met her face-to-face, he was not so sure.

Chapter 34

As Françoise disembarked from the Air France A320 at Heathrow airport, she wondered why she had accepted the invitation to her ex-husband's birthday party after her son's last-minute refusal to accompany her. His ducking out reflected the young man's ambivalent relationship with his father. She had considered not going but hated the waste of free first class flights. At least, she could squeeze in some business meetings for her expanding fashion label in London.

Over the years she had tried to be an impartial referee, encouraging Charles to spend time with his English father: when he was younger Charles revelled in Pete's generous Christmas and birthday gifts, and staying in his ever-larger houses with their exotic cars and expensive gadgets. Françoise considered herself lucky that Pete's new wife, Suzy, had been an attentive and kind stepmother to Charles. The two women got on well and she knew that Suzy spent more time with Charles than Pete, who was forever rushing to and from meetings. But as Charles matured the superficial novelties started to lose their sheen and, as Suzy's reputation as a successful barrister grew, her own free time became scarcer. The Hall's location, deep in the Sussex countryside, was another impediment to socialising and Charles became bored watching videos and ordering take-away pizzas.

'I will come to Dad's party if I can bring Danielle with me,' said Charles.

'Who's Danielle?'

'She's my new girlfriend.'

'Not another one? Charles, you know it's impossible to change flights at the last moment.'

'Danielle could take your seat?'

'You expect the girl's parents to allow her to fly to England for a party without a chaperone. How old is she?'

'Seventeen, very grown up. She's Parisian.'

'I don't care if she lives in the Élysée Palace, I'm not giving up my seat.'

'Well, I'm not going.'

'Your father will be disappointed.'

'I don't care. Anyhow, he'll be spending his time with his English friends. I'll be lucky if he deigns to speak to me.'

'Charles, stop behaving like a spoiled child.'

Françoise was unaware that Henri, had bribed Charles with five hundred francs not to go to England. With his new-found funds Charles had promised to take his new girl to dinner and then out to a night club.

~

Françoise mingled easily at parties. She was busily engaged chatting to the head of Pete's letting agency. He was politely surprised when she told them that she had once been married to Pete and had a seventeen-year-old son living in France. Pete's selective omission of chapters of his personal history from business colleagues was a mystery to Françoise. Was it shame, if so, why the invitation? Then it dawned on her she was just the bait to entice Charles to attend, a strategy that had failed.

Looking around the large hall, she noticed a tall man with long, curly hair. She excused herself from the group and searched in her clutch bag to find her glasses. As her eyes adjusted she was certain the man was Angus. She hurried across the hallway and removed her glasses as she approached him. He was still slim and his dark hair had gone partially silver-grey, it gave him a mature allure, and she was reminded how attracted she had been to him all those years ago.

'Good heavens, Françoise! What on earth are you doing here?'

'You remember, Pete and I were once married.'

'Of course, how could I forget.'

'Angus, how lovely to see you. It's been so many years...'

Angus was unable to contain his astonishment. 'Françoise, you are still ...' His words faltered, and he bent forward to put his arms around her, instead of the conventional kiss on both cheeks. She pulled herself back, embarrassed at Angus's bear-hug, but instead she held both his arms and looked up at him as if to survey him for fault-lines.

'Pete told me you might be here.'

'He never mentioned it to *me*.'

'You know Pete. Too busy with his business empire.'

'Is your son with you?'

'No, I'm afraid not. He's in France, playing in a tennis tournament.'

'Oh, what a pity, I would have liked to have met him.'

'Is he like you?'

'A little bit.'

'I'm Priscilla, Angus's wife,' said Priscilla. She held out her hand and Françoise had no option but to release Angus from her grasp.

'Oh, hello, I think we met many years ago at an art gallery, was it in Marseilles?'

'Did we?' said Priscilla, recalling it well.

'It was before we were married,' said Angus, trying to smooth things over. Priscilla said nothing.

'You're staying at the Hall,' said Angus.

'Yes, I'm just here for the weekend and then I am going to London next week, I've a couple of days' business.'

Angus raised his eyebrows in surprise.

'I have some womenswear boutiques in France, and I design my own casual clothes ranges. I hope to sell some lines in shops specialising in French clothing in London.'

Seeing Angus again, brought Françoise's memories of her wedding years ago. What a sad day that was: the suppressed anger of her Papa for getting pregnant and having to marry an English non-believer, the hypocritical family priest unable to hide his disdain at the whole occasion. She had never forgotten seeing Angus, he looked like a broken man, while Pete tried to make light of the whole occasion. It should have been a happy day, but it was more like a funeral.

'Do you ride horses, Priscilla?' said Françoise, as she tried to make polite conversation.

'Many years ago when I was young, but my daughter Chrissy, rides, she's sixteen and very keen.'

'Have you other children?'

'A boy age fourteen called Neale. He's clever, like his father.'

'I used to have a Camargue horse when I was young. He had a mind of his own, very difficult to control, but a beautiful animal. I kept him on a farm about twenty-five kilometres from Aix. I would spend my summer months with other young people, riding, grooming…you know at that age, it is a kind of love-affair. When I got older, I had to study more and didn't have the time.'

'I suppose you know my husband once wanted to marry you?'

'Oh, that was just a teen-age romance,' said Françoise, taken aback by this direct remark. 'I guess we were in love for a short time.' She hesitated, and looked at Angus. 'I remember your husband being kind, I am sure he's not changed. You're very lucky, Priscilla.'

Listening to this exchange, Angus shifted on his feet, embarrassed. 'We were all young and idealistic back then. Sadly, realism creeps into your life, particularly when you have the responsibility of children,' said Angus.

'I agree, bringing up Charles on my own has not been easy.'

'Yes, that must have been difficult having no father around.'

'His French grandfather played a big role and Pete always made certain that Charles lacked for nothing.'

'Except having a proper father.'

Françoise was startled by Priscilla's direct manner.

'It's good you've maintained a civilised relationship with Pete over the years for Charles's sake, if no-one else,' said Angus.

'Well, sometimes the *entente cordiale* gets strained, but we're all adults and Pete is Charles's father after all.'

'You never married again?' asked Angus.

'No, I never seemed to find the right one. As the years pass, the fussier I've become. My fashion boutiques keep me busy, and as I mentioned, I design some of my own clothes which are now being sold in England.'

'How very enterprising,' said Priscilla

'And what about you Angus, are you still working at the university? I hear you've become an authority on Shakespeare and have published books.'

'Oh, I don't know.'

'He's too modest,' said Priscilla.

Françoise wondered if Angus was secretly thinking of an acerbic observation about his abrasive wife, or whether she had beaten the humour out of him over the years with her steam-roller approach to cordiality.

'My father would be impressed with Pete's success, just look at all this,' said Françoise, as she looked around the massive hall and the thronging guests.

'We are all rather taken with Raisford Hall,' said Priscilla. 'I hope he's earned it legally.'

'Ouch! He is one of my oldest friends, you must not make slanderous remarks. After all, we are his guests.'

'Oldest friend? You've not clapped eyes on him in decades.'

'That's hardly the point.'

'Don't be so pompous, you told me Pete always sailed close to the wind.'

'I don't understand, "*sailed close to the wind*,"' said Françoise.

'Underhand business practices, perhaps bending the law a little,' said Angus.

Françoise said nothing but bristled at Priscilla's implication that her son's father was a crook.

'How is your father, still a bit grumpy?' said Angus, trying to change the subject. 'He was never very keen on us two. I think he regarded us wastrel Anglo Saxon hippies.'

'Do you know I never understood my Papa's animosity towards you and Pete. He warmed up after Charles was born. I did try to talk to him, he said it was to do with the war and his time in the Résistance. He wouldn't go further. I don't know why our parents' generation can't forget the war. It's more than forty years ago.'

'I didn't know Henri was a partisan,' said Angus. 'Although by the end of the war many Frenchmen and women claimed to be resisters. I think it was a way of assuaging the guilt about the Vichy regime and their cooperation with the German occupiers.'

'Perhaps there's some truth in that,' said Françoise. 'But your country never had to endure a German invasion, I am certain that they would have found sympathisers in Britain, including your exiled King.'

'Touché,' said Priscilla.

'Many people in France disassociated themselves with the German occupiers. But you try living in an occupied country and not be involved at some level.'

'But the Vichy Government just rolled over to cooperate with the Nazis.'

'Perhaps at the beginning, and some of Petain's followers did regret the Germans' departure.'

'Because they knew they would be punished by those who had been loyal.'

'Yes, some were executed by the *Maquis* in revenge killings.'

'Brutal justice.'

'You have to understand the occupation was okay for certain businesses, as long as you went along with them. The Germans needed materials for fortifications and local labour, although much of it was forced.'

'Difficult to say no when there was a gun pointing at your back,' said Angus.

'I know my Papa was an early member of the Maquis in the Aix region, he was barely an adult. Anyhow, enough war talk, isn't this supposed to be a party?' said Françoise, nudging Angus's arm. 'Don't complain about my father at least he gave you and Pete a job!'

'But we had the benefit of a family ally on our side,' said Angus, looking at Françoise. Priscilla looked stoney-faced. 'Is he still working?'

'Kind of, semi-retired, one of his employees sees to the business day-to-day and I am a sleeping director so I keep on eye on things. They have moved into building villas, more profitable than painting. Papa is still well connected in Aix. After the war there was plenty of work repairing war damage and ridding the area of the signs of the occupiers. In the latter years, I think the Church, the Masons and old wartime networks ensured he had enough business to keeping him going.'

'Sounds like the Mafia,' said Priscilla.

'Just old alliances, I think in England you'd call it, "The old boy network,"' said Françoise, determined not to rise to Priscilla's ire.

Françoise was surprised Angus had agreed to attend the party after everything that Pete had done to him. Her own selfishness did not bear too much scrutiny either, and she tried to drive the memory of her infidelity out of her mind. Her cheerless father correctly predicted the marriage would never last. But when she had agreed to marry Pete it was never her intention to separate at a later date. She had tried her best to love Pete and make it work but the combination of her father and her own lingering doubts haunted her. Pete knew he was never her first choice. She was never a convincing liar.

'Angus, why don't we arrange to meet and talk at another time? There's so much to catch up on,' said Françoise. It was obvious that the antagonistic presence of Priscilla would never allow her to speak openly with Angus.' I am staying in London for a few days before I return to Aix. Can you get to London for a morning?' She pulled out a business card from her clutch bag and scribbled her hotel telephone number on the reverse.

Angus looked taken back by Françoise's directness in front of Priscilla.

'Why don't you come along too, Priscilla?' said Françoise. She smiled at her and hoped her bluff would pay off. 'I would love to know what you two have been up to during these past years.'

'I can't make any promises, but I'll check my diary on Monday,' said Angus, flustered by Françoise's question. 'It will all depend on my lecture schedule,' said Angus. Priscilla remained motionless, no emotion registered on her carefully made-up face. There was a long pause.

'I definitely can't make Monday, I'm working.' said Priscilla.

Angus looked at Priscilla but said nothing, he turned to look at Françoise and smiled, and she returned the smile in tacit acknowledgement of an invitation understood.

'I must find Pete, I would love to speak to his parents again, I believe they are here somewhere,' said Françoise. She went forward and kissed Priscilla on both cheeks and turned to Angus. '*À bientôt*,' she said and touched Angus's jacket sleeve and moved off into the crowd.

Angus tried not to look shocked but what had occurred was like a scene from a Shakespearean tragic-comedy. Here he was in his old rival's enormous house, drinking his expensive champagne with Priscilla, the mother of his two adored children, while this glowing, impetuous, French woman, who should rightly have been his wife, had just signalled a reconciliation, and all that might entail. And all this after an unforgivable betrayal and decades of separation.

'Get a grip of yourself, you look as if you are going to have a heart attack,' said Priscilla, furious at Françoise's impertinence. Whatever Angus' doubts about having misinterpreted the Frenchwoman's invitation it was obvious to Priscilla that it was a thinly disguised message. Suddenly, for the first time in Angus' unequal marriage he felt vulnerable and exposed. Out of nowhere Françoise had emerged poised with a wrecking ball to once again throw his measured life into turmoil.

Françoise's presence had exposed Priscilla's brooding hostility and ruminating self-pity for all the world to see. Angus could not help wonder if the two women who had dominated his life, also sensed the release of energy in the lithosphere of their relationships. Was it just him, or had they failed to realise that the resulting seismic shock waves could culminate in untold damage?

In Priscilla's case, she had at the outset never wavered in her ambition of snaring her kind, handsome and intelligent man. Then she married the dream, and two children and two decades later, thought better of it.

Françoise had relit the blue touch paper but none of the parties were certain if it would fizzle out or explode.

Chapter 35

Charles suffered no pangs of guilt about not attending his father's lavish celebration of himself. He knew it would be over the top, like everything his father ever did.

His grandfather, Henri, never liked to hear about his ex-son-in-law's extravagant tastes, his success irritated him. "An English bourgeoisie," he would say when his name ever arose in conversation, which was not often. Henri wasted no opportunity to put down Charles's father, and the English in general. His five hundred franc bribe to his grandson had achieved his objective of diverting Charles and hurting Pete; it was a spiteful and childish gesture.

Charles had enjoyed his dinner and clubbing night with his Parisian girlfriend, but despite her attractiveness, she would be just another date. Charles's litany of girlfriends never lasted beyond two or three dates. He enjoyed having a girl on his arm to show off, but his feelings for them never excited him. He did not know why, and it puzzled him, maybe the next date would be the one that fired him up.

His failure to go to England had upset his mother, and he hated himself for defying her wishes. Despite his grandfather's manipulative ways, Charles had learned to filter out the old man's prejudices. He had recognised the five hundred francs was a bribe to score points against his father. For Charles a dinner date with a beautiful girl, or attending an English party where he knew few people, was an easy decision.

Yet Charles loved his grandfather who had been a guiding hand since his father abandoned him when he was only young. "Abandoned," was the favourite word that his grandfather liked to use in referencing his father. Henri's hypocrisy knew no bounds, and it would be only when Charles was older that he would fully comprehend the role his grandfather had in driving his father to England.

Despite his many faults, the closeness between grandson and grandfather grew as Henri aged. When his grandfather had one more cognac than his doctor recommended, he would confide in Charles with tantalising snapshot memories of his war experiences in the Résistance. Long buried facts slowly emerged: Charles learned he had an uncle who was killed about the time when the Americans invaded the south of France. Charles had read a little at school about the German occupation and the disgraced Vichy Government's collaboration. But recently it was being spoken of more openly in newspapers and in TV documentaries. It was no longer being air-brushed out of France's collective history.

'I was just eighteen, when I joined a local Maquis group, they were a communist inspired guerrilla force,' said Henri, one evening, while sipping his cognac. 'Of course I was not political in those days, I just wanted rid of *les Boches*.'

'When was that exactly?'

'In early 1944. Initially I was just a courier, taking messages to other members of the group who lived in the town, but many hid out in the woods in secret camps. I didn't meet them until I became a full-bloodied activist. It was an exciting time and we were all waiting for the expected invasion by the Allies. As the date grew closer, although we didn't know precisely when, our guerrilla activities increased and an English spy was parachuted in to help train and work with our group. The British arranged regular airdrops of weapons, ammunition and explosives to arm Résistance cells across France. It was dangerous work unloading and hiding armaments in the dark before the Germans discovered us. '*Les Boches* were always on the alert and they became very jumpy after the Allies landed in Normandy. Many German troops from around here were recalled north to support the fighting.'

Charles listened in awe to his grandfather's exploits of blowing up electricity sub stations and ambushing German patrols. 'By 1944 the Gestapo had become very vigilant and hunted out partisan groups with the help of the *Milice*, the French pro-Nazi militia. It was frightening, no-one was certain who was a friend and who was a collaborator. We lost a lot of resisters to informers.'

'What happened if you were caught?'

'If you survived the interrogations, and many didn't, you were sent to a concentration camp in Germany, but most were shot, everyone... men, women and children, younger than you. The Gestapo were merciless,' he said, and suddenly the old man's eyes filled with tears.

'How terrible, Grandpapa... weren't you scared?'

'Of course, but I was young. I thought they'd never catch me. The invincibility and foolhardiness of youth. I was lucky never to be found out, I came close to it on several occasions.'

'How close?' asked Charles..

'I have said enough already,' he said, and looked away. 'No more talk of the past, it tires me to remember it all.'

~

When Charles was young he remained a little in awe of his "part-time" father who came to France on flying visits, and later on, when he visited England, he witnessed at first hand, Pete's frenetic lifestyle. He missed having a constant father who was part of his daily life, like his other friends in Aix.

Charles worked diligently at school and showed a flair for science subjects as well as being a talented tennis player. He was rated an above- average student but his teachers commented that he could be reserved and tetchy when the mood took him. From an early age Henri had groomed Charles to be his successor. Pete would have made a good fist of it but he could not contemplate his English son-in-law running his business.

'I have built this business up over the years,' said Henri. 'It is here, ready for you when you have finished your university and business school training. I need young blood to take over the reins and you are my only family.'

But Charles was not going to be bounced into a career in which he had no interest. When he announced he had other plans, his grandfather was devastated.

'I am sorry Grandfather, but I have decided to train to become a doctor, perhaps a surgeon in the long term. I would like to be a specialist in orthopaedics.'

'But I always assumed you would want to follow in my footsteps and run the family business?'

'Assumed, you mean presumed, Grandpa. You know you never asked me if I wanted to be a house builder or a painter?' Charles was trying to hold his temper and let down his Grandfather gently but he was finding it difficult to maintain his cool.

'But Charles, you will be wealthy, this is a sound business with a reputation that has taken me years of hard graft to achieve. From the moment you were born I always wanted it to be yours.' As usual Henri could only see things through a one-way mirror.

'Stop being so dogmatic, Henri,' said Madame Delores. 'Charles has ideas of his own, he must do what he wants and not bend to your wishes all his life.'

It was the first time Henri had been defied and it came to him as a shock. He had spent his life getting his own way.

'You should sell the business and retire. Time to take it easy,' said Charles. 'My mind is made up, Grandpapa. I have already been accepted to study medicine at Aix-Marseilles university.'

Henri looked like a beaten man, but his mother and grandmother were delighted with his choice of a career in medicine.

'A more worthwhile pursuit than building rich people's villas,' said Madame Delores.

'Traitor!' said Henri.

Chapter 36

It was fortuitous that Angus ran into Mr and Mrs Jagoda sitting quietly in one of Raisford Hall's morning rooms at Pete's party. They remembered Angus from his time at school with Peter. Mr. Jagoda looked frail and his breathing was laboured, but he still had a warm smile. They were very proud of their son' success. Pete had bought them a beautiful retirement apartment in Harrogate that overlooked the famous Stray.

'It's only a few minutes walk to Betty's tearooms,' said Felicja. 'They make such a nice cup of tea, and the staff are so polite.' Mrs Jagoda looked sprightly and well, she was still a commanding presence, thought Angus. They chatted for a while about Charles's medical studies and Angus mentioned that Françoise was at the party, although Charles had not come.

'I didn't know Françoise was here,' said Felicja. 'I would so like to meet her again. She was a beautiful girl, I never really understood the reasons why their marriage broke up. It was such a shame, a boy should have a father in his life.'

'I think Pete does his best, but it is difficult with Charles being in France, and Pete being so busy with his work.'

'No excuses, Angus. The father should him see as often as he can,' said Mr Jagoda.

'When did you last see Charles?

'Must be nearly two years,' said Felicja.

'I don't think he liked the boiled fish we always served on Friday nights,' said Mr Jagoda.

'I'll try and speak to Françoise and suggest Charles comes to see you again soon. He should keep in touch his grandparents, whatever the circumstances.'

'That would be lovely,' said Felicja. The old man nodded in agreement.

'Françoise is somewhere here and I'll get her to come up to see you. Now can I get you some food from the buffet and bring it here? It's a bit of a crush out there,' he said, looking in the direction of the large hallway.

'That would be lovely, Angus, you were always such a thoughtful boy. We are a bit old for bumping about in crowds,' said Felicja.

It did not take long for Angus to locate Françoise and between them filled up two plates with cold salmon and salads for the elderly pair and made their way to the morning room. Felicja wept when she met Françoise again and her husband looked rheumy eyed as he hugged the elegant figure of their ex-daughter-in-law. It was a lovely reunion and their chat was only marred when Priscilla suddenly emerged into the room and looked about her as if she was weighing up the decor. In fact she was half-way through her own self-conducted tour of the house, assessing the Hall's value for her boss.

'Oh hello,' she said, as she wandered around the room. She noted the carved cornices and oak panelling in a small notebook. 'I hope I'm not breaking up the party.' Then without another word she strode off on her fact-finding mission.

'Who was that strange woman?' said Mr Jagoda.

'My wife,' said Angus. 'I'm led to believe.'

Françoise raised her eyebrows. There was an awkward silence before Felicja asked, 'Have you children, Angus?'

~

The post party journey home in the rattling VW did not go well. Priscilla was drunk and argumentative: 'How can we afford…' she started, warming to her normal theme of lack of money. Angus switched off as he thought about his unexpected meeting with Françoise.

When he looked back at their relationship, he likened it to one of his beloved Shakespearean tragedies:

"My bounty is as boundless as the sea
My love as deep, the more I give to thee."

Pathetic really, quoting Romeo and Juliet to himself, but in the moment his love for Françoise had been visceral. Perhaps that was the unescapable tsunami of a first love, an encounter like no other, never to be repeated. It had been heart-rending. He had to admit to himself that it was more than anything he had ever felt for Priscilla. Poor Priscilla, that was not her fault. As Priscilla yattered on, Angus felt an overwhelming sadness for his wife, she had loved him once and helped him overcame his bitterness when he was a broken man. He was mystified where all that affection had gone, it had drifted away like an early morning summer mist, atrophying over the years to be replaced by sour regret. He knew he was partly to blame, his absorption with literature and his passion for sharing it with his students had made him oblivious to Priscilla's call for help. Her complaints were not just about money it was a smoke screen for her overall discontent, money was an easy club with which to batter him. He thought about his own casual disinterest in her life and needs. He never set out to be cruel in the real sense of the word, but his inability to recognise Priscilla's horizons was a form of mental cruelty. It shocked him to admit to himself.

'Have you been listening to a word I have been saying?'

'Of course. We are short of money and it's all my fault.' It was the only answer he was prepared to admit. It was the wrong time of night to embark on a discussion about their failed marriage, particularly when Priscilla was drunk.

'I suppose you are mooning about that French woman?' she said. 'You seem to have forgotten she once broke your heart and it was me that put you back together again. My God, she was trying her hardest to ingratiate herself with you. You were lapping it up, like a cat who had got the cream.'

'Oh please be quiet Priscilla, I am trying to concentrate on driving us home safely.'

'She's got a nerve, turning up after all these years, when she'd discarded you for your alleged best friend. You were an emotional train crash when I found you.'

'You were a saint,' said Angus, humming an aria from Fauré's requiem.

'Now you've wrapped yourself up in your little academic world of books, lectures and conferences where the hell do I fit in to your cosy existence? Have you any idea what my life is like? Bloody cooking, looking after the children, and showing toffy-nosed people around expensive houses.'

'The problem is your job. It is filling your head with too many ideas about the material things that you hanker. Instead of fulfilling you, it's a disease that's feeding your envy for big houses, cars and clothes that your clients have in abundance. Do you really think a lot of money is going make you happy? It's so superficial.'

'I don't want a lot of money. I want more than your indifference. I want you to take notice of me. Yes, I'm fed up of not having enough money to buy some decent clothes and educate our children privately. But it's more than that.'

'By most people's standards we are comfortably off. You never used to be so avaricious. Perhaps, you should look for another job and re-evaluate your priorities.'

'Re-evaluate my priorities? I am not an exam answer. Don't you want the best for me and your family?'

'I wasn't aware the children wanted to change schools, and I had not noticed you were wearing rags.'

'Bloody hell, Angus. You're being deliberately obtuse, as usual.'

Angus felt nauseous with the stress of the row. The combination of the party's rich food and ample alcohol caused him to belch loudly which brought the argument to an end. Priscilla sighed in weary resignation and fell sleep, her head lolled like a doll against the car side window.

Fortunately, when they arrived at their Victorian house, the two children were asleep in bed. Angus woke Priscilla and gently pulled her from the car onto her feet. She stood upright and swayed slowly from side to side, took a deep breath and remembered her unhappiness. She shrugged off Angus's protective arm and staggered into the house and half-fell as she climbed the steep stairs. She wept as she battled her way up to the landing and eventually found sanctuary in the spare bedroom. The door slammed behind her.

~

Sunday morning was a favourite time for Angus. He awoke alone in the double bed, his head was mussy and he went down to the kitchen to make a brew. His daughter and son were both watching a video on TV in the sitting room.

'Have a good time, last night Dad?' asked his daughter, Chrissy. Neale remained glued to the TV and didn't turn around to acknowledge his father.

'Great party. My old friend Pete has a spectacular pad, and we were treated like royalty, the finest champagne all the way.'

'Mum would like that,' said Chrissy.

'She's got a bit of a headache this morning, so don't disturb her.'

'Okay, we'll keep quiet, promise. By the way I've got a riding lesson at two o'clock. Can you take me?'

'Of course, darling,' said Angus.

'What about me?' said Neale, managing to drag his attention from the TV screen.

'We could go bowling, while Chrissy has her riding lesson?'

'Great! Will Mum come?'

'I don't know, it depends on how she feels.'

'I'll get you two some breakfast before I take the dog for a walk. I need some fresh air.'

The river walk was always one of Angus's favourite strolls. He threw sticks into the water for Falstaff, his Labrador. It was a game the dog would play until Angus's arm grew too tired or when his trousers became too sodden from the animal shaking himself all over him. As he walked back to the house he passed a telephone box. On the spur of the moment he decided to call Françoise. He was not certain what he was going to say. He had not made his mind up whether to see her again but it would be nice to hear her French-accented English. The thought sent tingles down his spine, her voice was deliciously melodious and redolent of his youth.

He opened his wallet and took out her business card and involuntarily put it under his nose in the hope of smelling her perfume. He jammed himself into the phone box, the dog sat on his already wet feet. As he was about to lift the receiver to dial the hotel number she had scribbled on the card, he remembered that Françoise was staying at Raisford Hall overnight. He returned the card to his wallet and pushed open the heavy, red metal door of the phone box and squeezed outside. The dog looked up at him as if to say, what was that all about? Angus felt a guilty relief that his impulse of betrayal had ended in failure.

~

Pete's party was the apogee of his success, a last hurrah before his reputation was shredded and his glittering business empire was emasculated.

Matters began to go haywire in the early hours of the party. Councillor Jenkins retired to the Woodman Hotel accompanied by Sylvia the hostess. While she was bouncing up and down on his vast stomach, he suffered a catastrophic heart attack. The incident might have gone unnoticed if Sylvia had not screamed her head off and alerted the hotel's night manager. An ambulance was called and when it was clear Councillor Jenkins was no more, the local constabulary arrived on the scene. It didn't take long for the police to trace the Councillor's home address and later on that morning, a policeman and a female constable were on Mrs. Jenkins's doorstep to inform her, that at an unspecified time during the previous evening, she had become a widow.

Sylvia was designated as a "Hostess" on one of Pete's nightclub payrolls. She naively admitted to the police that her duties included "looking after the Councillor." Once it was discovered the hotel and champagne had been pre-paid by one of Pete's companies, more investigations followed. The deeper the police looked, the more their suspicions grew. It was not long before they discovered that the company has several "customer service hostesses" on their books. They were located in the various towns and cities where Pete had night clubs and student accommodation.

The complex strands of the saga took many months to unwind and had it not been for a diligent investigative reporter at Private Eye magazine, the story might have gone largely unnoticed. It was bad luck that the magazine has been undertaking a long-running investigation into the handling of dodgy housing contracts by councils and local authorities. A wide-ranging probe of council officials in each of the locations where there were expanding universities and polytechnics followed. It was not long before Pete's education housing customers smelt a whiff of scandal and began to distance themselves and sought alternative suppliers.

Pete sensed trouble ahead, and despite his denials of wrongdoing to anyone who would listen, he shrewdly transferred ownership of over half of his properties into his wife's name. He then created a network of new companies with different managers and the directors, all of whom enjoyed untainted reputations. But in the end, it was a personal catastrophe for Pete as the remaining properties, and many of his clubs, fast food outlets and other associated companies came under the hammer to pay the extortionate legal fees he had incurred attempting to defend the indefensible. It was the scandal of the decade and the trial received acres of media coverage and public opprobrium.

Priscilla's suspicions about Pete were proven to be uncannily prescient.

Chapter 37

England 1988

When Angus finally came to his senses and the initial jolt of excitement of meeting Françoise again became a reality, he began to question his own judgement. Had he misread her signals? He hesitated. What seemed so clear on Sunday morning while recovering from a hangover, appeared fanciful by Monday afternoon.

He had wrestled with the idea of 'phoning her all morning and could not concentrate on his academic work. His tutorial with his third year students was unusually lack-lustre. One moment he felt euphoric, the next terrified of the possible consequences if he made contact. It reminded him of his reluctance to approach Françoise twenty years before. This time it was conscience that held him back. He could not to put his relationship with his children in jeopardy. He could forsake Priscilla, but the children were another matter.

He felt rudderless to stop his marriage sailing into the abyss. His recent life had been characterised by bitter arguments followed by Priscilla's moody silences. His wife had single-handedly re-built his confidence after Françoise's infidelity. Now the words of his late, and unmissed father, came to him from the afterlife, intoning that he should not covet another man's wife, or even his ex-wife.

That late afternoon, Angus was with Falstaff on his regular riverside dog walk. As he approached the phone box he had not yet made up his mind whether to call. He had loaded his coat pocket with coins. Falstaff was unaware of his master's ambivalence and pulled impatiently on his lead to reach the river. The dog was perplexed, when unexpectedly, he was reluctantly dragged into the phone box.

'Oh Angus, it is you!' I didn't think would get in touch again. It's been such a long time since the Pete debacle and I imagined you had given up on me for ever.'

'I've never forgotten you, Françoise, although I have tried hard enough, believe me.'

'You have every right to forget me, dear Angus. I know I hurt you so terribly with my foolish behaviour and the consequences that followed. I don't deserve forgiveness.'

'You should always try to forgive, and accept forgiveness of others. Isn't that the credo of good Catholic?'

'You sound like a priest. I remember you telling me your father was a devoted Christian, have you become a believer since we last met?

'No, but I have my own guidelines on right and wrong.' He thought to himself how pompous he was being but he did not know what to say. It had been so long and he was like a nervous boy on his first date. Nervous of the betrayal of Priscilla and nervous for himself in making a mess of the conversation he desperately wanted.

'I was very wrong in the way I treated you. With hindsight we should have run way together as you suggested. Is that why you never tried to contact me again?'

'In part, yes. It did cross my mind, especially after I heard that you had split up with Pete. But by then I was married, and Priscilla was expecting our first child. What would you think of me abandoning my pregnant wife to try and resurrect a ruined romantic whim?

'Oh, Angus, our relationship was never just a romantic whim.'

'I couldn't face resurrecting what we once had, the memories were too raw. Anyhow, you might have changed your mind and turned me down again. I had not forgotten your threatening father, it would have been foolish of me to even try, it was out of the question.'

'It was me that was foolish. But it is too late for moralising now. It's in the past, we were both scarred by my actions. Actions I have regretted everyday since we parted.'

'Even now, after all this time?'

'Even now.'

'Why didn't you remarry after Pete?'

'Nobody ever matched you.'

'But you knew me well enough that I would never leave Priscilla to bring up a child on her own, not even for you, Françoise.'

'Angus, you were always so thoughtful of others.'

'And stupid.'

'Don't be angry, I can't bear it. Is there no place in your heart left for me?'

Angus remained silent. He could hear himself breathing, short breaths, his chest pounded. For a moment he contemplated putting the receiver down.

'Yes, there has always been a part for you but I have kept it hidden, dormant'

'Can you wake it up again?' .

'What are asking of me, what is it you want?'

'Can't you guess?'

'You can't just arrive in England, turn up at your ex-husband's party and proposition me as if nothing happened all those years ago. You broke my heart once, I cannot bear you to do it again. Surely you don't expect me to abandon Priscilla, my children, my life, after one brief reunion?'

'I am not propositioning you, Angus., God forbid.'

'What would you call it then?'

'So why have you bothered to 'phone me today?

Angus hesitated: 'I really don't know, perhaps it was curiosity? I wanted to know how you've filled the last twenty years. I hoped you were unhappy, it's a kind of schadenfreude. Those were years we should have spent together.'

'I don't believe you Angus. It is more than curiosity. If I had not met your wife at the party and witnessed your unhappy relationship at first hand, I would never have bothered to give you my number.'

'All couples can have bad nights together. It doesn't mean their marriages are finished.'

'Angus, can't you face what is obvious to all? You don't have to be a psychoanalyst to recognise that Priscilla no longer loves you. I can tell, and you know it too in your heart of hearts'

'That's a very speedy assessment of nearly twenty years of my marriage after a fifteen minute meeting with my wife.' Angus hesitated for a long time. He was annoyed at Françoise's presumptuous remarks, but he knew them to be correct, but he didn't want to hear it from her. His marriage had become a convenient facade, built on the pretext that his children had a balanced home life in which to grow up in. Angus did not answer. His silence said it all.

'I don't expect you to forgive me, but can we at least be friends?' said Françoise, he could hear the catch in Françoise's voice, she was silently weeping.

'I am not sure how that would work, Françoise. You are in France and I am over here.' He was silent again, he couldn't bring himself to reject the offer. 'Perhaps we could try,' he said quietly, not quite believing what he had said. Falstaff, pulled at his lead, he wanted his walk. 'Wait Falstaff, we'll go in a minute.'

'Who's that, have you someone else with you?'

'No it's my dog, he needs his walk.' Angus fed more money into the machine. 'I'm running out of money, I have to go in a minute. Can we meet tomorrow afternoon at your hotel, say four o'clock?' The phone went bleep, bleep, bleep, as the money ran out.

The next morning Françoise telephoned the university and finally tracked Angus down in his study. 'I'm so sorry Angus, I can't make our meeting today. I have to go back to France as I have had a break in at one of my shops. Someone has tried to set fire to the premises, it's an awful mess. I've managed to get a lunchtime flight to Nice, I will call you at the university when I'm next in England. I'll be back again soon. I have to dash, love you.' And she was gone, Angus was not quite sure if he had been dreaming.

On reflection, he felt a flood of relief mixed with disappointment at the cancellation. Perhaps it was for the best, he was not sure if the remnants of his Presbyterian upbringing could cope with a clandestine love affair.

~

As the shuttle bus rumbled its way towards Heathrow airport Françoise cursed the break-in and fire that had prevented her meeting Angus. He had been hesitant enough about meeting up and she worried, that after thinking it over, he might turn her down next time. Maybe she could write to him at the university?

She had surprised herself at the reservoir of feelings that she still harboured for him after so long. Meeting him again had brought it all back in a tsunami of memories and emotion. She had never stopped regretting her childish behaviour in sleeping with Pete. And my God, she had paid for it in spade-fulls. The only consolation was dear Charles. She had had a marriage of sorts but in reality it been a charade, little more than window dressing to satisfy the mores of the time. Poor Pete, he always knew he was playing second best, despite her half-hearted efforts to reassure him to the contrary.

Her mind returned to the conversation she had with Charles before she left for England. They were having breakfast together on her apartment terrace:

'Maman, you know when you met Papa, did he have another English friend with him?' he had asked.

'Yes, who told you?'

'Grandpapa.'

'Your grandfather is a terrible gossip.'

'What happened to him.'

'He went back to England and became a university professor.'

'Is he rich like Papa?'

'I don't think so. You have to realise that your father is exceptionally wealthy. Most people don't have a fraction of his money but you can be rich in other ways. Intelligence and learning can enrich your life, it is just a different type of currency. You can contribute to society in many ways, for example through the arts, science and medicine. It is just like you wanting to be a doctor, in time, you'll help other people lives by utilising your skills and knowledge to make them better.'

'A university professor doesn't sound like Papa's type at all.'

'They were very different characters but great friends when they were young. You've heard the phrase that opposites attract.'

'Grandpapa said you were close friends with him, went on dates.'

'I did for a short while.'

'Why did you stop?'

'It's a long story. We drifted apart. Look I have plane to catch, enough of this interrogation.'

'What was he like?'

'Kind, a gentle sort of man, quite serious.'

'Did you love him?'

'I was very young and it was a long time ago. Now enough of your questions.'

'Did he make you laugh.'

'Yes, he had a dry sense of humour. You could meet him if you could bothered to come with me instead of taking your girlfriend out.'

'Perhaps one day I will meet him and maybe he'll tell me what really happened between you two. I can always tell when you are lying,' he said, and banged his coffee cup down. Charles always became irritated when his mother shut him out of a part of her life. He wanted to share everything with her, even the past.

As the noise of jet engines grew louder and Heathrow's ugly buildings came into view, she made the decision that Angus had to become part of her life again. She knew it would not be easy prising him away from Priscilla and his children but the cracks in their relationship were wide open.

She knew instinctively that Charles and Angus would get on well together. Angus could become the guiding hand for Charles that she had never found in any other man.

She had already waited twenty years, she could wait a little longer.

Chapter 38

It was several months from the date of the party before Pete's misdemeanours began to fully emerge.

Unexpectedly, Pete 'phoned Angus at his home number. Priscilla took the call but forgot to mention it to Angus until three days later when she "suddenly remembered." Angus suspected the delay was deliberate but said nothing.

Angus has been following Pete's unfolding drama in Private Eye magazine. Surprisingly, he felt no pleasure over his friend's calumny. The revelations unravelled drip by drip each one more serious than the last. Initially, Angus thought that Pete would weather the storm until the bad news turned into a tsunami of accusations and once the national press got hold of the story, the writing was on the wall. The tabloid journalists fed on every lurid detail, like carrion picking over a carcass.

The headlines screamed: "*Prostitute Payroll;*" "*Disgraced Council Officials On The Take;*" "*Rich Industrialist's Daughter;*" "*One Million Pound Mansion*." There was no end of mud being thrown, much of it speculative, some plainly fabricated, but nonetheless, a very damning odour was spreading like a poison gas.

Angus called Pete back to offer any help he could. Despite their past differences, the bond of friendship, however fractured, still held. Pete was not at home when he called but he had a long chat with Suzy. She sounded breezy and relaxed, Angus was impressed by the chutzpah she was showing considering the stories flying about her husband. 'Pete's in Spain, briefing his barrister,' she said. 'Well, that's what he told me, he's probably cooking up some sort of explanation. He wanted to get away from all the media attention. They have been very intrusive, 'phoning, putting messages into our letterbox, sometimes they sneak past our security and arrive on the doorstep like vermin. Pete's confident this ghastly business will never come to court, he says the prosecution charges won't stick.'

'So, it's not as bad as it sounds in the papers?'

'No, I think there's a lot of hot air. Of course, once local Government officials are involved there's more prurient interest from the press. It's a terrible nuisance, there are photographers hiding in the shrubbery or camped outside the Hall gates. I can't go anywhere without cameras being shoved through the car window.'

'How awful,' said Angus, as he thought about Pete's elegant wife being put through the media mincer.

'It's as if I was about to go on trial. I love your old friend dearly, but Pete sometimes does go too far.'

'You don't think he's planning to bolt somewhere where he can't be extradited?'

'Good God, no!'

Then Angus remembered when he got Françoise pregnant, he did not shirk his responsibilities then – although marrying a beautiful French girl was more preferable than the current circumstances he faced which could end being a spell in jail.

'You're right Suzy, he'll tough it out, whatever the outcome.'

However, Angus was not reassured by Suzy's nonchalant assessment. She had to be keeping up some form of defensive screen, she was an eminent barrister after all. However, these shenanigans will be doing nothing for her own reputation or that of her illustrious father. He gave Suzy his university office number and asked Pete call him.

Two days later Angus received a call from Spain. 'Hiya, Angus. I hear you've been trying to contact me, have you got something on me too?' He laughed at his own gallows humour.

'How goes it?'

'The sun is shining and the media don't know I'm here. I have peace and quiet, and importantly, time to think.

'Is there anything I can do to help? From what I read in the press it looks like the barbarians are ready to pounce.'

'Thanks for the offer. You're right, the media are on the warpath, there will be bigger heads than mine to roll if they get their way.'

'Like?'

'The Home Office Minister is a non-executive director of Student Home Holdings?'

'Hell, Pete, you have been moving in exulted circles.'

'People, no matter their status, are the same the world over when they smell easy money - greedy,' he said, sounding his old ebullient self. 'You need to know there's some pressure being brought to bear from very high up for the case to be dropped.'

'I hope you're right.'

'You never know, once the press gets stuck in they are like terriers, they won't let go. I appreciate your offer of support, it's more than I deserve. I'll be back from Spain in a couple of days, perhaps we can we meet up, somewhere discreet. Could I come to your rooms at the university?

'I'd prefer not, but you could come to the house. I'll arrange a time when Priscilla's working.'

'Can you tell me what's it about?'

'Well, I might need to make some contingency plans. It's personal, just in case.'

~

Felicja and Piotr Jagoda were incredulous when they learned of the charges mounting up against their son. 'There has to be some mistake,' said Felicja. She was sitting in her favourite wing armchair while she read the reports in the *Yorkshire Post* of her son's alleged bribery of Council Officials. 'This cannot be my son. He was always naughty, but never a criminal. First, he makes girl pregnant and now this! Piotr, what do you say?'

'Well, he must have done something wrong otherwise there wouldn't be all this brouhaha. It's my fault, I should have been stricter with him when he was growing up.'

'Piotr! He's a grown man, forty years of age, not a rebellious teenager. He has a successful business. Look where we are living? We couldn't have afforded a luxury flat in this beautiful town. I'm beginning to feel it's tainted, as if we shouldn't own it. What if he stole the money?'

'Don't be ridiculous. Not all the money he's made over the years was made through illegal dealings.'

'How do you know?' she said, and burst into tears.

'Before the war in Poland, many Government officials were crooked. How do you think your father gained all those clothing contracts for uniforms?'

'How dare you blame my lamented Papa for our son's wrong doings. I don't believe that my father would do anything like that, I worked with him and travelled all over Europe. I never saw him do anything underhand. That's a dreadful thing to say, Piotr.'

'Do you think your father would tell you? You were an innocent young girl. He would have shielded details of deals from you. It's often the way businesses are run, here or anywhere else. The problem is in England if you get caught the authorities don't brush it under the carpet as they do in many countries.'

The thought that her father may have kept secrets from her reminded Felicja of her own wartime secrets that she had never confided to her husband. But somehow it was not the same, she had signed the official secrets act.

'What about these stories of him hiring prostitutes and blackmailing people? It's unspeakable, my dear parents will be turning in their graves. May God forgive his wickedness?' she said.

'Let's not jump to conclusions, he's not been found guilty. Yet.'

'There's plenty of smoke, there must be a fire somewhere.'

'If these allegations are proven, he'll go to jail.'

'Never, my son in jail. It's unthinkable, what shame he'd bring to our family. And what about his beautiful wife Suzy, and there's Charles to think about too.'

'It's lucky he's in France, away from all this publicity.'

'Suzy's father won't like this scandal. He will not want his precious reputation as a pillar of industry besmirched by his daughter's marriage to a criminal.'

'So, you are accusing your son of being a criminal already?'

Chapter 39

England 1989

Pete never did anything by halves, his downfall was spectacular. He was made personally bankrupt and given a ten year prison sentence for corruption of public officials, perverting the course of justice and prostitution. It was the maximum sentence he could receive. If he had pleaded guilty he would have received a lesser term, but Pete, unwisely, fought his case to the bitter end.

The company's architect was also jailed for giving bribes and various local authority officials, from leaders downwards, were eventually summoned to appear in court, disgraced, financially ruined and some sentenced to jail terms. Pete's reputation was shredded, his business empire shattered, and his second marriage destroyed. Lesser men would have lain down in the refuse dump of ignominy where they had been discarded. But that was not Peter Jagoda's style.

Angus visited Pete in Armley Jail, Leeds, two months after his sentencing. It would become a regular occurrence over the next few years. Pete looked better than he had anticipated. He had quickly become acclimatised to the large, antiseptic smelling, Victorian house of correction that was his new home. He was sharing a cell with a mild-mannered lawyer who had lifted vast sums of money from his firm's clients' account to fund a life of extravagant luxury. The lawyer was not coping vey well with his new surroundings, but nevertheless they got on well together. The pair became know as the "professionals" by their fellow inmates, whose crimes were often categorised as violent - bank heists, protection, gun running and other unsavoury activities. Pete had already lost some weight, appeared less bloated, and in better health for his incarceration.

By the time he had completed his first six months Pete had established a sought-after share-dealing service for his wealthier inmates, the lawyer provided legal advice where required. Pete's reputation grew for providing sound advice on buying shares in growing hi-tech US businesses, like Microsoft and Macintosh computers. His investment knowledge was a boon to long-stretch villains whose ill-gotten cash was being eroded by inflation. Their cash hordes, secreted up chimneys and dug deep into vegetable patches, was not earning money for them while guests of Her Majesty.

Pete's sage-like advice gave him and the lawyer a protective status within the prison community. They were useful assets and they both avoided being molested by any villains who might object to their presence. Pete quickly established himself as a financial authority, a beacon of probity in a den of thieves. The irony of his new status did not go unnoticed by Angus or the prison governor.

Pete forwarded Angus instructions on buying and selling stocks and shares on behalf of his inmate clients. Pete's broker was pleased with the sudden increase in business with Angus often acting as a nominee shareholder. The broker soon got used to receiving large bundles of cash in brown envelopes, sealed up with gaffer tape, for the purchase of shares.

Although Pete was a bankrupt and now divorced from Suzy, she still held half his property portfolio, and she supplied the necessary funds for Pete to make his own investments. Pete was shrewd enough to only recommend shares to his prison "clients" in which he was also investing, so he could never be accused of not following his own advice. It was a matter of honour in the circles in which he now resided. It was not long before the prison governor sought out his advice and agreed to turn a blind eye to the trades for inmates. He also ensured that Pete received a copy of the *Financial Times* every morning and the weekly edition of the *Investor's Chronicle*.

Before his conviction, Pete had asked Angus if he would act as a go-between with Charles. Pete was understandably worried the court case would drive a coach and horses through his already tenuous relationship with his son. On learning of Pete's crimes, Charles's grandfather's prophecies were realised and gleefully amplified. It provided Charles with the excuse to sever all contact with his father, guilt free. But Charles was upset for Suzy when she filed for divorce as she had been a caring stepmother to him over the years. He wrote her a long anguished letter, expressing his sadness for her, but failed to mention his father directly.

~

Françoise never wrote her letter to Angus but they did exchange a couple of telephone calls about meeting up. Françoise thought that Angus was stalling her. Then after some months, Angus said he was visiting Nice on a work trip and he would like to get together with her and Charles.

He explained that he had visited Pete in jail and he had asked for him to "keep an eye" on Charles in his prolonged absence. The following day after he had delivered his keynote lecture (with the help of a translator) on William Shakespeare to students at the *Université de Perpignan* they agreed to meet for lunch in Marseilles. The lunch was easily arranged by Françoise as Charles had expressed a desire to meet Angus and probe them both about their past relationship. Under the guise of accompanying Charles's mother on a nostalgic visit to the south of France, Angus, Françoise and Charles dined at the old established Miramar restaurant in Marseilles where they sampled their signature bouillabaisse.

It was the first time Angus and Charles had met face to face. Over the delicious lunch Angus was struck by Charles's intelligence and his inherited good looks from his mother. It was also evident he possessed some of Pete's hot-headed characteristics, particularly when he talked with angry passion about his father. Françoise remained quiet, save to say that Pete had provided for them both generously over the years. Angus was struck by Charles's almost child-like petulance in contrast to his more measured tones when he spoke of his desire to become a doctor. Angus thought that the absence of a father figure may have contributed to creating this slightly fey figure of a young man. It emphasised to Angus the maxim that money was no substitute for love and consistency in relationships; it was a sharp reminder of his own crumbling marriage and the damage it could cause his own children.

His weekend in Françoise's company exploring their old haunts in Aix enabled Angus time to renew his friendship at arm's length. Initially he remained guarded in his conversation but any anxiety he may have felt of being with Françoise melted away being hundreds of miles away from home. Meanwhile, Priscilla was unaware his visit to the south of France was anything more than a lecture junket. Angus pushed his Presbyterian guilt to the back of his mind and slipped into Françoise's easy company.

The irony of his situation did not escape him: not only was he back escorting Françoise but now he was playing nursemaid to Pete's son as well being a messenger for his old nemesis.

He silently cursed the wasted years.

Chapter 40

England 1990

Silver linings were too fanciful for Priscilla's hard-headed pragmatism, but if she had cared to think over the downfall of her husband's old friend, Pete, she would have realised that his demise was the catalyst that changed her life.

When Priscilla heard of Suzy's impending divorce, she had brazenly contacted her to ask if she could help with the sale of Raisford Hall and its contents. Suzy, who was overwhelmed by the downdraft from her husband's prosecution was mindful that Pete had treated Priscilla's husband shamefully over his first marriage. She had a regard for Angus and was aware of the support he was giving Pete in his hour of need. As a way of a favour, she decided to give his pushy wife a good turn. Carstairs-Palmer were awarded the prestigious assignment to handle the sale of the estate.

On hearing that his firm has secured the county's most important sale of the decade, Max Bulstrode-Palmer, the Managing Partner of Carstairs-Palmer, suddenly sat up and took notice of the forceful, and not unattractive, Mrs. Macintyre. Until then, he had barely acknowledged the woman's presence in his busy office. He asked his secretary to arrange a "bijou luncheon" at one of his regular watering holes reserved for special clients. It would be his special way of thanking Priscilla Mcintyre personally for her efforts in gaining this high profile, profitable commission.

Priscilla had long since disabused herself that a married life of "home counties harmony" she had once believed in, was an Arcadian illusion of her own making. The sensible, homely, love she had exuded when courting Angus was now exhausted with child rearing and trying to make ends meet. Money never seem to bother Angus, he was walled-off to such realities by his university work and love of literature. Their rattling old VW Beetle, his ridiculous 1950's bicycle, that was his preferred mode of transport to the university, was just part of his shabby, faded Viyella shirt, academic persona.

It infuriated Priscilla that Angus's lack of ambition took no account of her own needs. He was oblivious to her demands but remained steadfastly calm, despite her tantrums and moods. She often wondered why he put up with her. He was generous with his time with the children who both adored his amusing anecdotes, witty observations and attentiveness of their schoolwork. For all her animosity towards Angus, she was jealous of Angus's students who sat at his feet in adoration. She sometimes wondered if he had ever been unfaithful with any of them, in a masochistic way Priscilla wished he had. At least then she would have some ammunition for a divorce. She had often considered leaving him, but for what? She knew the children would never forgive her and she felt trapped by domestic dutifulness. Her decision to take a part time job at Carstairs-Palmer was her initial attempt at a break out. Although it had been some years since she had worked in an office, she relished the change of scene, the opportunity to meet new people, and quickly rose to the occasion. And of course the extra money was a bonus.

Just before the Raisford Hall auction, Max Bulstrode Palmer's invitation to what he described, in his rich baritone voice, "as a little light luncheon," was fixed. Some of the other girls in the office raised their eyebrows on hearing about the lunch appointment. The reason for the lunch was ostensibly legitimate, however, Priscilla sensed that Max might have other motives in mind.

~

It was a Friday and at twelve noon precisely, Priscilla was summoned by Max to join him in his large, deeply upholstered, piped leather-seated, car. They drove for what seemed like miles as Max drew heavily on a Monte Cristo cigar. As the car's interior became infused with the rich aroma of Cuban tobacco, Priscilla pressed a button to lower the window slightly.

'Sorry, if I'm fugging you up,' said Max, as he continued to puff away regardless. The luxurious vehicle glided along at a slow, self-important pace, its long, shiny bonnet nosing its way deep into the Sussex countryside. The car wound past country houses which Max claimed he had either sold, or wished he had. He articulated an extensive knowledge of the owners, although Priscilla suspected, many were totally unaware of Max and his relentless snobbery and greed.

Eventually, they came upon a beautiful inn by a river and as the car crunched its way across a deep gravel car park, Priscilla was reminded of the Potwell Inn from HG Wells' book, the "*History of Mr. Polly,*" which she read at boarding school. The likeness of the outward appearance of this literary manifestation ended as they entered the interior. There were acres of polished oak floors, antique tables and crisp white linen. It was immediately evident that Max was well-known in this fine dining establishment. An unctuous maître d' fussed around them as they were shown to a discreet corner table, conveniently shielded from the gazes of other diners.

Max had hammered his way through the majority of a bottle of Puligny Montrachet with the *foie gras* entrée and was well into the Margaux when they started their main course. He quizzed Priscilla about her husband and children, he probed relentlessly for pressure points in her marriage. Her unenthusiastic responses about her husband's professorship enhanced Max's confidence, and his breathing became heavier as he slurped his delicious claret. His first move came when he placed a surprisingly hairy hand over Priscilla's delicate and alluring paw. She paused before she took a sip of Perrier water and smiled diplomatically, as she waited for Max declaration of lust that she knew was heading her way. She allowed his hand to rest over her wrist as Priscilla quickly contemplated a suitable defence that avoided an embarrassing scene.

'I've been thinking about you, Priscilla. You'll go a long way at Carstairs-Palmer,' he said.

Yes, she thought, straight into Max's bed, if he gets his way.

'I need a woman of your tact and drive to ingratiate herself with the wives of the Sussex country house set,' Max said, warming to his pet subject of future house-sale fees. 'I think you could be the gel to do it for Carstairs Palmer. What do you say to a £1000 a year rise and the use of a company car during the week?'

Priscilla was taken aback by this surprise raid by Max, waving money and job prospects. 'Did you mean the Golf GTI?' she said, unable to think of any other question on the spur of the moment.

'Er...yes, that's the one,' he said, as a big grin spread across his crimson face.

'How do you anticipate me "ingratiating" myself with the wives of the country house set, Mr. Palmer?'

'Max, please,' he said, squeezing her hand. You could start by attending the sort of dos where they socialise, gallery openings, coffee mornings, point-to-points and the like. You know the sort of women's county stuff.' Max burbled on vaguely, clearly having little idea what he was talking about. Meanwhile, as Priscilla contemplated the thought of a £1000 a year raise and the use of the office Golf, Max thrusted his leg under the table and started to rub a suede shoe up her calf. She moved her leg out of the way and smiled sweetly at him, as if there has been some unfortunate mistake with their seating arrangements. At the same time, she squeezed his hairy hand in return, then removed it, returning her crushed fingers to her lap out of reach.

'I accept your kind offer, that would be wonderful, er...Max,' she said, raising her glass in a toast.

'Bloody wonderful, Priss, great to have you on board. Of course, I'll have to clear it with the other partners, I've got to be seen to be democratic and all that twaddle. But there won't be any problems,' he said, trying unsuccessfully to get his suede shoes back into action. They continued their meal as Max prattled on about country houses he was dying to sell, and particularly some that were being handled by a rival firm of agents in Horsham.

After the main course, an agreeable Muscat dessert wine accompanied an '*Ile Flottante* followed by a brandy *digestif*.

'No cheese Max?' said Priscilla, who was now feeling bilious.

'Love it, but it gives me bloody gout.'

As they left, Priscilla noticed he had not paid the bill or signed any account of their expensive lunch. She presumed they just sent the invoice to his office. As Max weaved his way unsteadily over the deep gravel towards his huge car, he suddenly grabbed Priscilla's hand. She incorrectly thought this was to steady himself, but he pulled her towards his bulky body. Priscilla was overcome by a sweet smelling, and undoubtedly very expensive cologne, which combined with the aroma of fine wines and Napoleon brandy fumes, resulted in a pungent odour that excreted from Max's pores. He clumsily placed his arm around her shoulders and thrust his fat body against hers, and placed a wet kiss on her left cheek. Priscilla tried not to flinch.

'We must do this again Priss, You're an absolute belter.'

Once released from Max's bear hug, Priscilla lurched towards the nearest laurel bush and vomited over its lustrous green leaves.

Chapter 41

Wartime France 1944

The boy reached the doctor's safe house before first light and was shown to a tiny attic room that would be his place of refuge for several days.

On the following day when he was found to be absent from the paint factory, the Germans re-arrested his father and this time took his mother for good measure. Before the terrified couple were transported for interrogation, they were forced to stand with revolvers pressed into their necks and watched as grey uniformed soldiers torched their farmhouse and barns. The few livestock they owned were shot and they watched their lives' work and meagre possessions disappear in flames. At that moment they believed everything they had ever held dear had ended. Their elder son murdered in his shop, and the younger boy, a partisan, now presumed dead.

Before the army wagon pulled out of the yard the old man was ordered to throw the two dead pigs and the few scrawny chickens into the back of the lorry. One of the soldiers took pity and helped the old man load the heavy swine onto the vehicle. The dead milk cow would be picked up the next day and sent for butchering. The officers mess would be well fed for a few days.

~

The Agent had arranged for the boy to live in the doctor's house until it was safe to join another partisan's group holed up in woods. He was to lie low as any new faces seen in the district, however brief, would raise suspicion. There were still collaborators who wanted to curry favour with the occupiers.

Every evening, the Agent brought him some bread and saucisson to his cramped hideaway. On the third day, after finishing his food, she had turned and kissed him. This time she embraced him with meaning. After ten days, the Agent arranged for the boy to go under cover of darkness to the new partisan cell she controlled.

The new group undertook several missions and together they succeeded in blowing up power lines, two electricity sub-stations and one night they ambushed a German patrol travelling in an armoured car and eliminated the occupants.

'What will become of us when this is all over?' the boy had asked, as he lay in the Agent's arms under a makeshift awning in the woods.

'Don't think about it,' she replied. 'You have to concentrate on surviving. Enjoy every breath and every day, tomorrow may never happen. We cannot plan when our lives are at risk.' She placed her hand over his mouth, smiled and kissed him gently on the lips.

The Agent had fallen in love with the young man's asymmetry of youthful vulnerability, fiery temperament and willingness to put himself in danger. His reckless bravery, which sometimes manifested itself like a death-wish, characterised the true spirit of French resistance. He was not like many other partisans who had communist sympathies, or who in civilian life had been on the outer fringes of the law. He did not see the struggle as something that would forward any political aspirations that would bring personal gain. The boy just wanted to throw the Germans out of his beloved country. And out of this maelstrom their strange and unexpected love had emerged.

The Agent had broken the rules drummed into her at the bleak Scottish training school where she had learned her craft. But she too had become war-weary, living precariously and starved of human affection. The boy's guileless, calf-love helped to temper the constant danger and fulfilled a deep need to have someone to cling to and care for. At that moment the boy was the only thing in her life now that her own adored family had disappeared. But she knew that her love for the boy could only ever be transitory, her transgression was an emotional convenience. The tragedy was that the boy was the repository.

'Was it the first time for you?' she asked. They were rested up in a hay barn after a raid. She stroked the boy's beaming face, and tears filled his eyes. 'I'll never forget our time together for as long as I live,' he said, as he rolled back on top of her. 'Will you marry me one day?'

'You're much too young,' she said, as she gently moved a piece of straw from his dark hair.

'But why not when we're older, when the war is over?'

'You will not want an old lady for a wife. Right now you have to use all your energies to keep alive,' she said, and gently kissed his forehead.

The Agent knew that she was playing with fire with the young boy in her thrall. She did not underestimate the emotional implications that went with love at first encounter, but she was unable to control him. Or herself.

It was a ragged, torn affair, born out of necessity of the moment. The boy's passion for her was strong and endearing, but deep down she regretted ever allowing it to take root. The Agent knew that soon she would have to leave, and that time was fast approaching.

~

It was to be expected that a member of the new partisan group informed him with some relish that it was they who had been responsible for the murder of his brother. Because of the filial association with the butcher the boy had been initially regarded with suspicion by his new comrades. It was only the trust shown in him by the Agent, and his manifest bravery on missions, that prevented him from being the recipient of a stray bullet.

The confirmation of his brother's killers made him realise the depth of Philippe's treachery. He suspected Philippe had a hand in wiping out many members of his old *Maquis* cell but he dared not ask the Agent if she had participated in murdering his brother. She must have been alerted to the urgency of shutting down a treacherous informer. He knew the Agent was trained in silent killing as he had seen her slit the throat of a German guard. Whatever, she would certainly have approved the order for the mission. The awful irony did not escape him that she had most likely eliminated one brother to save the other.

However, these thoughts did not diminish his love for the Agent, he knew her actions in getting him to the safe house had saved his life. If she was responsible, she showed no guilt.

Her training had taught her to understand the heartless rules of war.

Chapter 42

England 1990

After their initial meeting in Marseilles, Angus managed to maintain a dialogue with Charles over the telephone. It would take time to build a relationship with the young man and fulfil his promise to Pete. It would take a long period of rehabilitation as Charles remained seriously disillusioned about his father.

In an attempt to distance himself from the disgrace his father had brought upon his family, Charles reverted to using to his mother's maiden name. During one of Angus' regular telephone calls he had asked the young man about the change of surname. 'Trying to rub out the past won't change the shame you feel about your father,' said Angus. 'Your Papa's not a war criminal. You may come to regret it later in life, can you imagine how your father feels?'

'What do I care how what he thinks, it serves him right for the humiliation he's caused my mother and the family.'

'Do you really believe that's your mother's opinion?'

'Of course it is.'

'Why does she still style herself as Madame Jagoda?'

'What is it about my mother that makes you so interested in her views of my father?'

'It's because we are old friends. We all met when we were hitchhiking back in 1968. You know that Pete and I were best friends when we were your age.'

'Is that how you came to Aix?'

'Of course, we met while hitchhiking together. Your mother was a student escaping the riots in Paris.'

'The 1968 revolution?'

'Yes.'

'Why didn't you marry my mother? I would have preferred you as my father?' Angus blushed with embarrassment.

'We went out a couple of times, it was never anything serious,' he said, trying to make light of the question.

Changing the subject Angus asked: 'Talking of Aix, how is your grandfather these days? Does he still have a thing about trains? I remember your mother telling me he would never take a train anywhere, he'd rather drive or take a bus.'

'Granny Delores did mention his aversion to railways, but she's never offered any explanation. I took it to be just another of Grandpa's weird phobias like Brits and Americans. I never had the nerve to ask him, he can be very grumpy when the mood takes him.'

'I remember him being bad tempered when I first met him.'

'Granny is always trying to persuade him to sell the business, he tried to badger Maman into running it for him, but she was not interested. She said building houses was not as interesting as fashion. She has a point. When I told him I wanted to study to be a doctor, he went up the wall. He presumed I would take it on.'

'So his temper is not just an old age thing.'

'I've been doing some research about the family. Grandfather was in the Résistance. Occasionally he opens up about his experiences, but only when he's had too much cognac. He once showed me an old photograph of himself with a group of partisans, he was holding a gun.'

'Was it a rifle?'

'Yes, I think it was.'

'He pointed the bloody thing at me once and threatened to shoot me. He was livid with your father for making your mum pregnant. It was all in the heat of the moment. He was just taking his anger out on me, in his eyes, I was just another Englishman to get mad at. It was when I handed in my cards, he would never have shot me, but he did throw me out of the paint shop.

'*Mon dieu!* that sounds frightening.'

'Well, it's all forgotten now. Better to let that story remain in the past.'

'What else did your grandfather say about the war?'

'He said he blew up trains and cut power lines during the summer of 1944.'

'That was a brave of him, if he'd been caught, he would have been for the chop.'

'I also discovered that my father's elder brother, Philippe, was killed about the same time. Grandfather won't talk about it, he was a member of the *Milice*, the hated French militia, set up to root out resisters. I wonder if he knew his own younger brother was a partisan. Imagine it, your own family on opposite sides? I think that's why nobody will talk about it.'

'You're probably right. At the time, some French people were ambivalent about the German occupation, particularly in Vichy. War is an awful thing that drives wedges through people, families and communities.'

'It seems to have been a defining part of my Grandfather's life.'

'Did you know that your Polish grandmother, was in British intelligence during the war? Even your father doesn't know to this day what she did. She once told him she'd worked in some "boring" office reading German intelligence messages.

'I had no idea. Dad's never mentioned it.'

Chapter 43

Priscilla successfully removed most of the signs of regurgitated food from her dress during the long, ponderous drive back to the office. As she sobered up, Max remained unfailingly polite. It was if his lady companions were always violently sick after dining with him. With a flourish he produced a box of man-sized tissues from the dashboard's cavernous glove compartment to help restore her appearance.

When Priscilla tottered out of Max's ostentatious limousine her instincts were to bolt for home. She was certain the staff of Carstairs-Palmer were well aware of Max's proclivities. Despite it being after four o'clock she decided to tough it out and returned to her desk.

Mr Bulstrode's car was beautiful,' said Priscilla, to the girl on the next desk. 'But it did wallow a lot and made me feel rather queasy.' Her remark did nothing to dispel the knowing glances from the other girls in the office.

So what, thought Priscilla, she had just secured a £1000 a year pay rise, and the use of the Golf.

That was worth a few uncomfortable moments and she smiled to herself and savoured her triumph.

~

Priscilla worried how she could accommodate Max Bulstrode-Palmer's demands to her best advantage. There was a price attached to her pay rise and the use of the Golf. Somehow she needed to come up with a winning idea for his drive for more country house sales.

The task that Max had set her was not an easy one. She tried scribbling a few ideas down at home, but nothing emerged that would tempt the county's wealthy property owners through the doors of Carstairs-Palmer. In desperation, she confided in Angus who said in his normal good natured way, he would ponder the problem while out walking the dog. She did not hold much hope from a professor of literature, buried in sixteenth century texts.

As Angus strolled along the riverbank, he tried to put thoughts of what Françoise might be doing to the back of his mind and mulled over Priscilla's task. Intuitively, Angus thought that Priscilla was not telling him the full story about the ebullient Max Palmer, or her life at the estate agency. He never liked to probe too deeply as she became defensive which could escalate into a row. She had arrived home from the office the previous week, smelling of drink and in a disheveled, but nevertheless, cheerful state. She seemed a little drunk but he decided to say nothing. One moment she was elated about her work and then agitated and bad tempered. She had even muttered about looking for another job. Maybe she had cottoned on that he had been seeing Françoise?

On his return from his stroll, he cautiously approached Priscilla. 'I've had an idea about the challenge of reaching the county's big estates,' he said. 'It might not work but could be worth floating to your pal, Max.'

'Good heavens,' said Priscilla. She was genuinely surprised that Angus was capable of anything beyond academia. 'Anything you've got would be a real help. I feel stuck and I've got the Managing Partner breathing down my neck, asking me about progress. He's a very demanding man.'

'Well, try this out on your boss,' said Angus. 'It needs to be fleshed out but it might be just what you need.'

'Tell me more,' said Priscilla, not expecting any miracles.

'It occurs to me that most of the owners of these crumbling old country houses, whether they are impoverished landed gentry, nouveau riche footballers or pop stars, have egos as big as Winchester cathedral. Many of them would love to have their names in print?'

'Go on,' said Priscilla.

'Why not satisfy them by feeding their inflated sense of self-importance by producing a book featuring the owners and their beautiful houses? You might get some resistance from the Russian owners but others might take the bait.'

'What would you call it?'

'"*A History of Sussex's Great Country Houses.*" It would be a glossy book, like one of those on coffee tables that nobody reads.'

'Go on.'

'You could feature photographs of the houses with historical details of their past and a brief background on the current owners if they wish to be included. There's probably no more than a dozen or so worth including.'

'How would I go about it?'

'You will need to give the book an air of scholarship. I think I could persuade our History Department to do the property research as one of their projects,' he said. 'I'm also certain the County Records' people would be interested in chipping in and finally, you get Carstairs-Palmer to fund most of the costs and put their name to the book as sponsors. You will need to approach the owners to gain their permission but this could open some doors for you.'

'Priscilla thought about this idea for a moment. Then a broad smile lit up her face, the first one Angus and seen for months. 'Angus, that's a really good idea! Thank you. Brilliant Angus, I've always told you your talents are being wasted as a university professor.'

'Praise indeed. Thank you Priscilla, glad to be of service.'

Priscilla typed up a short proposal and obtained quotes from the design company who prepared the firm's advertising brochures. She then spoke to Carstairs-Palmer's retained property photographer about shooting the interior and exterior pictures. Finally she approached a local printer who specialised in printing short run, table-top books.

Angus's Head of History agreed to get behind the project if it could be undertaken in the autumn semester. Priscilla would project manage the publication and make contact with the property owners to persuade them of the importance of having their cherished properties in "*A History of Sussex's Great Country Houses*."

Priscilla, nervously outlined the idea to Max in his office and handed him the completed proposal to review. He grunted briefly, skimmed the pages. 'Good work Pris, this could fly. I'll see what the partners think.' He stalked off in the direction of the Head of Residential's office, slapping the proposal's folder on his ample thigh as he went.

At the next monthly partners meeting Priscilla's proposal was unanimously approved. Max boasted what a find he had made with Priscilla Macintyre. 'That woman has Gold Cup potential,' he said. He often drew analogies from his favourite pastime of horse racing. 'That woman is going to go far at Carstairs-Palmer, mark my words, gentlemen.' The partners exchanged knowing looks before moving on to debate the most suitable country houses to be approached.

All Priscilla had to do now was negotiate the delicate task of determining how much rope she could allow Max without hanging herself. Her attitudes towards the old rogue softened as he heaped praise on her for Angus's inspired country house book idea. Wisely, she turned down more 'bijou lunch' invitations until her promised pay rise materialised and the Golf keys were in her elegant, gloved hand.

Priscilla had not felt so pleased with herself since before the children were born.

Chapter 44

Angus was sitting at his large Victorian partner's writing table in his university rooms. The green leather desk top was filled with student papers and boring administrative demands. That morning he had not the energy to tackle essay marking. He looked at his mahogany bookshelves filled full of every conceivable study, analysis, comment and examples of medieval literature. Just thinking about the amount of study that he had squandered on this subject at the expense of living a normal life made him lightheaded. He tried to clear his mind, he had tutorials to prepare for that afternoon and he needed to telephone Pete's son, Charles. He had become increasingly involved with the young man and Françoise had told him he appreciated his calls with "Uncle Angus." Today, he wondered what he was going to say beyond the usual prosaic fluff of everyday life. Angus was concerned with Charles's new obsession about his family's war time history; he didn't think it was a healthy preoccupation while he studied for his medical exams. As the sun filtered through the narrow lead paned windows of his rooms, he picked up his desk telephone and called the usual French number.

After their preliminary greetings Angus raised the subject that worried him. 'I know Charles there are many wartime secrets locked away that you would like to unearth. But please remember that sometimes these memories are too painful to be revisited. It might be better if you go lightly with your grandfather and not press him further on his wartime past.'

'You are probably right Uncle Angus. I read in a medical journal that traumatic memories are now classified as a type of disease, a kind of delayed shock. The problem is that so much is unsaid about my family's history that it might help explain my Grandfather's behaviour.'

'Soldiers suffered from something similar in the first war. They were classified in those days as cowards. Thank goodness that medicine has moved on since then, but for now I think it is best to leave that alone until you've got your medical exams over.'

'I admit I do need to concentrate more.'

'I want talk to you about your visit to England in a few months time.'

'I'm looking forward to seeing you again,' said Charles.

'I'm pleased you are going to visit your English grandparents, they can't wait to see you again. How long since you last saw them?'

'It's years.'

'Grandpa Jagoda is not in the best of health, you should try and see them as often as time allows. One day they won't be around, and you'll regret it.'

There was a recuperative silence from Charles.

'I don't want you to dwell on this as it is more war time stuff. But you should understand both your father's parents had lucky escapes from Poland before the Germans invaded,' said Angus. 'Not many Jews got out before the holocaust, they're lucky to be alive. All your grandparent's relations were murdered, wiped out. Think how that must affect their outlook on life.'

'Dad only spoke briefly about it. I don't think he knows that much himself, although he did say that Granny's father had been very wealthy and had clothing factories in Poland.'

'Yes, I've heard about that too. Your Granny was tricked into coming to England on a cloth buying mission for her father's business. Wisely, her parents had spotted the danger ahead. That trip certainly saved her life.'

'How is it that my Polish grandparents lost everything they owned?'

'The Nazis stole all Jewish peoples' property, and I would imagine that the factories and shops were destroyed in the fighting towards the end of the war when the Russians liberated Poland. I have a theory that the terrible losses that your grandparents suffered was a reason your father worked so hard. He was desperate to be successful and emulate his grandfather.'

'Do you really think so?' said Charles, 'I never understood what drove him.'

'Underneath all his bluster and bravado your father is a good man. I knew him was he was young, he never had any malice in him, yes he was mischievous. But you must realise that sometimes people do things for reasons we don't always understand.'

'I've never thought about it like that, I was always so angry he had left Maman and me.'

'I knew your father at school, he loved the idea of doing deals. The end result wasn't important. In a way, he couldn't help himself, it is what we would call today, "a displacement activity." It means doing something to cover up something else.'

'What was he covering up?'

'Maybe having parents who were refugees, of being an outsider, being poor, not having a brother or sister? It could be any of those things, perhaps a psychiatrist could get to the root of his issues.'

'Did he have many friends?'

'No, but lots of acquaintances, you know what I mean, casual friends, not proper ones. I was probably his only one. Did you know it was my idea to go to France in '68?'

'No, why did you go?'

'For the hell of it. I dropped out of university and your dad gave up his accountancy job. We just wanted to be free, untethered, it was very selfish. By God we had some fun, we wanted to capture the spirit of the age. How naive is that?'

'I suppose you could call it liberating.'

'After a fashion.'

'You have made me think that I don't know much about my Papa. And I probably never will.' And for the first time, Angus could tell Charles was holding back tears.

'You mustn't be too hard on him, he's paid a heavy price for his wrong doings. He's lost a lot in the process: his wife, his beautiful house and most important, he lost you. That has been his worst punishment.'

Charles did not reply for a moment.

'You should not be so ashamed of your father, you need to try and bury your pride and learn forgiveness.'

'But he left us, and I had to grow up without a proper father.'

'That's not entirely true, he was generous, even if he wasn't always around.'

'I only had my grandfather.'

'And he didn't do you any favours, always trying to drive a wedge between your mum and dad.'

'You're right, he was unkind to my father. I think it was his anger about having me out of wedlock. Today it seems like a joke, but back then…'

'Times change, thankfully, for the better.'

'I admit, Maman was upset for Papa when she heard he was going to prison. But Grandpapa rejoiced at the news. It made me wonder why he was so bitter. I'm certain there is stuff we don't know.'

'I think his wartime experiences are the root of his negative outlook on life.'

'Thank you for talking to me, Angus. It is helpful to hear your side of the story about my father. I think you might know him better than Maman. She doesn't talk much about Papa, she is very evasive when I ask why she married him in the first place. Sometimes, I feel as if I am surrounded by locked doors: my Polish grandparents, my grandfather, my father and mother, and even you, Angus?'

~

It was some months later and Charles was staying at Françoise's London flat, his mother's base for her growing London fashion business. The flat was also a convenient cover for meeting Angus.

Charles was travelling by train north to have lunch with his Polish grandparents in Harrogate. Angus was already in Leeds conferring with colleagues from Leeds University ahead of a conference. He had agreed to pick Charles up from Leeds rail station and drive him to his grandparents plush Stray side apartment.

'Good to see you again,' said Angus.

'Nice car, Angus, is it a GTI?'

'I haven't the foggiest, it's Priscilla's, she's loaned me it for the day.'

On meeting Piotr and Felicia Jagoda again Angus was struck how much the couple had aged since they last met at Pete's birthday extravaganza. The strain of their son's downfall had taken its toll. After an emotional reunion, Angus left Charles to enjoy his lunch. 'I'll pick you up around 3.00. I'm off to view the Joseph Turner paintings at Harewood House. Enjoy your meal, your Dad told me your Granny is a legendary cook.'

'First we'll have a celebratory glass of vodka,' said Charles's Grandfather.

'Just water for me Piotr. You know that alcohol makes my heart go boom, boom,' said Felicja.

After the men had toasted one another, Felicja served a traditional Polish meal of "*rosół*," a delicious clear chicken broth soup. They sat around a carefully laid table with silver cutlery and fine china dishes. The soup was followed by "*kotlet mielony*," a minced meat cutlet with eggs, breadcrumbs, garlic and rolled into a ball and fried with onions and butter.

'This is delicious, Granny,' said Charles. His grandfather poured two glasses of Polish beer to accompany their meal. They rounded off their special lunch with crêpes made with cream, fruits and nuts, 'This was my old Grandmama's a favourite dish, she taught my mother who taught me, so it is a very ancient recipe,' she said, a crease furrowed her brow in momentary sadness.

'You must let me have the recipe, Granny, we cannot let that family tradition be forgotten, I love cooking.'

Charles relaxed in the warmth of his Polish grandparents' company and he silently regretted not seeing them more often, particularly since his father's fall from grace. At least they were prepared to talk about their son, although Charles could see the mention of his name upset them.

'Your father always possessed too much ambition,' said Felicja. 'He's brought disgrace upon himself and our family. When the court case was being heard we hardly ever dared leave the apartment because of journalists pestering us.' Her hand went to a string of beautiful pearls around her neck which she touched like a comfort blanket. 'You wouldn't believe it, they kept putting messages through our letterbox offering us money for pictures or any story about him. We felt so ashamed, and shame for you, dear Charles,' she said, her eyes filled with tears.

Charles has been so absorbed with his own resentment of his father's wrong doings he had never given a thought how his downfall would affect his grandparents. He felt guilty he had not considered their feelings.

'We sometimes wonder if our lovely apartment was paid for with dirty money? We feel like criminals living in our own home,' she said.

'But enough of him, he's paying dearly for his crimes now,' said Piotr. 'But our son, your father in jail, who would have thought it? He coughed and gasped for breath in distress.

'Enough Piotr, you mustn't upset yourself,' said Felicja.

Charles wanted to change the subject. Talk of his father was spoiling the lovely meal they had just enjoyed.

'You know Maman's fashion business is really taking off,' he said.

'Clothing is a good trade to be in, people always need good quality garments,' said Piotr. 'It has been my life's work.'

'And my own dear Papa,' said Felicja.

'What are you doing now, Charles?'

'I am studying to be a doctor.'

'That's a very worthwhile profession, good for you.'

After the meal, while Grandpa Jagoda was smoking a cigarette and sipping a strong black coffee, Charles brought up his French grandfather's experiences with the partisans during the war in southern France.

'I spent a little time there during the war,' said Felicja, as if she had just remembered it. 'It was before the Americans invaded St Tropez in the summer of 1944. I did meet people in the Résistance and helped them get arms from England. I had a secret radio to call up drop zones. They were very brave. It was a difficult time for French resisters, particularly in Vichy, not everyone supported the Allies.

'You never told me you were in France,' said Piotr. 'What were you doing, being a spy or something?'

Felicja did not reply.

'Good heavens, Granny,' said Charles, as surprised as his grandfather at this revelation. 'Do you remember any of the names, you might have met my French grandpapa?'

'I never knew any of their real names. They all had false identities in case anyone was captured, then nobody could inform on one another. It was bit silly as most of the partisans knew one another. I moved around a lot between safe houses in various parts of France and met many different people. It was a dangerous time, avoiding being identified. I was young and would do anything to get back at the people who had destroyed my family.'

'Of course,' said Charles.

'After the Germans went north, there was a lot of bad feeling, many of the French collaborators had to move away for fear of reprisals.' Felicja spoke quietly and with sadness in her voice. 'I remember when it was all over, seeing films of the French girls who had German boyfriends. They had their hair shorn off in public and were paraded around their villages like exhibits at a circus. It was medieval; humans can be very cruel. It was the people's punishment, the only way they could exact some sort of revenge.'

'I thought you worked in an office in London,' said Piotr, as he tried to come to terms with his wife's astonishing revelation.

'I was in an office, it was in Baker Street.'

'You kept your travels dark, Felicja.'

'I am still bound by the official secrets act. But enough of the war, it was a long time ago and best forgotten,' she said, and blew her nose. Yet more secrets, thought Charles, as he blinked back his own tears.

The flat doorbell rang and Angus was ushered into their dining room. The table was crammed with empty plates and the appetising aroma of Felica's cooking still lingered in the air.

'Dad was right, Granny's cooking was fantastic,' said Charles.

'Have you had any lunch, Angus?' said Felicja.

'I grabbed a sandwich at Harewood.'

'Can I make you a crêpe before you go? It won't take a minute.'

'No, it's good of you, I need to get Charles to the station to catch his London train.'

It was not long after their fond goodbyes that Angus and Charles were driving to Leeds in Priscilla's racy Golf. 'Thank you, Angus, for fixing the lunch, Granny's crepes were *formidable*.' She also told me some astonishing news about her work during the war.

'Tell me more.'

Chapter 45

Summer 1991

Angus was luxuriating in deliciously soft Egyptian cotton sheets of a super king size bed. Alongside the exclusive Knightsbridge hotel bed was a gilt side table with a half-finished bottle of Krug champagne, its remaining contents languorously sweated in an ice bucket.

It had been nearly three years since Angus was reunited with Françoise. They had maintained a friendly but platonic relationship in a way only very good friends are capable. They continued to have clandestine, social meetings - lunches, theatres, gallery visits and snatched coffees. They both understood it was a waiting game. Françoise had stopped dating other men.

Meanwhile, Angus had privately vowed to himself he would not divorce Priscilla until his children had completed their university education and could fend for themselves. During this time Françoise remained steadfast. Angus had always been the one ever since they first met at the filling station outside Troyes. She knew she had to be patient.

Then the dam burst. History repeated itself when one day Françoise said: 'Angus darling, it took you months before you would kiss me, and now we have been seeing one another for years and yet you never tried to seduce me?' Didn't you ever want to?

'You know why Françoise, Presbyterian guilt,' said Angus, as he cradled Françoise in his arms.

She lay her head against his bony chest, 'You're incurable!'

Angus's betrayal of his two children was the only emotion that tainted his surging happiness. He smiled to himself. 'Isn't it the French who coined the phrase a '*cinq a sept*' relationship,' he said.

'It's midday. I hope I'm more than a two hour relationship.'

'Of course you are, you're my life, the reason why I live. Believe me, it has tested the will of Job to contain myself these last few years. I wanted to sleep with you the moment I saw you again at Pete's party. I knew it would be inevitable one day. But I just had to be sure you were here to stay, I couldn't take another betrayal. And you've always known my feelings about splitting from Priscilla until my children were older.'

'I'm sorry you couldn't trust me enough. Angus darling, your late father's influence is still messing with your head after all this time, you have to let it go. I love you for your stubborn adherence to your principles of right and wrong, but your conscience has been a roadblock to our love and happiness.

As Angus lay back in the enormous bed, satiated by the voluptuous surroundings, the crisp pillows engulfing the lovers they had once again become he did wonder why it had taken so long for his life to become so satisfyingly and happily complicated. Françoise shifted her body up on one elbow, she pushed her auburn hair back and turned her oval face to his, her large brown eyes glittered with tears.

'Angus, I owe you two apologies: firstly, for messing up your life twenty years ago, and secondly, for doing it again now.'

Angus roared with laughter. 'Thank you,' he said, and slipped on top of her. It was time to catch up on the wasted years.

Chapter 46

England 2000-2004

It was on a warm summer's day in 2000 when Pete was released from Kirkham open prison in Lancashire. Angus picked him up and they travelled south to a furnished flat not far from Angus's university town. Pete was still on parole after his early release and had to report to a local police station on a regular basis.

'I need time to think matters over and get acclimatised to civilian life. I worked in the kitchens at my last prison so I know how to cook for myself, although it won't be for hundreds of inmates,' he said.

Angus was struck by Pete's calm manner as he looked around at the countryside and people as they headed back to Sussex. It was difficult to imagine how you must feel after nearly a decade of being locked up. They agreed to meet up for a lunch in a fortnight's time.

'I need to buy some new clothes. Suzy has kept my old stuff but I bet not of it will fit me now, I have lost so much weight.'

Angus's life also changed in many unexpected ways after Pete's release.

'So, Pete, what now?' The pair were sitting in the exclusive Comme Ca restaurant in Chichester.

'Firstly, I have to behave myself. I am on parole.' Pete seemed to have regained some of his old ebullience since Angus last saw him. He was wearing a smart, casual, Jaeger lightweight jacket, a light blue cotton shirt, Hermes tie and khaki chinos.

'Can you control yourself?'

'Of course. I can't tell you how peculiar it is to be free. Just being here with you in this super restaurant is like a dream. You easily get institutionalised: Sleep, get up, eat, work, exercise, eat, get banged up. I've done a lot of thinking over the years, and I have a lot to catch up on. Particularly with Charles.'

'He's a credit to you.'

'No, he's a credit to you, Angus. It's your influence that he has benefited from.'

'Rubbish.'

'Did you know he came to see me on several occasions while I was locked up.'

'Yes, he told me about it.'

'I suspect I have you to thank for those visits.'

'Well you've been away a long while.'

'You make it sound as if I had been on holiday.'

'I have been doing my best to counterbalance some of the poison his grandfather has been feeding him over the years.'

'Has it done any good?'

'Now he's a mature young man he's intelligent enough to see through Henri's prejudices. He's still fond of the old man, in a way I think he feels sorry for him.'

'He always was a bastard. But enough of Henri, I need to get back to work. Firstly, thank you for keeping an eye on things while I was away on "holiday,"' said Pete, with a grin.

'Your consultancy fees, for the little work I have done has been very welcome, thanks.'

'That's what I wanted to talk to you about, I've got a proposition for you, Angus.'

'Go on.'

'You know I am still barred from being a company director for another ten years.'

'Yes.'

'Well, and I need someone with impeccable credentials to head up my new company.'

'What company?'

'Macintyre Student Lets.'

'What?'

'Let me finish. You know Suzy has half of the original properties in her name, the ones you have been making sure the rents have been paid and the necessary repairs undertaken.'

'Yes.'

'Technically, they are still mine.'

'Will she hand them back?'

'Yes, particularly, if I pay her a premium for her stewardship while I have been on "holiday."'

'Pete, before you go on, there is something I need to tell you.'

'What's that?'

'I am in a relationship with Françoise.'

'Don't worry, I've known for ages, Charles told me. He seems very pleased about it. And so am I. Françoise was always meant to be yours. Why do think I invited her to my fortieth party!'

'You devious sod,' said Angus, as relief spread across his face. 'Charles admitted to me on one of his prison visits that he had never thought how his Polish grandparents must have felt about my litany of stupid mistakes - getting Françoise pregnant, and then being banged up.

'Angus, I owe you a huge debt of gratitude for what you have done for me, Charles and my parents.' There was a long silence as Angus lowered his head and stared at his bowl of *moules*.

'But don't get me wrong, Angus, I am not making this offer out of sentiment. I think you have the makings a damn good businessman. Your organisational skills, and calm demeanour, will be a great counterweight to my more impulsive ways.'

'It would be an enormous change for me, Pete. I am an academic, not a property tycoon. Thank you for the offer but I will have to consider how it would affect my university work. You'll have to give me some time to think things over.'

'The way you handled the property issues while I was out of circulation and dealt with my broker, made me think there was more to Angus Macintyre than I had imagined. Maybe some of Françoise's business savviness has worn off on you?'

'Let's have another bottle of this delicious Chablis,' said Angus. 'I presume you are paying.'

~

While Angus mulled over Pete's offer he was conscious that something was happening with Priscilla. Her change of demeanour could not be put down to her mood swings, she was more content with herself, and was taking extra care of her appearance. She had even joined a gym to keep trim. Her work at Carstairs-Palmer was now full time and she was earning a good salary which gave her the financial freedom she had always sought. The children were now off her hands: Chrissy was a qualified primary school teacher and newly married, Neale had graduated from university and was studying to be an Intellectual Property lawyer. Angus was galled to learn when his son completed his qualifications his starting salary would only be a little lower than his own as a university professor. It brought Pete's dangling offer into sharper focus.

So, with their parental duties coming to an end, Angus and Priscilla were like animals released from captivity, free to concentrate on their diverging lives. Angus was not sure if Priscilla had any inkling of his long-running affair with Françoise. He had always been careful to cover his tracks but even if she did know he wondered if she would give damn anyway.

Considering the balance of his life had shifted so much since the arrival of Françoise, it made the decision to take up Pete's offer easier. But he insisted with Pete on laying down some ground rules for his terms of employment.

'If my name is on the company's documentation as "Managing Director," that is what I must be,' he said. Pete was slightly taken aback by Angus's newfound assertiveness. 'I have no intention of sitting on the sidelines like a blindfolded, cheque writing dummy. My own reputation is on the line, and I need to keep a check that everything we do is above board.'

'What you really mean is that nothing is underhand,' said Pete.

'You've got it one. To that effect I'm taking a crash Business Master's Degree at the university's business school. I will be only able to work part time for a while as I need to fully understand how to read a balance sheet, draw up cash flow forecasts, and understand how to assess business risks.'

'Great idea, Angus. But be warned the politics of business is different from the theory. Spreadsheets don't always throw up business elephant traps, or opportunities.'

'That's why your advice will be vital,' said Angus.

Angus surprised himself with his newfound corporate confidence. He negotiated a visiting professor role at the university so he could keep a toe in academia.

The reality of working alongside Pete was, as his mentor predicted, very different to the theory of the lecture theatre and role plays. But his studies were not wasted. He soon discovered that decisions that took days of hand-wringing and procrastination in academic circles, were taken at break-neck speed in the world of commerce. He also learned that businesspeople had different definitions of the truth: sometimes it was a combination of obfuscation, wishful thinking and sometimes, downright lies.

One of Angus's first tasks was to negotiate a favourable bank loan to purchase a small number of run-down properties suitable for conversion to student accommodation.

'Your business plan was masterful, Angus,' said Pete, clapping him on the back. 'I have made some minor alterations and removed any areas where doubt had crept into your narrative. You don't want to frighten the horses.'

It was a good first lesson. Angus's detailed plans and unblemished credentials secured the loan. Pete undertook the negotiations when making purchases. It was not long before they started to slowly buy-back Suzy's two hundred and fifty properties.

Françoise was spending more time in London with her burgeoning fashion business and met Angus on a regular basis.

'Isn't about time you told Priscilla of your on-going affair,' said Pete. 'This charade should end, Françoise won't wait around forever. I bet Priscilla has a good idea of what you have been up to all these years. She's not stupid.'

'You're right. She leads a life of her own these days, she's married to her estate agency. It's ironic really, we've both ended up in the world of property: hers for rich fat cats, and us with impoverished students.'

'I know where I would rather be. We own properties, estate agents just ponce around selling other peoples.'

'You don't need an MBA to work that out.'

'Come on Angus, then when are you going to put Priscilla to the sword?'

'I'll tackle her this weekend when she gets back from a property conference in Moscow. Would you believe it, she is selling our finest country houses to Russian oligarchs.'

'Good luck with that my old friend, I would like to be a fly on the wall when you deliver that choice piece of news,' said Pete. He picked up a hard hat and threw it across the office at Angus. 'I'd wear that if I were you.

Chapter 47

'Angus, I'm leaving you,' said Priscilla.

Angus looked up from his *Sunday Times*. His boiled egg cup and saucer was smeared with dried red yoke intermingled with whole meal bread crusts.

'Oh,' he said.

'Did you hear me?' said Priscilla, annoyed that her statement hadn't elicited any more response than "Oh."'

'Where are you going?' said Angus, as if she was planning a trip to the Maldives.

'Stop being perverse, it doesn't suit you. I'm going to live with Rupert Henshaw-Smith.'

'Where's he from?'

'Berkshire.'

'I meant how did you meet him?'

'Have you never *heard* me say his name. Office, of course'

'I don't remember you mentioning him before.'

'Shows how little notice you take of me and my work.'

'Have you been seeing him long?'

'A few years.'

'Good heavens, you've kept that quiet'.

'You never bothered to take any bloody notice. Anyhow what about you and that French piece of fluff? You must think I am blind, I've known for years you've being seeing that woman.'

Angus did not respond to the accusation about François or that she was a piece of "fluff." 'Yes, I suppose you're right. We seem to have drifted apart.'

'Drifted apart, more like you've been bloody shipwrecked since that woman appeared at your jail-bird business partner's party. How long ago is that?'

'Ages.'

'It's a wonder she hasn't got fed up with you by now. I never knew why you didn't leave me years ago. Anyhow I'm doing it for you now.'

'The children, I suppose. I didn't want them getting upset.'

'That was big of you. You always were a coward, Angus.'

~

Priscilla's meteoric rise at Carstairs-Palmer was kick-started by securing the sale of Raisford Hall. After her pay rise and access to the Golf were confirmed the "bijou luncheons" resumed. But now Priscilla was forewarned and prepared herself for these outings. She was sparing with her alcohol intake and always wore a ferocious pair of corsets to ward off any straying hands. Max's attempts to escalate their meals into a full-blown smash and grab were thwarted. But they did talk about property opportunities and that distracted Max as money was second on his agenda after attractive women.

Priscilla's tactful circumnavigation of being ushered upstairs to the pre-booked bedroom suite required all her skills of tact, until Max, like an exhausted old stag tired, realised the attractive Mrs Mcintyre was not going to become one of his hinds. Shrewdly, Priscilla mitigated Max's disappointment by introducing an attractive, aristocratic, new client that she had netted with her successful Country House Book project. This lady was more amenable to "bijou luncheons" Max-style, and could not wait to check out the upstairs suite.

The office dynamics changed once Rupert Henshaw-Smith joined as a new partner from arch rival agents in Horsham. Rupert, in his early fifties and recently divorced, was well connected. He had applied for the position with his eye on the main partnership role at Carstairs-Palmer. It was obvious, even to the most casual observer, that Max's excessive lifestyle would eventually catch up with him.

This prescience proved accurate when after another one of his excessive lunches with an unsuspecting female companion, quite literally, went off the rails. Max was returning from a gourmet restaurant in a fog of brandy excess, and coupled with some in-car groping, had failed to notice railway level-crossing warning lights. His vast motor forged its way through the closing barriers and became stuck halfway across the track as the far barrier closed on the vehicle's bonnet. His lady companion sensibly fled the vehicle before the 100 mph express to Paddington ploughed into Max and his magnificent motor. Sadly, Max was too inebriated and did not possess the speed and agility of his female luncheon partner. He remained bewildered as he struggled to find his seat belt release among the detritus of the stranded vehicle's inflated air bag. His demise was as fast as the train that struck him.

It was only natural for Priscilla to devote her attentions to the divorce-scarred and handsome Rupert Henshaw-Smith as he took up the reins of the senior partner.

Rupert had married well but this had proven to be his downfall. His artistically talented wife (she painted), had inherited a fortune from an unmarried uncle, and succumbed to a cocaine habit. Her addiction resulted in a chaotic marriage and a tumultuous break up. By the time Rupert arrived at Carstairs-Palmer he was in need of rehabilitation.

A task in which Priscilla Macintyre was a past master.

Chapter 48

Angus and Françoise's wedding took place in a Mayfair Registry Office in early 2002. Charles was accompanied by his partner, Angus's children: Neale and Chrissy and her husband attended. There was more than a little irony in Pete being best man.

After a sumptuous and very liquid lunch at Le Gavroche restaurant, Pete made a short speech. He talked of enduring friendships and jokingly apologised for stealing Françoise from Angus decades ago. An embarrassed silence followed until Charles raised his glass in a toast to the bride and groom.

Finally, Angus rose to his feet: 'Friends, family, and of course my beautiful wife.' A ripple of applause trickled from the small group. 'We lead lives crowded with compromises, doubts, secret desires and self-interests. As a Scot, I, perhaps more than my French friends, have been held back by my Puritan upbringing exemplified by my late father.' Pete snorted in recognition at this description of Angus's domineering parent.

'My father's well-meaning but distorted views of right and wrong characterised my childhood and young adult life. I have spent a greater part of my time on this earth absorbed in the study of Elizabethan drama, cut off from the world, entranced by the mastery of Shakespeare's prescient insights into human nature and life's frailties, beautifully dramatised in his written prose. Until just a few years ago, my life had been like a modern-day Shakespearian tragedy. Stupidly, I nearly came to believe that it was my destiny to be betrayed by my closest friends.'

There was a collective gasp from around the table. Chrissy looked up, horrified, her hand was in danger of breaking the champagne flute stem as she gripped it in disbelief.

Angus turned first to look at Pete and gave him a long, slightly amused gaze, as if testing his reactions. Pete was sitting stock-still, his face frozen with remorse, thinking to himself: For God's sake Angus, shut up, you're going to bugger up your marriage before it has even started.

Angus's head slowly swivelled downwards to Françoise on his right hand side, her face was in her hands covering her ears, she could not bear to hear Angus's long withheld, cry of anguish. Why this confession now, she thought?

She remained immobilised by the terrible public exposure of her and Pete's long ago moment of shameful passion. Charles and Neale both seemed mesmerised, they stared hopelessly at the remnants of cheese on their fine china plates.

Angus continued speaking: 'But you see, it was by other people's betrayal, greed and foolishness that I have found love once again with my dearest old friends.' His voice was lighter now, more jocular. Françoise looked up at the composed, controlled figure of the man she loved. It was then she realised that his speech was not aimed at her or Pete. It was for himself, a cathartic public cleansing of his soul, his late father might have called it a baptism.

'The wheel turns,' he said. 'Had I not gone to Pete's extravagant fortieth birthday party I would probably never have met Françoise again. In fact, had Pete not invited her, my life would have been entirely different.' Heads were raised around the table, their attention once again focused on Angus.

'And without Pete's bombastic stupidity, and his resulting incarceration, his love for his son Charles, a love that through his own hubris, had buried so beautifully, would never have blossomed. And all of us would not be sitting around this happy table as friends. It has taken me a long time to understand how to forgive and shed myself of the self-flagellation of "duty" that has held back my life for so long. I am at long last free.

'Now I have had my brief say, allow me to finish with a predictable, but apt, if even corny Shakespearean reference. As always, the Bard manages to sum it up better than I ever could with his play written in 1604, a play the critics cannot agree whether it's a comedy, or a tragedy. I tell my students it's a tragicomedy. The title of course is: "*All's well that ends well.*" I toast enduring friendships, forgiveness, and love.'

As Angus raised his glass, the group around the small table rose as one to their feet: Françoise and Chrissy with tears rolling down their cheeks, Pete was hanging onto Françoise's arm to support himself, and Charles embraced his partner, only Neale was on his own, head bowed, but smiling at his father's reincarnation

Chapter 49

France 2008

By 2008 Charles was a well-respected orthopaedic surgeon working in a Marseilles hospital. It was a typical sunny Mediterranean morning, sunlight sneaked through the half-closed blinds of his consulting room, casting shadows across his stylish pine desk.

A dark-haired young nurse in a starched white uniform opened the door and announced his next patient: 'Madame Delores to see you,' she said, and held open the wide door to his consulting room. An elderly lady dressed entirely in black, entered with the help of two sticks. She shuffled with painfully slow steps, no close examination was required to determine her hips were in poor shape. His file stated her name was Madame Sylvie Delores. Charles glanced at her records on his computer and read that she was 88 years old and lived in a poor suburb of Aix-en-Provence.

The old woman brusquely refused the nurse's assistance in helping her into the chair on the other side of Charles's desk. She slumped down on the leather seat, her sticks clattered loudly against the desk's side. Charles noticed the old lady's dark brown eyes were scanning him closely and he wondered if she suffered from cataracts. The intensity of her examination was disturbing, as if she was looking for some sign of recognition. She said nothing.

'Without examining you I can tell your hips are giving you pain, Madame,' said Charles. 'Is any one of your hips worse than the other?'

She remained mute. Charles continued to scan her medical records. Are you by any chance related to Henri Delores of Aix, the painting contractor and builder?' He said, as he tried to elicit some response from the old lady swathed in a strange assortment of black apparel.

She continued to stare at him but remained tight lipped. Charles thought she had not heard him so he repeated the question, louder this time.

'I'm not completely deaf. What's it to you, to whom I am related?' she said. 'I am here because I can barely walk. I did not come to the hospital to be cross-examined. My relations are none of your or the hospital's business.'

'Of course they are not, my apologies for raising a personal matter. Can you come over to the examination couch behind the screen I need to take a closer look at your range of movement,' said Charles, as he pointed to a curtained corner of the room. 'Please remove your outer garments as I will need to examine both your hips. The reason for my enquiry is that we maybe distantly related. My grandfather mentioned he had lost a brother in the war and he had lost touch with his widow. As you share the same surname, I thought there might be some connection.'

The old lady did not get up as requested but instead stared at him a little longer. Then her beady eyes widened in recognition. 'Are you Henri's bastard grandson?'

'I am Henri Delores's grandson. My mother was Françoise Delores.'

'Ahh, I thought as much, so you're the son of that whore of a daughter.'

'Madame, may I ask you to please moderate your language,' said Charles, taken back by this vitriolic old woman. There is no need to be rude. Don't you know it's against the law to slander someone.'

'Bah, don't try and hide your illegitimate birth.' Then she raised her hooded head and spat, a weak dribble of spittle fell on Charles's desk smearing his mouse mat.

Charles stood up in alarm as the vituperate old woman grappled with her two sticks and tried to get up from her chair. 'I don't want to be seen by you. Get me another doctor,' she said, before she slumped back down again into the expensive Italian chrome chair.

'But Madame, I'm the senior orthopaedic surgeon in this hospital.'

'I don't care who you are. I don't want any member of Henri Delores's family touching me. Get me another surgeon. I don't want to be murdered at your hands.'

'Murdered Madame? What on God's earth are you talking about? This is a hospital, we save lives, not end them.'

Charles, was on his feet, and wondered if his patient had some form of dementia. He picked a tissue from a roll on the wall and wiped clean his mouse mat before bending down to scan the medical records on the computer screen. There was no mention of mental illness or any age-related dementia. 'Are you sure you don't want me to examine you? I was going to arrange an x-ray of your hips today. You'll have to wait for perhaps another week or more if you don't have it done today? ' he said trying to return to his unruffled, professional self.

'I don't want your damn x-rays, don't come near me. Didn't you hear what I said, I want another doctor? She glared at him with real hatred, her old eyes glittered with malice.

'Can I ask, what's wrong with me?'

'I don't trust you. I don't trust any Delores.'

'But you don't know me.'

'I know your family, and that's enough.'

'How do you know my family?'

She said nothing and continued to stare at him malevolently. Charles gave up, trying to reason with the mad old crone. He had a queue of other patients to see. On the very rare occasions when patients did not take to you they could seek an alternative opinion. But this old woman was in different league. She was openly hostile about some past and unknown family issue. He could have perhaps understood someone refusing him earlier in his career when it became known he was gay. But thankfully, today times were more tolerant. There had been a brief time when the threat of Aids had patients running for the door after a mere handshake.

'I'm going to refer you to my junior colleague, Dr. Guillaume Rostern. He's not on duty today so you'll have to come back when he's free.' Charles scribbled on a card which she snatched out of his hand. 'Give this to the lady on the reception desk, she'll fix you another appointment.' Charles got up from behind his desk to help her onto her feet. This time, in a major effort of willpower, she grasped her sticks and got to her feet unassisted. She shooed Charles out of the away as he held open the door. The old woman tottered out into a waiting area, muttering, 'Murdering Delores, murders all of 'em.' The other patients waiting to be seen looked up in alarm as she staggered past, her sticks clacking on the marble-tiled floor. 'Nurse, nurse, get me a proper doctor,' was the last Charles heard of her utterances as she disappeared down the corridor in search of the receptionist.

Charles would have liked to broach the subject of this unwelcome relation with his grandfather, but they were no longer on speaking terms. Henri had yet to come to terms that his only grandson was gay. To him it was the final betrayal.

The old woman knew all about the Delores family, she had to be his Aunt, Phillipe's widow. There was obviously a dark story attached to her husband's demise, something never spoken of in the family. The phrase, "murdering her husband," kept resonating in his mind for the rest of the day.

The following weekend Charles decided to do some research on Aix during the latter years of the war. There had been a spate of books published recently about the British involvement in helping Résistance groups during the conflict. Many wartime records were becoming declassified, lifting the lid on the German occupation, some of which did not make comfortable reading. Charles bought a couple of books and scoured the internet for information on both the British Intelligence Services (SIS) the British Special Operations Executive, or the SOE, as it was known.

Much to his partner's annoyance, Charles spent the weekend assiduously studying his purchases reading anything he could find about the secret agents who had worked in the Cote'd'Azure and Provence regions.

One story told of the fear the partisans had of informers and how members would be suddenly picked up and never seen again. Later, the narrator described the murder of a suburban Aix butcher who had been a part-time member of the *Milice*. This individual worked with the Gestapo, using intelligence gained in his shop, to help identify resisters. The butcher's shop was a good source of idle gossip leading to arrests of Résistance members and subsequent executions.

The murderers were presumed to be partisans, but it was never proven. The butcher had his throat cut and his body strung up on a meat-hook in the shop window. It was designed to serve as a grim reminder to the locals what happened to informers. The German's retaliated with widespread arrests, torture and executions. They also torched number of shops in the town including the butcher's shop.

Could this be the husband of the angry old woman? If so, why was she so angry with his Grandfather?

Chapter 50

England

After Priscilla's divorce from Angus, she settled down with Rupert in an elegant Georgian house near the Cathedral.

Their final parting had been remarkably equable. A relief on all sides. They had both recognised their relationship, born in the heat of Angus's crushing betrayal, had matured and finally stagnated over the years into an unhappy compromise.

Angus' wilderness years when he was lost in academia, and then his latter, surprising, metamorphic dive into commerce, combined with Priscilla's ambition to be her own woman, were the final stakes that drove them apart. Priscilla had been brought up in the mould of home counties middle class England but she had always wanted more, exemplified by her bolt to Monaco.

'You look happy,' said Priscilla, rather miffed that her once impecunious ex-husband was now driving a large Mercedes Benz and wearing Hugo Boss suits. It was one of those rare occasions the two of them lunched together to discuss the children and arrangements for Christmas.

'Is that the FT under your arm? Whatever happened to the Guardian, you've become quite the tycoon? she said. "Whatever do they say at the university when you grace them with your presence.'

'I don't go in much these days,' he said, ignoring Priscilla's jibe.

'And what about you and your dodgy Russians?'

'They're a vulgar lot, a bit frightening to be honest. Most of them have bodyguards; fortunately we rarely meet them. We deal with their beautiful Ukrainian personal assistants who seem to have more taste, and the most expensive lawyers that London has to offer.'

'You've become a bit of a cynic, Priscilla. What ever happened to the home counties girl I once married?'

'That was a childish dream, Angus. It was a chimera of my own making. Reality crushed that notion stone dead.'

'You mean I did?'

'Oh, stop being so sensitive. Getting married, having children, and never having enough money finally put paid to my fantasies. It just took a long time for me to realise it.'

'And are you happy you've the trappings you craved for when we were together?'

'In the main, yes.'

'You know it has taken me a lifetime to shrug off my Scottish Presbyterian upbringing,' said Angus, in a rare moment of candour.

'Your father was a bit of an ogre. He looked me up and down when we first met. Do you remember he asked me which church I attended?'

'And you told him you were an atheist,' said Angus, laughing at the memory.

'How is your ex-con business partner these days?'

'You would hardly recognise Pete these days. His tumultuous downfall and spell locked up has made him fiscally chaste. He's become a much more caring human being. He's reconciled with his son and made it up with his parents. They went through hell during his trial.'

'Perhaps some good has come out of his comeuppance.'

'It definitely has. He still has a shrewd nose for sniffing out properties and he's a canny negotiator, knowing exactly when to bid at auctions. It's an art form that comes naturally to him.'

'Isn't he still a bit of a risk.'

'Not any more. I keep an eye on him. He can't make any decisions without my say. But these days he's happy to work behind the scenes, he no longer seeks the limelight.'

'He's probably had enough limelight to last a lifetime.'

'Some of the characters he met in prison still write to him asking for investment advice, he ran a sort of investment club for long term inmates.'

'He never stops does he?'

'When he's not thinking about property, he devotes his time to his parents and Charles.

'Making up for lost time.'

'I think we are all doing a bit of that.'

'Chrissy and Neale both seem happy and settled in their marriages, so we have achieved something worthwhile together,' said Angus.

'It's us the baby-boomer parents that have taken a lifetime to sort out our respective relationships,' said Priscilla, laughing.

Chapter 51

Pete's mother had taken time to come to terms with her son's rehabilitation. As the bonds of family were slowly renewed, she began to understand her son better, and finally accepted his frailties.

Pete's introspection and new calmness enabled him to maintain a cordial relationship with Suzy, but neither of them expressed any interest in getting back together. He struck up a relationship with a divorced girl in the sales office, but their dating was only half-hearted. His passion lay in new quarters: cooking and family. He purchased a penthouse apartment in the same city as Angus's university and exercised his newfound skills holding gourmet dinners for family and friends.

Pete visited Marseilles and stayed with Charles and his partner at his apartment in *Le Quartier du Panier*, just behind the old port. Charles's partner was a gourmand and there were plenty of restaurants on their doorstep. It was typical of Pete he had arranged that his half of the company's shares were in Charles's name. One day Charles would discover he was a wealthy man.

Françoise and Angus visited Aix to see her parents and occasionally dined with the elderly Henri Delores, whose antagonism for the English had been briefly replaced by a bewildered fury that Charles's wife was a man not a woman. Old age had only brought a partial mellowness. He was pleased that his daughter was finally happily married, albeit to an ex-hippy employee. Charles had become the focus of his malcontent. It was a rejection of all the hopes he had invested in the boy from early childhood. It was as if his old nemesis, Pete, had had the last laugh. The old man had not spoken to his grandson for over a year.

~

The visit to Charles's clinic by Philippe Delores's widow triggered a renewed interest in getting to the bottom of the family feud. Her naked hatred of him, or any Delores, had been disturbing, particularly as she had carried the grudge for more than sixty years. He mentioned the incident to Pete on his last visit to Marseilles, but he had no recollection of her ever being discussed while he was married. Françoise was equally opaque.

'Papa was always reluctant to speak about the war time in Aix,' said Françoise. 'He would close up like a book if it ever came up in conversation. He positively avoided veterans' reunions and never wanted reminding of anything about the war years.'

'Why don't you speak to your Grandfather about it,' said Pete to Charles. 'It would be a good idea if you two put an end to this silly stand-off about your private life. It has gone on far too long.'

'It's him that can't accept I'm gay.'

'You have to rise above it. You just need to prove it to him that you are just the same grandson he always loved. What you've told me about the bad-tempered old lady that came to your clinic might be the clue why he won't open up about his wartime experiences,' said Pete. 'His bad temper has affected family relations for decades.'

'He hated your success and revelled in your troubles,' said Charles. 'I became inured to his prejudices. However, on other matters he was kind to me. In the end, I just blocked out the negative bits. But it is sad to go through your life carrying resentments, it's not healthy.'

'I thought at the time, he just couldn't come to terms with the idea that his lovely daughter had been made pregnant by the son of Polish Jews,' said Pete. 'But despite the obvious, I always thought there was something else feeding his paranoia. I could never put my finger on it. During the few years of my marriage, your grandfather only once touched on the war years. He opened up one evening after too many glasses of cognac. He told me that he had been in the Maquis and had "killed plenty of Germans."'

'Go on,' said Charles.

'He fished out an old, faded photograph of a group of scruffy-looking men holding rifles, on the back row was a pretty girl wearing a headscarf and holding a pistol, I couldn't make out her features, but she was slim, and I guess she must have been in her early twenties. The picture had been taken outside a farmhouse somewhere. Your grandfather pointed out himself as a young man. He was kneeling at the front of the group with a rifle held upright in his right hand. He was no more than a boy of about eighteen or nineteen, but I could still recognise him. He was good-looking young man.'

'I'll have to ask him to show me the photograph,' said Charles.

'Let's hope he's more chilled. I think he's finally got over his resentment of me now Françoise has married Angus,' said Pete. 'At least he's learned to accept Angus, which is a step in the right direction. I hear they meet quite frequently with your mother.'

'Well, let's hope he'll see me again,' said Charles.

~

Before attempting a reconciliation with his recalcitrant grandfather, Charles decided to look into more of Aix's wartime history.

As the distance between the end of the war lengthened more volumes of memoirs and historical research had emerged. Many were written by British and foreign agents, including female spies, smuggled into France to work with Résistance groups. Charles was surprised that after sixty or more years since the end of the war, it was only recently that many of these secret exploits had finally been made public. He knew that both the British and French Governments were still holding back some of the most sensitive material. Charles read with disbelief about the rivalry, double-crossing, and deception among the allies own secret service organisations.

Charles eventually stumbled across an English memoir that had been translated into French that detailed the activities of the *Milice* in Vichy France. Their collaboration with the Gestapo made uncomfortable reading. It was then he discovered a newspaper story about a butcher in Aix being murdered by a partisan group. The butcher's shop owner had been a collaborator and an active member of the *Milice*. His shop had been a valuable source of intelligence from other informers. Piecing together this oral conduit, the butcher had built up a valuable picture of the local inhabitants to feed to his German masters. The memoir went on to describe the thriving black market, particularly the shortage of fresh meat, in which the butcher was fully engaged. Such subterfuge trade was excellent cover for understanding the populace's attitudes towards the German occupiers.

Within the narrative Charles read the butcher's name was *Monsieur Philippe Delores*. His own surname. He felt shocked and deeply ashamed by the association. The jigsaw pieces finally fitted into place. The rude old lady in his surgery must have been Phillipe's widow. She probably knew that Henri was mixed up with the partisans and blamed him for the murder. True or not, that would be the reason for her bitter hatred, thought Charles.

This was the information that he had been seeking and which he now had to confront his recalcitrant grandfather. He had to know, had his grandfather murdered his own brother?

Chapter 52

Armed with the knowledge that his Great Uncle had been a member of the *Milice*, and had been murdered by persons unknown, Charles knocked on his grandfather's cottage door.

It was answered by Madame Delores who immediately threw her arms around him and hugged him tightly. Tears flowed down her wrinkled cheeks, she had feared that the impasse with Henri would never end.

'Charles is here to see you, Henri,' called a tearful Madame Delores.

'Who?' came a voice from the small sitting room where Henri was reading a copy of "*La Provence*."

'What does he want?'

Charles did not wait to be ushered in but marched the into the room and embraced his grandfather before he could protest. Henri did not have time to put down his newspaper. When he had recovered, Charles handed him a bottle of his favourite cognac. It was as if nothing had happened between them.

'You'd better sit down,' said the old man, as he examined the label on the bottle. 'Make some coffee will you,' he called to his wife. 'And bring the cognac glasses.'.

Charles took the cognac bottle and pulled off the seal and was uncorking the top as Madame Delores came in with coffee and two glasses. Charles poured a generous portion into each glass.

'Henri! It's not midday,' she said.

As they swirled the amber liquor around in their glasses and sipped their brandy, Charles talked about his work as a doctor in Marseilles.

'How's your arthritis, Grandpapa?'

'Bloody painful,' he said. Henri showed his grandson his swollen knuckles.

'Can you do anything for me?'

'Not a lot, but a change of diet might help. This stuff probably isn't helping,' he said holding up his glass. You should cut down on your red wine and meat.'

'I would rather die,' said Henri, and smiled for the first time.

'I'll look into some drugs that might help you, but arthritis isn't my speciality.' Charles' past difficulties about his private life seemed to have been forgotten, and topping up his grandfather's glass Charles decided to quiz the old man about his late brother.

'Now Grandpapa, I have some questions for you.'

'I hope you're not going to give me a medical examination?'

'Nothing of the sort. I have done some digging into our family's wartime history and it seems there is a lot unsaid.' Charles watched his grandfather bristle and he let out a large sigh.

'This is worse than a medical, Charles. The war was a long time ago and best forgotten. Many of my memories are too hard to talk about, they still haunt me,' he said, his voice low.

'But partisans and resisters are revered as heroes in France these days. Aren't you proud that you fought to free our country from *les boches*?'

For a long moment they both savoured the heady aroma of the Napoleon brandy, in the bowl of their glasses.

'War is not like it is portrayed in films or books. It is frightening, cruel and grossly unfair. Your friends become enemies.' His voice trailed off and there was another long silence as the old man stared into his glass as if seeing the past.

'I didn't know that your brother was a butcher, Grandpapa?' said Charles. There was another long pause and Charles thought he was not going to reply.

Then his grandfather looked up at Charles. 'You are right my boy, my father was a farmer and we bred cattle before the war. Philippe always wanted to have a *boucherie* and sell the meat from the farm. He was very proud of our cattle, but of course our little farm could not supply all the meat for the shop. He bought the business off a retiring butcher in the town in about 1934 or '35, I can't quite remember now. My brother was a good bit older than me.'

'Was it successful?'

'Yes, he did well, and gained a reputation for good quality meat, he supplied restaurants and hotels along the coast.'

'So what went wrong?'

'After the Germans invaded he became active politically. He supported the Vichy government under that damn traitor, Marshall Petain. And that's when we really fell out. A lot of people, particularly down here in the South went along with the collaboration. People took a wait and see attitude, initially, we thought the Germans might be here for ever. That was until Hitler invaded Russia. The problems of northern Europe: England, Netherlands, Belgium, didn't bother us southerners, people wanted the quiet life. But I didn't agree with him, I hated *les boches* lording over us, telling us what to do, stealing our food, using forced labour. I supported the Free French movement under General de Gaulle.'

'How did you feel about your brother being a part-time member of the *Milice*?'

'How did you find that out?' said Henri, annoyed that this piece of history had come to light.

'It's public record, Grandpapa.'

'Really.' The old man fell silent for a minute. 'I tell you, it was disgraceful. Philippe brought shame on our family. My parents never really got over it.' The old man paused again. Charles could see he was recalling some past time. 'You see, I was young and idealistic, but my brother got on okay with the Germans. He was flattered by their interest in him, it sounds simplistic, but he was a narcissist. He liked parading around in his stupid blue uniform and the Germans were good for his butchery business.

'Was he like this from the beginning of the occupation?'

'He liked the idea of cleansing France of Jews and communists. He swallowed the Nazi propaganda about making France part of the Greater German Nation. He was taken in by it all. He loved the idea of conquering the arrogant British, taking over their empire. He fell for the whole ideology. Stupid idiot, and he paid for it with his life.'

Henri paused again contemplating whether to go on. He took another sip of his cognac. 'At first the Germans were okay but after they disbanded the Vichy government and took control in November 1942, life changed. Up until then many people just rubbed along with them. There were not many German troops stationed here then, Petain took his orders from Berlin.

'Everybody hoped it would get better as time went on, but of course it didn't. It got worse as the war turned against the Germans. I was at school and they started interfering with our lessons and text books. They tried to indoctrinate us, portraying Hitler as our saviour, it was like a form of religion. Brainwashing. Even at our young age we could see through the lies, but some of the kids were taken in, most of us couldn't care less. When I got older I could tell that our country and its values were being subsumed by Fascist thinking. It was alien to everything France stood for.'

'It must have been a frightening time,' said Charles.

'It was, but at the same time, it was exciting, particularly after the Allies landed in Normandy. At last we felt we could throw *les boches* out. It shook everything up, we could see the end in sight.'

'I read that your brother was murdered?'

'You are well informed, how did you find out?'

'It was in a book, an English memoir.'

'It was a bloody business, very sad.'

'Who killed him?'

'I don't know. I was told it was members of another Résistance group to mine, but it could have been a British or foreign agent. They sometimes acted alone if they received some specific intelligence. London would most likely have ordered the assassination; they were involved in a lot of the partisans' activities. As my brother was a member of the *Milice* he was already betraying his fellow Frenchmen. He was a sitting-duck.'

'But he was your brother,' said Charles.

'Maybe, but the *Milice's* role was to hunt out Résistance cells and I was in one, the *Maquis*. We were on opposite sides.'

'Do you think he knew about your links with the partisans?'

'In the end, he must have known. My group had been penetrated and I had to go underground to avoid being arrested. I had made a terrible blunder when my rifle was discovered when the Germans raided my parents farm. Because of my stupidity my poor father was tortured, and my mother arrested,' he said, his voice choked with emotion. The old man was silent for a moment and Charles filled up his glass.

'That's a terrible story.'

'The British agents were very brave, but they were arrogant too. They never fully appreciated the work the Résistance had been doing long before their spies were flown in to help us. They treated us as if we didn't know anything about clandestine fighting.'

'Did your brother's murder make you question being a partisan?'

'Never, he was a traitor, he deserved what he got.'

'Even being strung up and hung from a meat hook in his shop window.'

'I know it was gruesome. But he was an informer, and killing him was meant to send a message to other collaborators.'

'As your brother was a traitor weren't your comrades suspicious of you?'

'I was aware of being watched closely by my fellow *Maquis* members in case I was a German stooge. Everyone was scared stiff of informers, if they had suspected I was a stool-pigeon, I would have been murdered on the spot, no doubt about that. It was very unpleasant to have your fellow partisans doubting your loyalty. I had to be doubly brave on missions to prove my worth. But I was trusted by the British spy that led our cell and that saved me.'

'It must have made your position very tenuous.'

'When our group was compromised, I was moved to a safe house to avoid arrest. When I disappeared the Germans burnt my parents farm to the ground and they were thrown into jail.'

'That sounds like a lucky escape.'

'Not for my parents, although somehow they survived being shot.'

'You must have felt very guilty about it.'

'Of course. I fled into hiding. If it hadn't been for the British agent who took me to a safe house, I would have been shot. That was a certainty.'

'Did you ever hear from the Agent after the war?'

'No, nothing, not a word.' His grandfather looked wistful for a moment. 'All this happened a few months before the Yankees and Free French invaded the South coast in August '44. Aix was liberated, and by a miracle my parents survived. The Germans shot a lot of prisoners before they cleared out, but somehow, they cheated death'

'A bit like you Grandpapa.'

'I suppose I did.'

Now Charles knew for certain why his great aunt believed Henri had murdered her husband and why she had showed such a manifest hatred towards him in the hospital.

However, it still did not explain why his grandfather was still resentful of the Americans and the British.

Chapter 53

War Time France 1944

Every day the boy lived in a perilous heaven, an interlude that he hoped would never end. The danger and violence of their nighttime activities enabled him to forget whatever agonies his parents might be suffering. With every German he killed he felt a vengeful satisfaction he was eradicating his brother's treachery.

On 13th August, two days before Operation Dragoon, the American and Free French forces invasion of southern France, his partisan group completed their last mission laying explosives at St Raphael railway station. They were timed to explode in the early hours of the invasion morning.

It was after the raid that the boy's four-month Valhalla came to an abrupt end. He was unaware that the Agent had received top secret orders from London. Her remaining *Maquis* group was to link up with three other cells for the expected fighting to liberate Marseilles, Toulon and other coastal towns on the south coast. Once the arrangements for the various partisan groups' dispersal onto different assignments had been made, she was ordered to immediately withdraw. From then on the partisans would come under Free French military control. She did not tell the boy this as she was afraid that once she had departed, he may be shot by a vengeful partisan.

The Agent had other plans that would safeguard him when she had gone.

~

'The party is over, I have orders to leave,' the Agent announced. 'The group is to be disbanded and you must go into hiding immediately.'

'In God's name, why?'

'It's great news, the Yankees and the Free French are coming.'

'Another invasion?'

'Yes, right here, and very soon,'

'Why can't I come with you?'

'You can't. Orders,' she said, dispassionately. 'I know a safe spot you can hide for a couple of days. It's not far, but you must go there tonight.'

'Tonight?'

'Take this.' The Agent unbuttoned a pocket of her green tunic and took out a tiny map printed on a handkerchief. She thrust it into the boy's trembling hands. Study this carefully to avoid the patrols from the German coastal gun batteries. Your hiding place is perfect, it has dry caves with soft sand you can sleep on. I've reconnoitred it myself, it was one of my secret escape routes, for a submarine pickup.'

'Are you coming with me?

'No.'

'Where are you going?' She did not answer.

'You have to keep out of the way until after the invasion has been accomplished. There is going to be lot of fighting for a few days, it will be chaotic and very dangerous. But you won't have to wait long. If you stay hidden until a bridgehead has been established you will be safe.'

'My God, are they coming by sea?

'Yes, along the coast across the bay of St Tropez and by air and there will be shelling from ships offshore. If by any chance you're captured, say nothing about what I have told you. It's top secret.'

'You must tell me where you are going?' He was nearly shouting.

'I can't tell you, I'm sorry. I have work I must do elsewhere.'

'Why can't I come with you?'

'If you do as I've told you, you'll be safe. In a few days, the war will be over for you,' said the Agent. She turned her back on the boy as she tried to control her emotions.

He tried to pull her around to face him. 'Why are you telling me all this? I want to help kick the Germans out for myself.'

'Don't be stupid. What have you been doing ever since you joined the partisans? You have to let the professionals take over now. It is no longer a guerrilla war. The Americans and French forces are backed by an invasion army. They're not like us with just a few guns and explosives. Our work is finished now. Your duty is to stay alive.

The boy looked aghast. He could not believe what he was being told. The excitement he should have felt about the invasion was blotted out by the realisation that the Agent was leaving. He had no idea when he might see her again.

'Now promise me, when you see the invasion vessels offshore, stay in hiding for at least another forty-eight hours as there will be mayhem until the Allies establish a beach head. The soldiers in charge won't know whether you are friend or a German collaborator. Just keep out of the way and don't be impatient. If you do as I say, you will be safe,' said the Agent. The Agent was determined to show no emotion, she knew this would be the last time she would see him. The boy had been her companion on many dangerous missions, he had been an anchor for her own self-doubts. She had witnessed him fledge from a hot-headed youth to a heroic young man. She hoped that after the war, his bravery would be recognised.

'When will I see you?' he asked again, his voice quavering, as the Agent was about to dispatch him to his refuge. She ignored his questions.

'You must go now,' she said, and kissed his cheek gently, her lips brushing his light stubble. It was a repeat of their first encounter in the Rognac forest.

The boy felt it was a lifetime ago.

~

The boy had been in two minds to ignore the Agent's instructions but remembered her insistence that it was an order to be obeyed. He had located the hiding place after negotiating thick vegetation and scrambling down a steep escarpment. The Agent had been true to her word, his temporary new home was dry and safe.

On the next morning he ventured to the mouth of the cave when he heard the thundering engines of the USAF B.17 bomber aircraft flying inland, wave after wave they came in the grey, half-light. The ground shook as their high explosive bombs struck targets in the coastal hinterland and he was glad he had followed the Agent's advice and was sheltered in relative safety.

Very early on the following morning he saw an armada of DC3 transport planes flying inland packed with airborne troops ready to be parachuted behind German lines. Some were towing gliders containing more infantry. It was not long after he heard the whistling of naval shells overhead as they pounded the shore batteries nearby. He retreated further inside the cave as pieces of rock fell from the cave roof onto the sandy floor as shells struck nearby German gun installations.

Again he agonised about the whereabouts of the Agent as the terrifying barrage was unleashed. Later, he spotted on the horizon a fleet of grey ships approaching the coastline. The boy ventured outside his cave and sat on a rock looking out at the azure, calm Mediterranean Sea. He could see smoke arising from the shore and the towns along the coast the results of the naval bombardment. But still the sun shone and the water looked inviting enough to swim, despite the coiled barbed wire along the shoreline. How lovely it would have been if the Agent had been with him, they could have slipped naked together into the clear waters.

Then from nowhere, swooping out of a cloudless sky, came Thunderbolt P-47 aircraft as they screamed towards the coastline at sea-top height, strafing coastal gun installations with rockets. He shrank back into his cave once again for fear of being hit. It was fortunate that most of the ordnance was targeted away from him in an easterly direction.

As the ships drew closer he could see grey landing craft packed with men, their metal helmets just visible as they headed for the sandy beaches in readiness to storm the defences. He could see bullets whipping up the sea's surface from the German defences.

He prayed for the safety of the brave men as they approached the shore line. He felt powerless and wished he was on board one of the craft.

Chapter 54

England 2008

Piotr Jagoda's death was not a surprise. His lifetime's dedication to Caro cigarettes, a popular brand from his native Poland, had left its calling card of emphysema. Eventually, his smoking habit and a dose of winter pneumonia caught up with him and he died fighting for breath in Harrogate District Hospital.

Pete was with him in his last moments and he regretted the wasted years he had spent working like a mad man and then languishing in jail. Whilst he had tried to make up lost time with his father in the latter years, he had never managed to penetrate the man's inner self. He had been irreparably scarred by his family's loss in the war, memories he kept locked up and which contributed to his reticence.

'Look after your mother, when I'm gone.' he had said, in between gasps of oxygen, while lying prostrate in his hospital bed. 'She's a more remarkable woman than you could ever imagine.' His father looked worn out, beaten down by life, and Pete thought he was probably ready to give up the struggle of living. His brief conversation had been a few days before the light of life left his eyes. Pete put his father's remarks down to death-bed whimsy and soon forgot them as grief overwhelmed him.

After selling his little tailoring business, one of his father's retirement pastimes was to take the bus from Harrogate to Leeds and spend happy hours in the Polish Club on Chapeltown Road. His weekly visits enabled him to meet with other Polish émigrés, gossip about times past and play dominoes, a game in which he'd become an ace practitioner.

Piotr's funeral was held at New Farnley Jewish cemetery. It was a bitterly cold February day with a biting easterly wind, and after the service the mourners retired to the Polish Club for the wake. It was here that Pete saw his mother greet an elderly gentleman, someone of similar age to his late father. His mother had quickly fallen into an animated conversation with the stranger, it was clear he must have been an old family friend. Pete did not recognise him and wondering if he might learn something about his late father's past he went over to introduce himself.

Despite his age, the old man stood tall and straight and spoke clearly with only a faint hint of a Polish accent. Pete introduced himself.

'Your father and I were friends back in Poznań,' he said, 'we left for England together, but I lost touch when he went into the RAF, and I joined a British army regiment of Polish émigrés.'

That would account for the old man's military bearing, Pete thought.

'By chance, I met your mother before your father did. She was a beautiful girl, just like today,' he said, smiling as he took her hand. 'To my regret, I let her slip through my fingers.'

'Oh Jakob, don't be silly,' said his mother, as her free hand reached for the pearls she wore around her neck.

'We first met in 1943 when we were training to be special agents. Do you remember that gloomy big house we were sent to in Scotland?'

Pete's eyes opened wide in astonishment. 'Mother?' Then he remembered his father's last few words.

'Of course, I didn't know your real name then as we were only addressed by our code names. Yours was… let me think, "Warsaw" wasn't it?' Jakob said.

Felicja ignored her son's questioning expression. 'I remember it well, it was on the West coast wasn't it, Arisaig, I think? My God it was remote, it took an age to get there by train from London. It never stopped raining for all the time we were there,' she said.

'They trained us very hard. Your mother was as tough as any of the men,' said Jakob.

'Do you remember that Dutchman who blew himself up practising with explosives,' he asked.

'Yes, I remember, it was very sad.'

'Our instructors just dismissed it as a casualty of war. They trained us to be unsentimental, we had to focus on our training, nothing else mattered.'

'I enjoyed it, I couldn't wait to go and bash those bloody Germans. I suppose we were conditioned for it, but I didn't need much encouragement.'

'Oh Felicja, beneath that beauty you were ruthless in those days.'

'No point in training me to be parachuted into France if I was not going to be effective.'

'Parachuted? Is this true Mother?' said Pete, even more astonished to hear of his mother's exploits.

She turned and looked at him. 'There was a war on, it was what we did in those days.'

'Not everyone parachuted into enemy territory, and you were Jewish too. If you'd been caught, you'd be shot, or at best sent to a concentration camp.'

'Correction. I would have been tortured for information and then shot,' she said. 'We were told by our trainers what the consequences would be if we were uncovered. And many sadly were. We were issued with suicide pills, just in case.'

'Have you still got your medals?' asked Jakob.

'No, I threw them away. I didn't want to remember what had happened to my parents, and what I had done to avenge their murders. Then I met Piotr and I fell in love again.'

By now Charles had joined the group. 'Granny, what do you mean fell in love again?' he said.

She hesitated. 'We all have pasts we'd rather forget, which is where that story will remain,' she said, looking at her grandson.

'But who was he? You can't leave a casual remark like that hanging for us to guess,' said Charles.

His grandmother hesitated.

'Come on Felicja, you have to tell your son and grandson your story. You should be proud of what you did, there's no shame. C'mon, it's more than sixty years ago and we were fighting for the survival of our way of life.'

'I am saying no more, it's in the past, over.'

'Everything we did in the field was extreme, you never knew when you might be found out. You risked your life every day as a secret agent,' said Jakob.

'When we had finished our training we never met again until after the war. You went to Holland if I remember correctly, and I to France. So how do you know anything about what I did?' she asked.

'Because men talk about their pasts and their wives. You can blame Polish beer and dominoes,' he said.

'Piotr, my dear departed husband, I never told him the half of it. I did not want to burden him with my history. I wanted us to build a new life in England.'

'Well, if you won't tell them, I will. The younger generation should know what sacrifices we endured for their futures,' said Jakob.

'Don't you dare say a word,' said Felicja, looking at Jakob and wagging her finger at him.

Jakob knew better than to defy his old friend's wife. He lowered his head and brought a finger to his lips in respect of her wishes.

After all, it was her husband's funeral.

Chapter 55

France 2008

In mid January, not long before Piotr Jagoda's death, Madame Delores had a sudden heart attack. She was preparing lunch in her kitchen when she keeled over and fell heavily to the kitchen floor hitting her head on a heavy fruit- wood table as she collapsed. Henri heard the crash and came stumbling through from the sitting room where he had been reading the newspaper. He found the crumpled heap of his wife on the floor, blood oozed from an ugly gash on her forehead. By the time the ambulance arrived she was dead.

Her sudden death affected Charles more than he had anticipated. He was aware she had a heart condition, and at the age of eighty-three, he knew as a doctor her life expectancy was not long. Françoise was more stoical and rallied around her father, who was stunned by the loss. They had been married for over sixty years and whilst it had never been a passionate coupling, they had rubbed along together in a companionable way. She had tolerated his bad tempered moods, and he finally accepted her antipathy for more children. Henri supplemented his rationed sexual congress by maintaining a series of mistresses into his early sixties.

Mysteriously, Henri organised with Françoise's approval a live-in house keeper to ensure he had regular meals and the house was kept clean. What Françoise never knew was Henri's choice of companion was one of his past lovers.

That spring Henri Delores celebrated his eighty-fifth birthday. Françoise and Charles decided to cheer him up, (although outward appearances suggested he did not need much cheering up), and mark this milestone with a lunch party. Family, old friends, and colleagues were invited and even Pete made the guest list.

The lunch conformed to typical French standards: a festival of delicious food and wine stretching through the afternoon in a noisy milieu of good humoured company, all washed down with plentiful fine wine. The food was largely prepared by Henri's new housekeeper who bustled about importantly in a colourful cotton dress.

It was a beautiful day in early May and the apple blossom was in bloom, the sun was pleasantly warm but not excessively hot. The meal was served outside in the orchard at the back of the Delores family home, where a large awning had been erected that extended over the rows of trestle tables for sixty guests. Angus had donated the Chablis and the Chateauneuf-Du-Pape, and Pete had brought some excellent vintage champagne.

Pete and his mother Felicja were staying with Charles at his Marseilles apartment. Since her husband had died she had decided to travel again and the offer of three weeks in the south of France with her grandson was the first step in a new found desire for adventure. They were both invited to Henri's party. They arrived slightly late as Felicja had asked Charles to drive her into the Rognac Forest.

'Why here?' said Charles, 'It's just forest.'

'It holds some special memories,' she said.

They crossed a railway line and Felicja asked Charles to stop the car. She got out and looked up and down the railway line. Looking west it curved downhill and eventually was lost from sight. She got back in the car.

'Happy?' said Charles.

'Yes thanks. Let's go to your grandfather's party. Pete will be wondering where we have got to.'

When they arrived Henri was surrounded by Françoise and other friends and neighbours seated at one of the long tables and no formal introductions were made.

Charles and Felicja sat down at an adjacent table and Charles introduced his English granny to some of the guests. He was amazed at her fluent French.

'I didn't know you spoke French so well,' said Charles. 'I speak fluent German too,' she said. 'I was well educated in Poland and travelled all over Europe on business with my dear Papa. Of course, that was before the war.' During the meal Felicja kept glancing at the adjoining table where Henri was sitting, there was something about the old man that was familiar.

Once the feasting drew to a close and the last of the cheeses had been consumed, some of the elderly guests started to drift away exhausted by the rich food and lively company. A small group of immediate family had gathered around Henri's table to listen to anecdotes and chat about the influx of Russians and other Eastern bloc visitors to the south of France. It was agreed they were changing the character and tone of the Riviera, and, despite their vast wealth and spending power, their presence was damaging the magic of the Cote.

Charles related the tale of meeting his great aunt at the hospital. 'She's the first patient in my career who has refused treatment, just my luck it should be a member of my own family!' Everyone roared with laughter.'She was always a stubborn woman, even when she was young,' said Henri, who had listened to the story. Whether spurred on by the wine or the talk of the past the old man continued. 'Looking back, it was very sad, my oldest friends knew that my brother and I had never seen eye-to-eye since we were kids. When the war came we held diametrically opposing views. Philippe and his wife, thought the occupation was a positive move for France, to become an integrated part of greater Germany. They were very devout Catholics and agreed with many of Hitler's extreme views. They wanted France free of Jewish influence, something I vehemently opposed.'

Pete's eyebrows shot up with surprise.

Henri turned towards the two Englishmen sitting together. 'I know you both thought I was an anti-semite, but you were wrong. A couple of my fellow partisans were Jewish, somehow, they'd avoided being transported.'

'I never thought that,' said Angus, affronted by the accusation.

'But even before my marriage to Françoise you were antagonistic towards Angus and myself. Was it was because we were British?' asked Pete.

Henri threw up his arms in a typical Gallic gesture, then pausing for a moment: 'Was I so bad, I gave you two hippies some work?' he said.

'We were cheap labour, and we got you out of trouble,' said Angus. 'I admit we were happy to go along with it.'

'What you English never understand,' said Henri in a more serious tone, 'is our two countries' histories have been marred by conflict. We've had more wars with the Anglo Saxons than anyone else.' Henri rolled his head back recalling the iniquities inflicted upon his beloved country, 'Crecy, Agincourt, arguments over Gascony…'

'Oh come on Henri, it's ancient history, centuries ago,' said Angus. 'Have you forgotten it was the Normans who invaded Britain in 1066.'

'They weren't French, they were Vikings that settled in Normandy.'

'What about Napoleon, he wanted to rule Europe?' said Angus.

'Another bloody Hitler,' muttered Pete.

'Surely you can't still feel embittered about us Brits after all this time?' said Angus.

'I thought my great Aunt had a grudge, this beats them all,' said Charles, in an aside to Françoise.

'We've fought alongside one another in two world wars, doesn't that count for anything?' said Pete.

'But you English forget France is a proud nation. We have always considered the English as uncultured barbarians, like your soccer hooligans.'

'Stop being stereotypical,' said Angus, getting irritated. 'It's like me saying that all French people smell of garlic and eat frog's legs.'

'Oh come on Papa, you are being extreme to provoke an argument,' said Françoise. 'You know most French people don't think the English are like that. I married two Englishmen, so I should know.'

'It's a Gaullist view of the world,' said Angus.

'During the war we resented having your spies telling us how the Résistance groups should operate, it was as if we were incapable of doing it ourselves.'

'Ah, is this your real gripe with the Brits? And where did all the arms come from?' said Angus. 'Flown in by brave RAF pilots.'

'Of course, we all hated *les boches*,' continued Henri. 'The British did send us good men and women of many nationalities, and yes, they did provide much needed arms and ammunition. But they often operated on their own, without reference to the partisans they were meant to be helping. This annoyed us, we thought they were arrogant, bossing us about as if we didn't know anything. After all, it was our country that had been invaded.'

'But these people were risking their lives to help you, it seems churlish to criticise their efforts,' said Françoise

'I cannot believe that this was the only reason that has fed your anger over the decades,' said Angus.

Henri paused again, choosing his words carefully. 'Did you know one of your spies murdered my brother,' said Henri, very quietly.

There was a silence as the small group took in in what Henri had said.

'A spy murdered, him?' said Angus.

'How can you be so sure it was a spy. It could have been anyone with a hatred toward your brother. He was an active member of the Milice. Philippe was an obvious target,' said Charles.

'Do you dislike all Englishmen because of that one act. Is that the reason for your long-standing bitterness?' asked Pete.

'No,' Henri answered. 'Definitely not.'

'Why not, you have a reason if your assertion is correct?' said Angus.

'Because at the time I didn't know that my brother had information on members of my Résistance cell. The English spies received intelligence that a member of the *Milice* in Aix had information that could blow the whole group open. The Brits knew my brother had been informing so he had to be removed before the whole network was compromised.'

'And your brother had no idea you were a member of this cell?' asked Pete.

'I'm certain he did, in the end. If the Getsapo had caught me I would be finished. Can you imagine it, my own brother? But I was lucky and managed to escape before they could arrest me.'

'So why were you so angry with the English spies? They probably saved your life,' said Angus.

'They did,' Henri paused before going on. 'But if I had known that my brother had been informing on my comrades, I would have killed him myself. It would have been my patriotic duty,' he said, his voice cracking with emotion. 'He had brought shame on the Delores family, and shame on France.'

The small group was stunned into silence at the admission that nearly sixty five years ago, the frail old man before them, surrounded by his close family, was prepared to murder his own brother.

'The consequences of the past never go away,' said Angus.

A champagne cork popped in readiness for the birthday toast.

Chapter 56

War Time France 1944

It was two days after the invasion, on a starlit night, when an RAF piloted Lysander light aircraft flew out of a field near Marseilles. The small plane's cargo carried the boy's dreams. The Agent's mission was completed and other Résistance groups would take up her clandestine work as the invasion spread. The Agent was being flown the short distance over the Spanish border where a ship would take her home to England. As the light aircraft bumped its way westwards, the girl took off her soft leather gloves and unbuttoning her tunic pocket, she removed a string of pearls. They were cool to touch and as she ran them through her fingers she remembered her mother who had entrusted them to her. It was her mother's last gesture of love for her daughter before she left home for the last time.

Meanwhile, crouched in his sandy cave, the boy thought about the last few blissful months of danger and love with the Agent. In retrospect it felt like a mirage, a figment of his youthful imagination. His only record was a crumpled monochrome picture of his original Maquis group. It was a bitter, heartbreaking end to his life-changing love affair.

"I have work I must do elsewhere."

Chapter 57

France 2008

The champagne glasses were handed around in readiness for Charles's birthday toast to his grandfather. He appeared to have calmed down after his tirade about the British and his revelation that he would have murdered his brother if he had known about his treachery. The conversation returned to the war.

'Did you know the spy's name who undertook the assassination?' Pete asked Henri, as he filled his glass.

'I had my ideas, but I never knew for certain. We only knew the spies by their code names. There was a very brave young woman who lead our group. She helped me escape to a safe house. One of the spies I met was called "Cheltenham," the other was a young woman, not much older than myself. She was very special, fearless and skilful, a ruthless operator.

'Do you remember her code name?'

'Oh yes. I have never forgotten her.'

'What was it?'

'Warsaw.'

Pete's eyes widened in astonishment. 'Can you repeat that again?'

'Warsaw,' he repeated, more loudly.

'Are you absolutely sure that was her name?'

'Of course I am, how could I ever forget it.'

Pete turned to look at his mother who was seated at the back of the group, and not in full view of Henri. She was listening intently to the conversation.

'I was deeply in love with her,' said Henri.

'Good heavens,' said Pete.

'We were lovers for nearly four months, and then one night she disappeared. She gave me orders to go into hiding just before the invasion on the south coast. I was completely heartbroken.' Henri's eyes filled with tears as he spoke the words. 'She left a few months after my brother was murdered and I've never set eyes on her since.'

'Oh Papa, how sad,' said Françoise. 'Why did you never mention this before.?'

'I didn't want to upset your dear mother. It was a long time ago and I was very young.'

'A tragedy,' said Charles.

'I hated that lovely girl for leaving me in the way she did. We never even said a proper goodbye. There was no message from her after she'd gone. I didn't even know if she had survived the American invasion.'

'Maybe she'd been uncovered by the Gestapo and had to get out in a hurry,' said Angus.

'After the war I did discover she'd been airlifted to Spain by the RAF,' said Henri, his voice cracked with emotion again. There was another awkward silence.

'Can I propose a toast to Grandpapa on his eighty fifth birthday… and er…to absent friends,' said Charles, trying to break the sudden embarrassed gloom. Everyone raised their glasses and as they drank they contemplated the abrupt ending of this wartime romance so many years ago.

'Why were you so interested in the girl's code name Pete?' asked Angus.

Before he could answer Felicja rose to her feet and stepped closer to where Henri was sitting. The old man looked up and something in his face registered recognition. Before Henri could utter a word, Felicja spoke in French:

'My code name was Warsaw. I'm very sorry Henri, I had no alternative but to leave you. I had orders from London. I couldn't tell you at the time, you'll remember how everything we did in those days was top secret.'

Henri looked up in disbelief. 'Warsaw? I cannot believe it really is you…you after all these years. Why are you here?'

'Because Peter is my son?'

'What! I cannot believe it. Am I dreaming?'

'Dear Henri it's no dream, it's really me, and Pete is my boy. Now you can call me by my real name: Felicja.'

'Good God!' said Henri.

'We were in love you and I. The war threw us together and tore us apart. It maybe a small consolation but I never forgot you, Henri.'

There was a gasp from the small gathering as Felicja stepped forward and Henri rose unsteadily to his feet and they embraced. Tears poured down Henri's cheeks. 'I can't believe you really are my darling Warsaw,' he repeated, sobbing. Felicja held the old man tight as it looked as if he might collapse. She managed to remain calm but dewy eyed. The housekeeper, who was fussing around clearing the plates, stood still, and watched this reunion with less affection than the family.

'My God, how did you know your mother's wartime code name was "Warsaw"?' said Angus, looking at Pete.

'One of her old comrades, who trained with her, told me at my father's funeral. He mentioned she had been a spy in the south of France during the war. She has never ever spoke to me about it before, not the slightest hint. I did learn at the funeral that my mother had thrown away her war medals. She said she wanted to forget everything. I think that might have been the reason why she refused to attend my marriage to Françoise, too many memories of her time spent here.'

'And that included poor Henri,' said Angus.

Henri, regained his composure but did not let Felicja out of his arms. 'I always thought there was something familiar about you, Peter,' he said. 'It's been troubling me every day since you walked into my yard all those years ago.'

Reluctantly, the old man let go of Felicja and walked unsteadily towards Pete who had also risen to his feet. Everyone was uncertain what was going to happen next. The people around the table instinctively leaned back in their chairs, as they waited to see how the old man would react to the astonishing revelations that had just unravelled.

Henri stood in front of Pete, raised his grey head and grasped Pete's shoulders with his bony veined hands and kissed him on both cheeks. Then, holding Pete at arms length he studied his face for a long moment.

'Now I recognise your mother's features. She was a brave, beautiful woman, you should be very proud of her. Peter, you are the son I never had.

'I owe you an apology.'

ENDS

About the Author

D A Adamson is an advertising copywriter who has published two comedic crime novels set in the 1960s based in his native North Yorkshire: *The Windelton Absurdities* and *Windelton and the Bavarian Incident*. His first children's chapter book, *Rubbish: The Little Dog That Became A Street Cleaner* is currently being published. He is a regular contributor to radio for the visually impaired, a prolific short story writer and has a Substack, *Diary of a Baby Boomer*. He is married with three children, three grandchildren and seven hens. He lives in Lower Wensleydale.

Printed and bound by CPI Group (UK) Ltd, Croydon, CR0 4YY
08/12/2025
02014710-0001